THROUGH THE EYES OF DESPERATION

THE BLACK VERSION

DANIEL J. VOLPE

BAD DREAM BOOKS

ISBN: 978-1-961758-14-8

Cover & Interior Art by Anton Rosovsky

Cover wrap design by C.V. Hunt

Edited by Jason Parent

Printed in the USA

WARNING:
This book contains scenes and subject matter that are disgusting and disturbing; easily offended people are not the intended audience.

FOR SIGNED BOOKS, MERCHANDISE, AND EXCLUSIVE ITEMS VISIT:

www.DJVHorror.com

To the lucky ones.

"Oh, I don't lose. People who bet on me to lose, lose.
And they lose big."

– Al Pacino in *Ocean's Thirteen*

SHADOWS

Vinnie Sable was fucked.

Always a gambling man, he'd found himself in some tight spots before, but this time was different. As he and his teenage daughter, Cee, walked through the underground casino, Vin had a feeling his luck had run dry.

He guided Cee through the crowded casino floor. Men gazed upon her teenage body with lust in their alcohol-soaked eyes. Cat calls came from a group of older men—men old enough to be Cee's grandfather. If she heard it, she didn't care, at least not enough to show it.

"Don't listen to them, hun," Vin said. He put his hand on the small of her back, ushering her past the men. Vin glared at the perverts. But he couldn't afford to hate them, considering what he was there to do. Hate wasn't justified, but it felt good to direct that anger anywhere besides into himself.

The casino was a whirlwind of noises, lights, and smells. Their impacts to his senses were, in some cases, uplifting, like the joyous shouts of a man winning the jackpot on a slot machine. Others were things of nightmares: the stench of vomit or spilled entrails; the shrill cries of a player who lost everything. It was an overload.

They weren't inside any ordinary casino. This was Shadows.

Vin moved Cee along, not stopping to watch any of it. He'd seen it all before, and unfortunately, so had she.

"Don't look at it," he warned. A high-stakes roulette game was getting gory. Blood ran down the man's face as he wept and prayed. Vin glanced at Cee, who was watching the violence. The wheel spun; the bettor had his head down in despair. The wheel hadn't even stopped yet, and already the man was defeated.

"Red," the croupier shouted. Two brutes in tight-fitting suits grabbed the man with his hand over his blood-drenched face, escorting him away. He didn't fight, but his cries grew louder and more childlike.

"Huh, fucking dummy," Vin said. He pushed Cee forward. "Always bet on black." He moved toward a lone security guard. Vin looked at Cee and stooped down slightly. The teenage girl was almost his height, but he made it a point to lower himself. "Listen to me, Cee. I have a meeting with a very important man, okay? A meeting that'll make or break us. One that can ensure we're never on the run again." Vin smiled. "Don't wander far, and just remember, everyone's here because they want to be. Don't forget that."

Cee nodded. "Okay, Dad."

Vin squeezed her shoulder. He forced a smile but knew she could see right through it. He turned and walked away, melting into the crowd.

A DEER IN HEADLIGHTS

Cee knew they were in trouble when they walked into the casino. Shadrick, a thuggish loan shark, had mentioned the underground casino years ago. Meeting him that fateful night had been the first time Cee had seen a man maimed. She didn't know why, but the name of the casino stuck with her over the years. So, when she'd overheard her father talking with someone, mentioning the casino, the old memory rocketed to her forebrain. As a girl, she'd imagined what the interior of the casino might look like. Was it a place of fun and joy, like every gambling ad? Or would it be a sad place, filled with smoke and drunken people full of despair? Now that she was standing inside, she knew it was the latter.

The journey to reach the strange place was unsettling. A mine shaft in the middle of nowhere—a long tunnel of darkness that seemed like it would never end—eventually led them to the entrance. When they'd first walked in, the games seemed somewhat normal. But the more Cee watched, the worse they became.

A craps table where the losers had to eat crap. The three-card monte table where the cards were replaced with used maxi pads. That was just in the first few steps into the hellish casino. As her father led her deeper and deeper, the sounds transitioned. The bells and whistles of winning slot machines or the cheers of a great hand of poker began mixing with screams and groans. Mangled players sat at tables. They were betting bits of flesh when their money ran dry. Black-clad security and pit bosses stalked the floor like wolves on the hunt, watching and waiting.

As vile and obscene as the games were, there was something almost alluring about the casino. The power and desperation on display were staggering. To watch a man cut a finger off or a woman flay her breast just to play a game was sickening.

Cee wandered around, even though her father had warned against it. She wasn't one to listen, especially to him. Their relationship was strained after her mother left when Cee was only eleven. That had been six years ago, and her father never quite recovered. Every person had their vices, and Vinnie Sable was no different. Whether it was making poor investments, betting money on races, or just gambling in general, when he decided he was going to do something, he went for it. Including drugs, mainly cocaine. And when Cee's mom left, things just spiraled out of control.

Vinnie's gambling took on new heights, and payouts became staggering. First, he'd lost all his mother's jewelry betting on football games. Not a big deal. She'd been dead for years. Then he lost their car, the only mode of transportation he or Cee had. Again, not the end of the world, with public transportation being so accessible. His job was next.

Coked out of his mind, Vinnie would often find himself at the off-track betting building until the wee hours of the morning. He'd sit there, hoping his luck would change. It never did. When he had a job, he'd roll in late, drunk, or high. Sometimes it was a combo of all three.

Unemployment was common for Vinnie but always concerning for young Cee. She'd be left alone for days at a time, which could be a blessing, especially if her father had been drinking. He wasn't violent, not in a physical sense. Cee was never hit with his fist, but he wasn't above throwing insults her way, often blaming her for the disappearance of her mother.

The casino staff paid her no attention, even though she was underage. Shadows wasn't a business that played by the rules of society. She was certain there was a strict line of parameters set in the establishment, and being underage wasn't a concern. It was welcomed.

The leers of older men—and even the occasional woman—followed her around. Whispers hissed from their mouths when she'd pass, and more than one obscene comment came her way. She ignored them, but part of her liked the attention.

Cee knew she was attractive, but she had no interest in the men. Even the boys in school had a hard time getting her attention, and they were her age. She wasn't interested in sex but instead reveled in the power of her persuasion. Boys would drool over her when she'd show up wearing a tight pair of shorts, with just the hint of her ass cheeks at the bottom. Even some teachers would get caught looking as well. Men were easy, and Cee had no problem playing them like a fiddle.

She stopped at a card table, standing far enough back to avoid being mistaken for a player. She'd seen the desperate men and women at the bank getting their palms branded with the symbol of the casino. An 'S' meant they were playing with their flesh.

"Come play, darlin'," a man said from behind Cee. His hand found her lower back just above her ass.

Cee turned around. An older man with a head full of gray hair stood close to her. His mustache was wispy, and his breath reeked of cigarettes and whiskey. She pushed his hand away from her.

"No, I'm just here to watch," she said. Cee wanted to back up farther but didn't want to hit any of the other players.

"Watchin' is no fun." The man stepped closer and put a hand on her shoulder.

Cee looked at it with disgust. She dug the ball of her foot into the ground, preparing to knee the old creep in the nuts.

"I gotta room nearby," he said, looking at her young breasts that had filled out her shirt for the last few years. "Maybe we can do more than watch." He moved closer still. "I'll make it worth your while." He pulled a hundred-dollar bill from his pocket. "Give this old man a taste of that young cunt, and you can have this."

Cee's muscles were tight. She loaded up, thinking of how wonderful it was going to feel to destroy this old man's withered cock.

"Charity Sable?" a deep voice said next to her. It belonged to a black-clad security guard.

She snapped her head to the side, brushing the old man's hand from her shoulder. "Yeah, that's me." The security guard was a hulk. His shoulders were wide and his face hard. His haircut and clean shave screamed ex-military.

"Come with me," he said.

THE HALLWAY TO HELL

The security guard's eyes drifted to the old man. "And you, leave the fucking girl alone. We have plenty of whores in *The Doll House*. Now, get the fuck out of here."

The old man scurried away without another word, melting into the crowd.

The security guard looked at Cee. "You shouldn't be wandering around. This isn't a place for a young girl."

As he started walking away, Cee followed. "That might be so, but I can handle myself."

The big man grunted. "Sure you can, sweetheart. I've seen many a dead girl who thought the same way. Strangled, raped, and with their piss-soaked panties stuffed in their mouth."

Cee stepped up next to him. "Yeah, I'm sure it happens, but I was ready for him. You just saved that old pervert's nut sack."

He looked at her with a smirk. "Oh yeah? You were gonna hit him?"

"My knee was about to make him sing soprano," she said.

"Hmph," the man grunted. They walked through the casino, passing multiple games of chance and gore. A set of double doors loomed in the background. He stopped and turned to her. "I'm Marty."

Cee looked at his meaty hand and took it. "Cee," she said. His hand enveloped hers. "But I guess you already knew that." They walked through the doors. "This is about my dad, isn't it?"

Marty led her down a long hallway. The rough-cut rock walls were lit by overhead drop lights. He didn't look at her but spoke. "Yeah."

Cee felt like her heartbeat was visible through her shirt. Marty's footsteps echoed through the empty chamber, giving the tunnel its own heartbeat.

"Bad?" she asked, already knowing the answer. This wasn't the first time her father had been in trouble with dangerous people. She still remembered years earlier when she'd come home from school, after dealing with a pair of bullies, only to find her father in shambles. That was the first time they were truly on the run, but it wasn't the last.

Marty didn't speak, he just looked at her and nodded.

Cee wanted to stop, to turn and run away, but knew it was no use. She was in too deep—dragged into the dangerous underbelly by the one man who was supposed to keep her safe. The hallway continued into pure darkness until they came to a stop in front of a red door.

"He's in there with the boss," Marty said.

"The boss?" Cee asked.

"Gianni Lito. He owns the joint—this is all his baby."

As Marty's hand pounded against the door, Cee's heart pounded inside her chest. The horrors inside the establishment went beyond anything Cee had ever seen. She wasn't sure she was ready to meet the architect of such sinister proposals.

DADDY'S BET

The red door opened slowly, revealing a room of torment. Vinnie lay strapped to a table that was reminiscent of an old lethal injection contraption.

Cee walked in and almost burst into tears.

Her father was a bloody mess. He was shirtless—his chest covered in open wounds. His left ear was missing—a ragged hole was all that remained. Three fingers had been removed from his left hand and two from his right. They lay in a heap of blood and meat piled on the floor. He moaned but didn't scream.

"Cee," Vinnie croaked. "I'm-I'm sorry, Cee. I fucking lost again." Some of his teeth were missing. Spit and blood spilled from his mouth and down his cheeks.

"Daddy!" Cee yelped. The urge to run to him nearly overpowered her.

"Ah, so this is your lovely daughter," a man said.

He was tall and thin, with a head of gray hair that contained too much Pomade. His cheeks were clean-shaven and droopy. Ice-blue eyes glared in the fluorescent lighting of the room. They were watery but clear. His suit was ash-gray and perfectly tailored, with a black pocket square and matching tie.

A toad of a man stood next to him. He was squat with a thinning head of hair. His nose was two sizes too big and displayed a road map of broken blood vessels. Every one of his fat fingers held a ring, each more garish than the last.

"Welcome, my dear," the older man said. "I am Gianni Lito." He stepped forward and extended his hand.

Cee was quivering but reached out to shake hands. "I-I'm Charity, but everyone calls me Cee." His hand was clammy, but his grip was strong.

Gianni yanked her forward, almost dislocating her shoulder. He pulled her hand up to his face and licked the back of it. His tongue slithered over her flesh, causing Cee to break out in goosebumps.

"Mmm, I can't wait to taste the rest of you," Gianni said.

Cee pulled—shocked at the strength of the old man. Finally, he released her. She wiped the back of her hand on her pants.

Gianni smiled. and his toad bodyguard laughed. Even the noises he made sounded amphibian.

"She didn't like your kisses, boss," the bodyguard said.

"Oh Geno, you know these young cunts are like wild horses. Ya gotta ride 'em hard a few times until you break 'em."

Geno croaked out a laugh. "She'll be a fun one to break."

"Daddy, what's going on?" Cee asked.

Vinnie's tears mixed with the blood on his face. "I'm sorry, baby. I really am." He lifted his head from the table and looked at Gianni. "Fucking flip already. Just get this shit over with."

"My, my, someone is quite impatient," Gianni said. He leaned in close to Vinnie, his purplish lips near his ear. "Don't worry, pops. If you lose, we'll take real good care of your little girl." He sniffed hard. "Mmm, I can smell that pussy already. Stinky and scared, just how I like it."

"What flip? What's going on?" Cee shouted. She looked back at Marty, who stood by the door like a statue. The big man wouldn't make eye contact with her.

"Well, let me fill you in on something, Cee," Gianni said. "Your daddy is a bad man. And not only that, but he's a shitty fucking father to boot. He likes to make bets he can't make good on and bet things that aren't his."

Cee furrowed her brow. "What are you saying?"

Gianni grinned. "You, Cee. He bet you."

Vinnie's sobs broke into downright wails. "I'm so sorry, Cee. I had to do it. They'd kill me if I lost. I'm in too far, honey. This is the only way."

Cee's eyes burned. The tears fell fast and free, running down her cheeks. "Y-you bet…me?" It was a question to which she already knew the answer. She looked at Marty. "Am I going to die?"

The big man didn't respond. His casual friendliness had been left at the door.

She turned to Gianni and Geno. "Are you gonna kill me?"

Gianni shrugged. "Probably not, but that's up to you. This is a very profitable business, and there's lots of money to be made. Play your cards right, and maybe that money might find its way into your pocket. Or cross me and…" he ran a finger across his throat. "But that's neither here nor there. We still have one last game to play." Gianni reached into his suit pocket and pulled out a battered red and black poker chip. "As you can see by his condition, Daddy hasn't done well. Let's hope, for his sake and yours, he does better on this last one."

"Black. I fucking choose black," Vinnie spat. Snot ran down his face and into his mouth. "Now flip the goddamn coin and end this!"

Gianni's smile wavered and faltered. His hand shot out and grabbed Vinnie's remaining ear, twisting it into an angry shade of red. "Listen here, you slug. I make the fucking rules. Me, not you. Keep running your mouth, and I'll let Geno take your daughter apart with a fucking hacksaw. You hear me?"

Vinnie shuddered, grimaced in pain, and nodded.

"What? I can't fucking hear the marbles rattling around that empty skull of yours."

"Yes! I-I hear you. I'm sorry, Gianni… ah, Mr. Lito."

"Much, much better." Gianni sneered. He released Vinnie's ear, which remained red and angry. Gianni rolled the poker chip over his knuckles, letting it dance. "Okay, let's do this." He stopped the coin and held it up for everyone to see. "The bettor has chosen black."

Vinnie nodded enthusiastically.

"Okay then," Gianni said. He flipped the coin into the air. Red, black, red, black, the coin spun.

Time slowed as Cee watched it flip over and over while her life hung in the balance.

COLLECTING PAYMENT

Gianni snatched it out of the air and slapped it on the back of his left hand.

Cee thought she was going to puke.

Gianni smiled at Vinnie and peeled his fingers back, revealing the chip. The red side faced up like a bloody hole in the back of his hand. "Oh, what terrible luck, Vinnie."

Vinnie's sobs turned to blubbering. His glossy eyes fell on his daughter. "Baby, I'm so fucking sorry."

Cee's head was spinning. Her world closed around her as the edges of her vision faded to black. Her focus snapped back when Gianni spoke.

"Geno, get me the ice pick."

"With pleasure, boss." Smiling wide, Geno grabbed the tool. The ice pick was long, thin, and sharp, perfect for piercing flesh.

"Wha-what are you doing with that?" Vinnie asked. He pulled against the bonds holding him down. The leather straps held fast.

"Marty, help Geno and flip this cocksucker onto his side," Gianni ordered. "I got something for him."

"No, I'm free now, you fucking promised!" Vinnie shrieked. He was raving and thrashing.

Marty grabbed Vinnie's balls through his pants and squeezed them. "Now listen here, this is fucking happening, you hear me? The boss says it's happening, so it's fucking happening." He put his lips close to Vinnie's remaining ear. "What kind of piece of shit brings his daughter to a place like this?"

Vinnie took shallow breaths—appearing to be in pain. "Fuck you," he muttered through gritted teeth, but he stopped fighting.

Marty released his scrotum and unstrapped one hand while Geno handled the corresponding leg. Together, they flipped Vinnie onto his side.

"Please, Gianni, don't do this. Whatever it is, please. I paid my debt. You have her now. Just let me go!"

"Oh, I'm gonna let you go," Gianni said. He ran the icepick down Vinnie's spine, stopping just before his lower back. The tool left an angry red mark on Vin's flesh. "But you ain't walking out of here. In fact, you ain't walking ever again." Gianni plunged the icepick into Vinnie's spine.

Vinnie screamed and tried to thrash, but his limbs ceased to work. His world went numb—each limb was now just a memory.

"Get him the fuck out of here," Gianni said to Marty. He tossed the icepick back on the table.

"Yes sir," Marty said. He keyed up his radio, which was connected to an earpiece.

"Bring a wheelchair to The Red Room ASAP." A jumbled voice replied, but only Marty could make it out. He unstrapped Vinnie's paralyzed body from the table and pulled him off.

Cee shuddered when her father's limp frame hit the stone floor with a thump. He didn't cry out in pain—that was a lost sensation. His tears still flowed.

Marty dragged him to the door. He pulled it open and yanked Vinnie into the hallway.

The door slammed behind him.

Cee felt like a caged animal.

The two remaining men stared at her like predators. Their gazes roamed her body and smiles formed.

Gianni began rubbing his crotch through his suit pants. He framed his cock with his hand, stroking it erect.

"Come here," he said.

Cee shuddered in revulsion. "Fuck you."

Gianni laughed. "Feisty, I like that." He was hard and well-hung. "I fucking hope you struggle. I do. It's only gonna hurt worse." He unbuckled his belt. "Now get over here before I make Geno bring you to me."

Cee had her back against the wall. Geno's sadistic grin perked. "Listen, cunt. You don't want me to grab you, so listen to the boss. You're our fucking property now, so get that sweet ass over here and take care of the boss."

She knew he was right—there was nowhere to go. Marty—the only person who *may* have been an ally—was gone. Cee's knees shook as she staggered forward. The table was between them, but Gianni moved to intercept her.

"Atta girl," he said. His pants fell to his ankles, revealing his swollen prick.

Cee wasn't a virgin, but she was far from experienced. She'd only had sex a few times, and it had been less than enjoyable and with less-endowed men.

"Turn around and bend over," Gianni said. He grabbed her shoulder and spun her, his bony fingers digging into the muscle.

The air rushed out of Cee as her stomach hit the stained leather. Small puddles of her father's blood pooled on the table. She quivered.

"Take your fucking pants down," Gianni commanded.

Cee lowered her pants. She was sweaty, yet cold, as her ass broke out in goosebumps. She left her panties—a plain white thong—on.

Gianni grabbed her underwear and pulled it. The fabric bit into her vagina as he yanked.

"Oh, you wanna be cute, huh?" Gianni tugged harder,

but the thong didn't rip.

Cee writhed in pain. "Sorry, I'll take them off; just give me a chance." She grabbed at the sides of her underwear, but the tension was too much.

"Stay still," Gianni said.

Cee heard a click as a pocketknife locked in place. With one swipe, Gianni cut her thong off, letting it drop to the floor. Cee looked down and saw blood on the front of her ruined garment.

"Just stay bent over and don't fucking piss me off again," Gianni growled in her ear.

Cee bent over the bloody table. She closed her eyes as the old man's fingers entered her sex.

"Yeah, this is a good little pussy, all right. But I'm not taking that." His thumb, wet with her secretions, played over her snug anus. "No. To break a wild horse, you need to ride it rough." Gianni hocked a loogie on her asshole.

Cee cringed as the warm saliva ran down her crack. Both of Gianni's thumbs spread her open. She took a deep breath then screamed.

***

Marty stood outside of the Red Room, listening to the screams and laughter. His fists clenched and unclenched. But this wasn't his fight.

Yet.

THE SEED OF TOMORROW

Two years had passed since Cee had been bet away to Shadows. A lot had changed for her. She'd learned more than she could've imagined but never forgot that first day. The feeling of Gianni's slimy member inside her was something that gnawed at her.

Cee walked the casino floor, dressed in a black shirt and matching slacks. After Gianni had broken her, Cee accepted her fate. She hated to admit it, but part of her embraced the casino life. Thanks to her old man, it was all she'd known.

A deep, dark recess of her damaged mind came alive in the neon lights inside Shadows. Seeing the life and death of the bettors, the screams and shouts of winners and losers—it was all perfection. Each day was different. Different players, different circumstances.

In the beginning, Cee was passive aggressive toward the new arrangements. But she soon grew to love the casino life, becoming a valuable member of the crew. Her brutality and cunning were always on display, earning her a bloody reputation. She'd never forget the violations committed against her, instead learned and watched.

The first time Cee witnessed a man die in the casino, she didn't know what to feel.

It was nerve-wracking, but oddly, she wasn't scared. The only other time she'd seen someone die, it was out of necessity.

In Shadows, death came through choice and greed. It intrigued her. To see life fade from someone's eyes was magical. It filled the room with an uncanny power unlike anything she'd ever known.

Shadows was an underground orchestra of chaos, bloodshed, and money. Gianni Lito was its conductor. The vile man had a finger on the pulse of his domain, and no one would speak out against him. His staff scurried underfoot, afraid of him sending his goons or Geno, after them. The first time she'd seen him shoot another staff member at the orders of the boss, she knew things would never be the same for her.

Cee hung back at a roulette table, watching a woman tear her fingernails from their weeping beds.

"Put these all on red, please." She handed the chewed nails to the croupier.

Peggy, a senior employee of Shadows, took the bet without flinching. Over the many years of her employment, Peggy had things much worse than fingernails in her hands. She dropped the nails on the large red rectangle on the felt and picked up the white ball. With trained efficiency, she tossed the smooth piece of ivory into the spinning wheel.

"Anything good?" Marty asked.

Cee didn't jump. She'd seen him coming out of the corner of her eye. "Eh, some broad just bet her fingernails. Nothing major. Now, if she loses and puts up an eyeball, then our night might get more interesting."

Marty nodded. "We haven't had one of those in a while. At least it seems that way."

The ball spun, slowly losing its momentum. It bounced in the slots of the wheel, seeking its ultimate resting place.

"I'm sure the old bastard would like that," Cee said. "I feel like the only person to see the Red Room in the last week was Jasper, and he was one of us."

Marty popped a cigarette into his mouth and lit it. He blew the smoke into the air and offered one to Cee. She plucked one out of the pack and accepted his light. Her smoke mingled with his as it drifted toward the high stone ceilings.

"Yeah, that was fucking rough alright," Marty said. He squinted as smoke went into his eyes. "I get it. He thought Jas was stealing from the house, but to let Geno cut him up like that? Especially with no solid evidence? Just wrong, in my opinion."

Cee smiled as the ball landed in a black spot on the wheel. She smoked, letting it flow out of her nostrils. "It seems like Gianni has been making more and more accusations of late. Most are unwarranted and, frankly speaking, bullshit."

"Scary times, indeed," Marty said. He put his cigarette out in an ashtray on the table nearest to him. "Luckily, he still let me make some new hires." He checked his watch. "In fact, they should be here soon."

"Oh yeah? More muscle, I assume?" Her cigarette joined his in the ashtray alongside half a dozen others.

"You can never have enough muscle, especially in a joint like this."

"True. And he let you pick them and not Geno? I'm shocked." Cee put a hand to her chest in disbelief.

Marty chuckled. "Yeah, that fucking guinea meatball wouldn't know a good hire if it bit him on his fucking nose."

Cee sucked her teeth and licked the sourness inside her mouth. "Loyal?"

Marty nodded. "Absolutely. I wouldn't have it any other way."

"Hmm, interesting," Cee said, locking eyes with the big man.

"Don't even fucking say it. Not again, never again, especially in here."

Cee batted her eyelashes in innocence. "Whatever do you mean?"

Marty wasn't smiling, and he didn't think it was a joke. He leaned in close to her. "You know what I mean, Cee. Don't fuck with this guy. I'd think after two years you'd get it by now."

Cee got it, yes she did. She understood better than anyone.

It had been three weeks ago when she'd asked Marty what he'd do if something happened to Gianni. Something bad and permanent, perhaps—like a trip to The Red Room. Marty shut her down almost immediately, but she'd seen the chink in his armor. That seed, the seed of a coup, had been planted. It wasn't hard to do, especially with Gianni at the helm.

The old man had become even worse over the last few years. Even more so than when Cee had been given to him. Killing in The Red Room was always vile, but his attitude toward the employees—the degrading things he'd do to them or make them do to him—was uncalled for.

Chrissy, a blackjack dealer, had a few awful nights in a row. Every hand she played was beaten, losing the house a substantial amount of money. And that was just poor luck for Shadows. But to Gianni, he saw it as theft and disloyalty. She must've been doing *something* to cause the consistent losses.

After Geno worked her over with a pool cue, she'd admitted to not using the auto shuffle. It was laziness, but she was six months pregnant with a four-year-old son at home. Her sleep had been shit, and the sound of the auto shuffle was grating to her battered brain. She'd lost the baby in the employee bathroom; a bruised and deformed fetus was stillborn in the toilet. Chrissy had nearly died that day and hadn't returned since.

That was one of the worst incidents Cee had witnessed, but she knew there were plenty of others. It was taking a toll on them, and this wasn't a job you could just put in two weeks' notice and quit. You were there for the long haul or you disappeared altogether.

Cee and Marty perked up when their earpieces came to life. There was static and a squeal of feedback over the little speakers. Each of them reached to adjust the volume on their radios, awaiting the message.

"Cee, come in, Cee," Geno said.

She shot a glare at Marty and keyed up her radio. "Go ahead," she said.

"The boss needs to see you in his office. It's urgent, so don't fucking dally around."

The line went dead.

"What's that about?" Marty asked, his brow furrowing.

"Beats the shit out of me," she said. Cee's mouth went dry, and her brain raced to figure out what the impromptu meeting could be about. "But I don't want to keep him waiting."

"Good luck," Marty said.

DISGRACED

Cee walked through the crowd of gamblers, many of them giving her a wide berth. Her reputation had preceded her, and anyone thinking she was an easy target for an ass grab would be sorry. Cee scanned her badge inside the elevator, lighting up the 'O' option on the button panel.

The elevator car rumbled through the old mine shaft then stopped with a lurch. Gianni's office door was open, and he was leaning against the large desk. His disheveled hair was longer than usual and rested on the nape of his neck. Geno stood next to him, looking rather greasy. A fresh crop of blackheads littered his bulbous nose.

"Ah, Cee, thank you for joining us," Gianni said. "Please, shut the door."

Cee pushed the large door shut and stood waiting.

"Yeah, sure, no problem," she said.

Gianni's pupils were wide. "Come closer." He flashed his teeth. "I won't bite." With a wink, he added, "Hard."

Cee moved closer, standing in front of both men. "Better?"

"Oh yes, much," Gianni said. "Now, if you wouldn't mind, get down on your knees."

Cee's face scrunched up. "My knees? What for?"

Gianni, without the slightest hint of jest, said, "Because you're gonna suck my cock."

"Are you fucking joking? I don't have time for this. I need to be back on the floor. Marty has two new hires and he'll ne—"

Cee froze when Gianni pointed a gun at her face. "I'm not fucking joking. I'll paint the walls with that smart fucking brain of yours, you little cunt." Gianni's finger caressed the trigger of the Glock.

Thanks to Marty, Cee knew the semi-auto had a five-and-a-half-pound trigger pull and the old man was squeezing. "So, you can blow me, or I'll blow you."

Cee looked at Geno, hoping the toadish man would give her an inkling this was a joke. a sick fucking joke she couldn't fathom. No humor lived in his eyes—none. For the last two years Cee worked alongside them, becoming part of the crew. At least, she thought.

The gun wavered in Gianni's hand as he inched the trigger back a little further.

"Fuck, alright, I'll fucking do it!" Cee kneeled in front of the old man's crotch. The cool muzzle of the gun kissed her forehead. She knew she'd have a .40 caliber indentation in her flesh when this nightmarish ordeal was over.

"Atta girl. Now get sucking; I want to watch the magic show soon."

Cee undid his fly, working his semi-hard cock out of his pants. Gianni's foreskin was around his glans. The putrid stink wafted toward her as she rolled the flesh back. She tried not to gag when his cock touched her lips. The gun barrel moved with her rhythm, always keeping pressure on her forehead. Gianni—for an older guy—could still pack a solid erection. It grew in her mouth as the paste from his fetid foreskin coated her tongue.

"Geno," Gianni said, "she's doing okay, but it can always be better. Help our girl out, would ya?"

Cee watched Geno move out of the corner of her eye. With the muzzle of the gun pressed firmly to her forehead, she didn't dare stop. Gianni had snapped. Years of maiming and torturing people had rotted his old brain. It didn't help he'd grown an affinity for cocaine. She knew if she slowed or stopped, he'd put a bullet in her head. He might still do it anyway.

Geno stepped behind Cee and grabbed either side of her head. "Yeah, you really gotta get in there, honey."

Cee almost puked when Geno forced her head forward, shoving Gianni's entire cock down her throat. She gagged and put her hands on Gianni's thighs, hoping to limit the depth.

Gianni pushed the gun harder into her head. "No, no, no. Keep those hands down, and let Geno show you what to do. Broads these days don't know how to give a proper blowjob."

Cee let her hands fall to her sides as Gianni fucked her face. The sound of sucking and gagging echoed through the office.

"That's it, that's it." Gianni groaned. He rose onto his tippy toes and clenched. A torrent of cum burst from his piss slit and into Cee's waiting mouth.

Cee choked as the thick load shot down her throat. Tears ran down her face, smearing her mascara. They weren't tears of pain or sadness but unbridled hatred.

Gianni plucked his cock from her mouth. A final pearl of semen clung to his tip before it fell to the ground. He brushed his dirty hair back and wiped his nose with the back of his hand. He holstered his gun and smiled.

"Ah, that was nice." Gianni tucked his cock back into his pants. "Thank you, Cee. I forgot how young and supple your mouth is. We might have to make this a new routine."

He bent down close to her. The smell of semen on her breath was strong, but Gianni didn't seem to care.

"And don't fucking forget, the walls have ears, my dear. I know everything." Gianni zipped up. "Next time, I'll let Geno have his way with you, and he's not such a nice guy. Now, get the fuck out of here."

Cee staggered to her feet and wiped her eyes with the back of her hands. The black streaks remained. She knew she looked like microwaved shit but didn't care. This had to end. If Marty wouldn't help her, she'd do it on her own. She was done being the victim. Even if it cost her life.

AN UNSPOKEN AGREEMENT

Marty stood with the casino's two newest employees, Manx and Rachel. Their tour was brief—they were both well-versed in violence and knew how to take orders. Something that was beyond important in a place like Shadows. The elevator lit up and the doors parted. Marty caught his breath when he saw her exit.

Cee made a beeline toward him. She stopped and looked at the new employees before bringing her attention back to Marty.

"This is happening with or without you," Cee said.

Marty couldn't take his eyes off the young woman. She didn't look injured—just a red dot on her forehead. But there was something in her eyes, something that had changed. There were no more words; they'd already been spoken. Marty knew the girl would act with or without him, and he couldn't let her go of it alone.

"Okay, Cee. The Red Room tomorrow. We'll end this, once and for all."

Cee sniffled and looked at each of them. "No, Marty. Tonight."

Marty sucked air through his teeth but knew she was right. This was like tearing off a bandage—fast and violent.

"Okay, tonight." He looked at the other two. "Welcome to Shadows. I hope neither of you forgot how to kill."

Manx and Rachel smiled. Apparently, they hadn't.

SKIN IN THE GAME

Cee's makeup was fresh, and she'd gargled enough mouthwash to drown a rat. The phantom taste of Gianni's cock was still on her tongue, masked by mint.

Marty gave her a nod, and Cee nodded back—they were ready.

Marty keyed up his mic. "Geno, copy," he said.

A bit of feedback ran down the line with a hiss. "Go ahead."

"Let the boss know we're heading to The Red Room, and his services are going to be required." He paused. "We have a live one, that's for sure."

"Copy that," Geno replied. "The boss has been notified and we're en route." The line went silent.

"Okay, it's now or never," Marty said.

Manx and Rachel nodded. Each knew their role in the event things went south.

"Let's roll," Cee said.

She was already heading to the double doors. The Red Room lay at the end of the lights. For most people, it was the end of the road, but to Cee, the room represented a new beginning. It would be her room—a haven where she could do what she wanted when she wanted.

The lethal injection table sat empty, but it wouldn't be that way for long. She hoped she would not be the one occupying it anytime soon. If Marty got cold feet, Cee would be dead, and dead horribly.

The sound of keys in the lock grabbed their attention. Marty touched the pistol on his hip. He knew it was there and fully loaded, but he had to make sure.

"Okay, who do we have here?" Gianni said. He walked in with Geno directly behind him. Rachel slammed the door shut, locking it.

Gianni looked around, his eyes squinting at the empty table. "What the fuck is going on?"

Cee leaned against the table full of tools. Her hands were empty but her eyes were debating which wicked instrument she'd be using shortly.

"It's over, Gianni. You're fucking over," she said.

Gianni laughed and smacked Geno on the chest. "Can you believe the stones on this cunt? Eh? I take her in, feed her, clothe her, pay her, and for what? A measly blowjob here and there? That ain't shit. I could have put your fucking ass in The Doll House and made some real money off you. But no, this fucking bitch is never satisfied. You don't like a cock in your mouth? Too fucking bad. You fucks don't like being talked down to? Too fucking bad. I gave you everything! Things most people would kill for! And this, *this* is how you repay me?"

Cee studied his outburst. He was raving now. Rage and betrayal drove his face to a mask of madness.

"You know what?" he asked. "Fuck it. You're all done. I can get more goons like you anywhere. You're nothing special. I have a small army of pit bosses and other muscle upstairs." He looked at his bodyguard. "Geno, waste these cunts."

Geno went to draw his pistol, but Marty was faster. Marty's Glock was already in his hand and pointed square at Geno. The gun barked twice, both rounds hitting him in the chest.

Geno no longer seemed concerned with drawing his gun, rather he tried to hold in the flood of gore pouring from his body. He was going down, but Marty wasn't done. He emptied the gun into Geno's head. Marty's teeth were gritted, and every muzzle flash was like a picture in time. Each bullet deformed the ugly man's face even more. The hollow points tore through flesh and bone, filling with meat as they exited into the wall and floor.

Marty dropped the spent magazine and rammed home a full one, sending the slide forward.

Gianni pushed his suit jacket out of the way, going for his gun.

Cee knew Marty wanted to kill Gianni, to empty the fresh line of bullets into his body. But she had different plans.

Gianni drew his gun and Manx moved.

The new bodyguard was lightning quick, pulling a K-Bar from behind his back. He swung it, aiming for Gianni's upper arm. The fighting knife plunged through Gianni's flesh, pinning his arm to his ribcage.

"Ah, fuck!" he screamed.

Cee stepped up to the wounded man and fished his pistol from behind his back. She wanted to say something clever—to shout at him and say it was her that was undoing his legacy. But she didn't. He wasn't worth her breath.

"Get this sack of shit on the table," Cee ordered.

Marty and his two goons yanked the bloody old man onto the lethal injection table. Manx pulled his knife free, unleashing a gout of blood. Together, they strapped him down.

"Please, Cee, don't do this," Gianni cried.

Cee wasn't even listening. The time for crying was over. She'd shed enough tears for two lifetimes and had no more left. Especially for this piece of human garbage. Quietly and with purpose, Cee began cutting off Gianni's clothes.

"God fucking dammit, Cee," Gianni said. "Stop it now, before it's too late."

For a moment, she stopped. "I think we're past *too late*." Cee cut and ripped until the old man was nude. His cock was shriveled and hiding in a thatch of salt and pepper pubic hair. Cee flicked his nuts. "Not so big and bad now, are we?" She grabbed a fillet knife off the table. Like a butcher, she ran it over a sharpening steel until the edge glimmered.

"You don't know what you're doing," Gianni squeaked. "I have friends—investors that will be fucking pissed. They'll come for you." He looked at all of them. "They'll come for all of you. You think the games are bad? Huh, these savages will rip you to shreds! They'll put you through a blender and mash your useless bodies to a pulp! And then they'll find your families, every bit of your fucking bloodline and do the same! Fuck, you'll never make it out of the casino alive. I have loyal people here, lots of them. Cut me free and take Geno's spot. He was a useless piece of shit anyway. You can be my right hand. I know you're smart and ruthless." Gianni's chest thrummed with each beat of his heart.

Cee stood by his legs, looking at his cock. The phallus that had violated her years prior in that very room and hours earlier that very day. Her throat was still sore from the most recent invasion. She squeezed the handle of the knife and eyed up his nude flesh. Stepping closer, she allowed the blade to lead the way.

Gianni strained his neck, trying to look down at her. "Stop! Don't do this."

The tip of the blade entered his taint.

"Ah!" Gianni screamed.

Cee pushed the blade deeper. Blood and piss ran from the wound, wetting the table. The violence wasn't too much for her. She grinned and cut upward.

"Does that hurt?" Cee toyed. Her eyes were narrowed and focused on pain. "Good, I fucking hope it does." She sliced, freeing his scrotum. It hung like a discarded lump of gory flesh. "You know, I like to hurt too."

Gianni wailed like a newborn baby that had just been slapped on the ass.

Cee twisted the knife and continued on. "Actually, I love it. Ever since I was a girl, I've been in love with it. But you showed me a new world of torment. Watching the games, the torture, the look on the faces of the condemned. And you? Huh, you knew how to hurt them. This was your art studio, and you were Monet, painting with blood and pain. But now you find yourself here."

As the cuts ran farther, loosening the skin above his penis, Gianni serenaded her with a barrage of guttural moans.

Cee watched the blood surge from under his flesh. "You pushed too far, harming those who served you. You kicked the dog too many times, and now you're getting bit."

Another long slice slid around his pubic hair. She severed his cock at the base and crimson ran down his ass crack.

She shook her head. "You had it all and could've reigned for years, but you had to push it." Inspired, she drove the knife deeper. The smell of shit permeated the air as Cee punctured his bowels. "And guess what? You pushed too fucking far." Cee grabbed his dick and pulled it taut. She sliced the few remaining strands of flesh holding his manhood to his body.

Gianni wailed and watched his genitals come off in Cee's fist. The young lady held them aloft like a macabre trophy.

"Here," Cee said, holding the severed cock and balls out to Rachel. "Find a jar and put it on his desk. Correction, *my* desk."

Rachel didn't flinch as she took the genitals from Cee. She grabbed a piece of plastic from the table and wrapped it like deli meat.

Cee wasn't done with Gianni, though—not by a long shot. She moved around the puddle of gore that had formed at the bottom of the table, stopping at his head.

Gianni was semi-conscious; the blood loss was getting to him. She wanted him alive and awake for what came next—at least for most of it. Cee grabbed his gray hair and pulled.

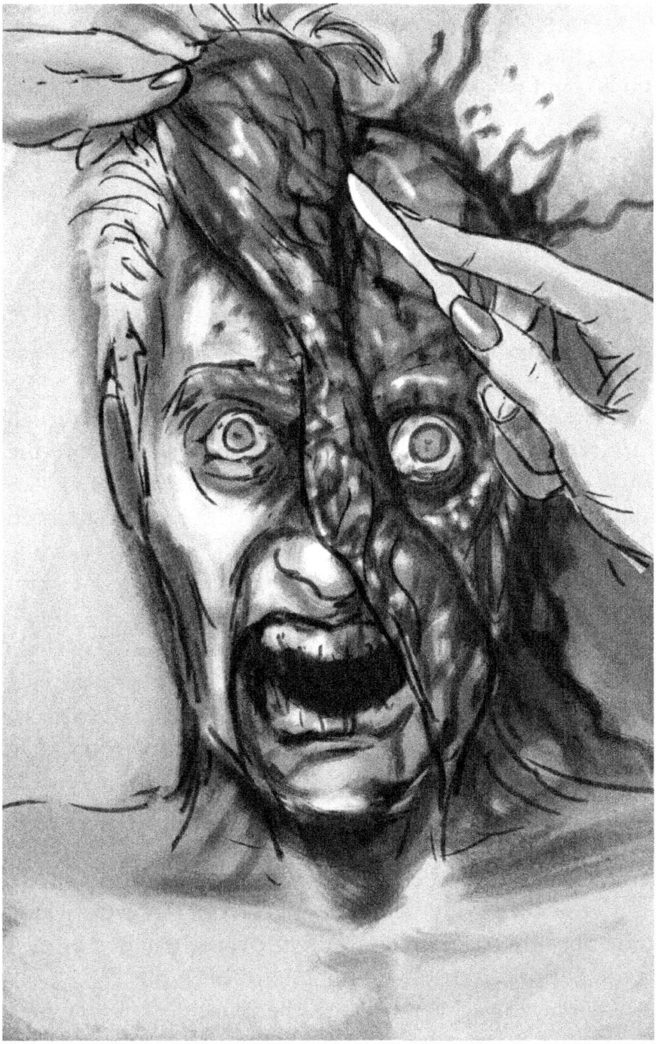

She placed the edge of the blade at his hairline and cut. The flesh split, forming a crimson line followed by a cascade of blood.

Gianni moaned. He tried to thrash and scream, but his elderly body was giving up the ghost.

Cee dug her fingers into the opening and pulled, freeing the skin from the bone. The knife worked, skinning the rest of his face.

"A little help," Cee said. Marty stepped forward and grabbed the skin flap. He pulled as she cut—the perfect team.

Gianni vomited, his bile and partially digested food covered the exposed muscle of his face.

Cee and Marty didn't slow down. The knife worked its way around Gianni, and Marty pulled and pulled. Each inch of flesh that was removed cried like a tearing canvas.

Gianni seized and bubbled more sputum from his mouth.

Cee was sweating but smiling. Her blade slid and cut, reaching Gianni's legs. Marty worked the flesh free, keeping it intact. Cee never told him to do that; he just knew.

Gianni died with a wet fart and a burst of liquid shit. Cee didn't stop, only increasing the fervor of her cuts until it was finally over.

Marty pulled the skin free, holding it up to show Cee her handy work.

She could've wept at the beauty. With shaking hands, she took the warm, old skin. "Perfect." She spun and looked at Manx. "Take this." She pushed it into his arms. The skin-feet dragged on the ground. "I want this pinned like a fucking bug on black velvet and cased in glass. This will be the first thing the guests will see when they enter Shadows. They will know better than to cross me."

Manx rolled the skin up and wrapped it in plastic. "Consider it done, boss."

Marty wiped his hands on Gianni's shredded suit pants. He stopped when he felt something in the pocket.

Marty pulled it out, holding the battered red and black poker chip in front of his face. Cee's eyes lit up and, without asking, Marty tossed it to her.

Cee snatched the chip out of the air. Her bloody fingers caressed each side, her heart racing from the memory of that fateful day two years prior. The last time she saw that chip get flipped she was on the wrong side of it. But next time around, she'd be doing the flipping.

Her former boss—the man who'd imprisoned her and tormented her—lay dead, the front of his body skinned.

"What next?" Marty asked.

Cee pocketed the poker chip, knowing it would spin soon. "Round up the rest of the security and pit bosses and bring them to my office. We'll find out who's loyal to me, and who wants to die." The gory knife was still in her hand, dripping blood onto the floor.

Marty nodded and smirked. "Consider it done."

THREE YEARS LATER

DEFORMED DOLLS

Cee snapped awake, allowing the memories to drift away like a gambler's life savings. It had been five years since her father had bet her away. Five years since the one man who was supposed to be her protector gambled her away like she was nothing. A glorious three years of her running the casino that made so much money and drank so much blood. At first, she feared repercussions from the investors, but her profits were more than Gianni's. The shadowy men and women behind the casino were only loyal to one thing: cash.

She was sweaty, wrapped in her sheets. Cee tossed them off and stared at the ceiling. She didn't enjoy sleeping at the casino, but it was a necessity. Calypso the Cunning was performing later that night, and Cee wanted to be around to ensure the act went off without an issue. She slid her feet into a pair of slippers and put on a silk robe—black, naturally.

She walked out of the small bedroom and into her spacious office. A computer rested on her desk with a wide monitor showing the vast array of cameras placed about the casino.

Cee dropped into the chair and scanned the cameras. She removed a pack of cigarettes from the desk drawer. The monitor flickered as she lit her smoke. Shadows was bustling, even early in the night. Dregs from all over the world would come to the underground casino for a chance at riches or to feed their deepest perversions.

Smoke rose from the cigarette clenched between her fingers. Cee's gaze bounced back and forth from one hellish game onscreen to the next.

A bettor lost a hand of blackjack. He must've bet with flesh because he was getting one hell of a beating. Cee smiled, watching her employees smash the bettor's face repeatedly.

To Cee, there was something erotic about violence. She'd been baptized in blood. Sex and murder went hand in hand. The reverberations of her younger years shaped her, nudging her toward a wicked lust. Her dream, even though it brought back harsh memories, had awoken a primal urge.

Another camera, one of her favorites, gave her a perfect view of The Red Room. Cee enlarged it, gazing at one of her prized possessions: the severed manhood of Gianni. His severed cock and balls floated in a jar of murky liquid on the table in the hellish room. Bits of flesh had long since settled on the bottom of the glass.

Shadows provided everything: sex, drugs, and all the violence Cee could gorge herself on. Warmth flooded her vagina, burning between her thighs. She crossed her legs and squeezed them tight, grinding.

Cee took a final drag on her cigarette and crushed it out. She grabbed the mouse, leaving her view of The Red Room and ran the pointer over another screen.

The Doll House was her personal treasure trove—one part strip club, one part whorehouse. Black lights and neon strobes danced, revealing stains of random DNA on almost every piece of furniture. The girls of The Doll House were hers to choose from. Each one of them told a story, and most of them displayed their tales in flesh. Whether it was an amputated limb, a missing eye, a patch of burned skin, or any other penalty for losing a bet, almost all of them were marked. Most of them didn't come to the casino to be whores, getting fucked by the wealthy. No, they started as gamblers, betting on themselves. Betting on the fact they could beat the house. Well, they found out the house always wins. And for the last three years, Cee had been the house.

Akari, a legless Japanese woman, rolled by in her wheelchair. Her black hair was trussed up, and she had just enough cleavage showing. Cee grinned at the memory of taking the woman's legs from her. The bite of the hacksaw blade…

Just because her legs don't work doesn't mean her pussy can't.

Cee squirmed in the chair, relishing the slickness growing between her thighs. Akari had been a favorite of Cee's for a while, but like everything else, she had grown tired of the Asian woman.

Maya strutted by, her wide ass cheeks parted by a G-string. Her dark skin was smooth and unblemished. At least on her behind. Her face was another story. Maya had a bit of a problem with Pai Gow, a problem that had caught up to her as she bet away both ears and an eye. When she'd lost the final game, it was her last eye or The Doll House. She'd taken the latter, becoming one of the most popular girls in the club.

Cee opened her legs and pushed her panties aside. She could smell the sweaty musk as she caressed herself. To her, watching The Doll House was like shopping. One of the girls would be joining her shortly, but she hadn't picked yet.

Her smile faltered as her eyes landed on Lilly.

Lilly was far from perfect, as everyone in the casino had demons, but there was something about her that Cee loathed. Lilly wasn't like the other girls. Her risk-taking was non-existent. While her body wasn't the best, she didn't bear any deformities from debt. Cee couldn't stand her.

Fucking, bitch. Thinks she's so much smarter than everyone else.

Porsche came into view, talking with Lilly. She pulled an oxygen tank behind her. A long tube ran into the mask fitted over her face.

Porsche was a girl who liked to gamble. A bad loss at the craps table had her eating some rather nasty stuff. On one occasion she was forced to drink a shot of gasoline. Not thinking straight, Porsche sparked up a cigarette, torching her throat and lungs. Luckily for her, she survived, but she'd lost most functionality of her lungs. The only thing that kept her going was the tank she wheeled behind her.

This handicap didn't stop men from fucking her. Some men got off on it. Those men that had an elder kink, but still wanted the semi-firm body of a thirty-year-old. Porsche wore a blue teddy, with a pair of boy shorts peeking from underneath. Her saggy ass hung out, showing cellulite dimples.

Cee continued to touch herself and made her pick. She pressed a button on her phone, and Marty picked up in one ring.

"Yes, boss," he said over the speaker.

Cee grinned. "Go down to The Doll House and bring me Porsche."

BUCKING BRONCO

The oxygen mask hissed as Porsche walked into the office. Cee sat behind the desk still clad in her robe watching Porsche breathe deeply. Her mask fogged as she exhaled hard.

"Anything else?" Marty asked.

A fresh cigarette burned between Cee's fingers. She took a drag and exhaled through her nose.

"No, I'll call if I need you," Cee said. She put the cigarette out in the ashtray, maintaining eye contact with her bodyguard.

Cee knew Marty hated leaving her alone with anyone, especially a girl from The Doll House. The rumors about what Cee did to some girls weren't all fake. Some of the worst accusations were real. Marty saw it all and cleaned up every mess she made. There was always a chance a girl would fight back, attacking and maybe killing Cee. That was unacceptable, but Marty followed her orders, even if they were flawed. A trait that carried over from combat, Marty had seen his fair share of piss-poor command decisions. Some of which cost men, like him, their lives. It seemed, lately, Cee had been making more messes for him to clean up.

Marty left, shutting the office door.

"You wanted," Porsche breathed, "to see me?" Her blonde hair was down and looked like it hadn't been washed in weeks. Bangs that were at least a decade out of style, curled on her forehead.

Cee stood. "Come, follow me." Without waiting, Cee walked to her bedroom and opened the door.

Porsche followed behind, dragging her oxygen. The wheels on the tank squeaked and squealed, as if in protest.

Cee stood at the foot of the bed, arms crossed beneath her breasts. Finally, Porsche joined her.

"Strip," Cee demanded. She looked the prostitute up and down.

Porsche didn't hesitate. She took a deep hit of oxygen and pulled her mask off. Quickly, she yanked the teddy over her head. Heavy tits lined with blue veins, dropped out. Gasping like a fish out of water, Porsche grabbed her mask and strapped it over her head once again. She then removed her underwear. Her labia drooped, looking like a pair of pink elephant ears. Black stubble covered her pubic mound and surrounded her lips.

Cee sneered in disgust. It was no wonder Porsche didn't get more customers. Her pussy looked like a cold-cut massacre with a 5 o'clock shadow. It didn't matter; Cee wasn't concerned with the appearance of the woman's snatch.

"Here," Cee said, reaching behind the door. She pulled out a strap-on dildo. It was thick and stout, made of quality latex. "Put this over that mess you call a cunt." She threw it at Porsche, striking her in the chest.

Porsche bent and picked it up. Obeying Cee, she strapped the sex toy to herself, positioning it on her pubic mound.

"Good," Cee said. "Now get on the bed."

Slowly, Porsche crawled onto the bed. Unsure of what Cee wanted. The rubber cock stuck out jauntily from between her legs. Porsche positioned her oxygen tank next to her, puffing away.

"No, lie on your back. I'm going to do all the work. If I

waited on you to fuck me with that thing, I wouldn't cum until next week," Cee said. She dropped her robe and peeled her moist panties off.

Porsche looked relieved. The exertion of just walking to the office was enough to get the disabled prostitute breathing heavily. Cee helped Porsche uncoil some of the extra tubing on the oxygen tank, making it long enough that she could lie on the bed.

"Put your arms back," Cee ordered.

Porsche was slow to listen, but did. She knew the penalty for disobeying.

Cee cuffed Porsche's wrists to the bed frame. The oxygen mask fogged up as Porsche panicked.

"Shh," Cee said, rubbing the other woman's face. "I just like a little role-play from time to time." Moving to Porsche's feet, Cee secured them as well. Porsche's heartbeat was visible in her chest. Her breasts hung near her armpits, as she tried to control her breathing.

Cee opened a small nightstand and removed a bottle of lube. She sprayed the sex toy with a generous amount. "See, easy night for you," Cee said as she mounted Porsche. "Just lay there, and let me do all the work." Reaching between her legs, Cee grabbed the greased-up tip of the dildo and positioned it under her sex. Slowly, she descended, impaling her pussy with the rubber phallus.

Cee didn't consider herself a lesbian, but she would rarely fuck men. It wasn't an attraction thing; it was about power. She didn't feel weakened by men, but there was always the fear of getting pregnant. Abortions were an option, but that wasn't a route she wanted to take.

Even though the sex would be consensual and she'd insist on controlling the tempo, there was just something demeaning about getting fucked. Having a man coat her tits with his cum could be a fun time, but it was something Cee found submissive. And she was far from submissive.

Porsche gasped as Cee lowered her full weight down onto the rubber cock.

Wet slurping noises echoed in the room as Cee found her rhythm. Faster she rode, arching her back to hit all those perfect angles. She put her hands on Porsche's stomach, leaning forward so she could grind her clit against the raised nub of the strap-on.

Porsche's oxygen mask fogged up as she fought against the added weight. Instinctively, she pulled at the cuffs, but they held fast.

"You like that?" Cee asked, slowing her fucking. The dildo squelched as she descended to the base. "If you think that was fun, wait until I do this." Cee grabbed the clear tube running from Porsche's oxygen tank to the mask on her face.

The prostitute's eyes went wide, and she tugged at her restraints. Her face scrunched in primal fear as the realization that she was trapped set in.

"You girls know how to eat pussy like no man, that I'll give you. But when it comes to fucking, even from the bottom, you're clueless. Most of the others will give it their all, really ramming me with this, or whatever other toy I tell them to. But you, you're a dead lay."

Porsche struggled as Cee pinched the line shut, cutting off the flow of life-saving air. "But, but…" Porsche tried to plead her case, to explain to Cee that she didn't even have the opportunity to fuck. As if Cee didn't know that. Like this wasn't all part of the plan when she'd called the disabled woman to her room.

It had been a few seconds since Cee cut off the air supply. Porsche pulled at her cuffs and strained her feet. There was nothing she could do. As a last act of desperation, she bucked, attempting to throw Cee off her.

"Mmm, there you go," Cee moaned. Porsche's hips thrust up, as if she were trying to impale Cee. Instead, she gave her what she wanted: a good, hard fucking. "Atta girl." She raised her hips higher, allowing for a greater range of motion. Soon, she was able to get Porsche's rhythm down and began riding her again.

Porsche was turning blue. The oxygen line was wrapped in Cee's hand and pinched tight. She bucked and thrust, but the only thing she accomplished was fucking Cee even better.

"Fuck me, you crippled bitch!" Cee screamed. The wetness of her pussy and the fear-piss that Porsche had sprayed, made the bed squelch with every thrust. Cee was almost there. With a free hand, she grabbed her breast. Kneading the soft flesh, she pulled at her swollen nipple.

Porsche whipped her head side to side, desperately trying to get the mask off. It was useless, and she needed to breathe.

Cee leaned into the sex toy, teasing her clit once again, sending her over the edge. She came as Porsche finally stopped moving. Shuddering breath escaped Cee's mouth as she felt the whore go limp. She braced herself, digging her fingers into Porsche's flesh, as she leaned forward. Dark hair hung low as the last pulse of the orgasm ebbed out of Cee's body. A final groan escaped Porsche's lips when Cee put more pressure on the dead woman's ribcage, forcing the remaining air from her lungs.

Cee rocked back, releasing the bent oxygen tube. She whipped her hair back out of her face, looking down at the dead whore.

Porsche's eyes were bloodshot. Burgundy streaks ran down her abused wrists, cut by the handcuffs. Bloody foam was still popping inside of the useless oxygen mask. It released a subtle hiss as the air flowed from the tank once again.

Cee braced herself and slid the rubber cock from her pussy. She stood on wobbly legs. A mixture of lube and sexual secretions ran down her thighs. Her room stunk of sex and piss, but luckily Porsche hadn't shit herself. Cee grabbed her robe and left the room, heading back to her desk. She popped another cigarette into her mouth, lighting it before grabbing the phone.

It hardly rang once. "Yes, boss," Marty said on the other line.

Cee exhaled smoke. "I need a cleanup in my room."

"I'll be right up with a few cleaners," Marty replied.

Cee rested her ass against the edge of the desk. "Thank you. Oh, and Marty?" she asked.

"Yes."

"Dump the body, but leave her oxygen tank in The Doll House. I want them all to see it. Just as a reminder who runs this place."

"Consider it done," Marty said.

Cee hung up. She blew a cloud of smoke toward the black ceiling, watching it vanish into the darkness. Electricity coursed through her veins. The night was just starting, and Cee needed a shower. She had a feeling there would be more death before sunrise.

THE WIDOW'S WEB

Cee felt like a new woman. Showered and dressed, she emerged from her room and went into the office. The corpse of Porsche had long since been removed and was being disposed of as she spritzed herself with two-thousand-dollar perfume. Cee's dress was snug, accenting her curves. Her cheeks were flushed from the warmth of the shower and the still-fading effects of the orgasm. She checked her make-up and hair one more time in the mirror before exiting the room.

Normally, she wouldn't walk around without Marty or another one of her guards, but she wasn't going to the casino floor. She was heading to the place where she'd been reborn—The Red Room.

Cee entered the private elevator, selecting the desired floor. Moments later, she stepped into a glum tunnel of rough rock. Her high heels clicked as she walked to a red door.

The Red Room: The Black Widow's lair. Lights popped on as Cee entered. She walked past the lethal injection table and her various instruments of torment. A small desk sat against the wall, and on it rested two items: a computer, and a jar. On the wall, additional monitors showed the view from multiple cameras in the casino.

Cee picked the jar up and looked at the mutilated cock and balls of Gianni. The meat floated and bobbed in her hands. She smiled, thinking back to that day.

Cee set the memento back down, ensuring it was on display. Most of the condemned focused on the tools of torture, but she wanted them to see the genitals. If at any point they thought it was all for show, that grotesque jar would snuff out their hope.

The monitors on the computer were lit, displaying the growing crowd at her casino. Cee lit a cigarette and watched the gamblers filter through. In they came, with smiles upon their faces. Some of them would never leave, especially not whole.

For every excited smile was a corresponding look of desperation. Men and women with pit stains on their shirts and faces that hadn't seen a good night's sleep in weeks. The dark-rimmed eyes of gamblers who had one last shot at glory. If only that bet could hit.

Winning big was the story of their lives, chasing the high of hitting a parlay or praying to the gods of roulette to stop the marble at the right time. But time and time again, the bets would miss, or the marble would bounce out at the last second. and the chips would land in the house's pocket, leaving the bettor destitute.

In most casino's, a loss like that would leave the players scraping together change for their next meal or pawning an heirloom to make rent. Not at Shadows. At Cee's casino, if you had flesh, you had a bet. It was a matter of how far you were willing to go. And she'd seen plenty of people go all the way.

Cee watched through a cloud of smoke as a bettor ripped out his fingernails at the poker table. Ears, noses, teeth, tits, dicks—they were all severed and bet. A few nails that would ultimately grow back were nothing.

Play was another thing that kept the casino moving and the money flowing. And for most bettors, playing with sex was almost as fun as money or skin. The Doll House was getting busy, with more and more bettors taking breaks from the machines and tables.

Cee brought up a main bank of cameras, showing the whorehouse from dozens of angles. Two brutes stood at the entrance. There was rarely any trouble with the patrons, but on the off chance someone got rowdy, they wouldn't like the outcome. Cee watched with a smirk as men and women filtered into The Doll House. Each one was a bag of money, there to release some stress and empty their wallets. The girls in the club would do anything for Shadows. Absolutely anything. They knew the consequences if they didn't.

Cee flipped between cameras, looking at the girls. There were many black globes and obvious cameras set up in the ceiling, but the hidden cameras were Cee's favorites. Each private room had one, including the dressing room. It was her little bit of voyeurism, a guilty pleasure that she couldn't help but indulge in.

Almost all the private rooms were occupied. Cee's pulse raced as she switched between each one, peeking in on the sins of the flesh.

One camera revealed Akari suspended from the ceiling by a harness. She was gagged and her arms were drawn behind her back. The john, a rather tall man with a potbelly, swung her back and forth. He held the scarred stumps of her legs, pulling her back, impaling her on his cock. Akari squealed with each entry into her ass—a girlish, stereotypical sound that drove the johns wild.

Cee clicked, finding another prostitute hard at work. Bonnie was repulsive to most men—morbidly obese, with smooth patches of scar tissue. Lumps of her fat had been scooped out—a nasty bet she'd lost years prior—leaving her mushy body resembling the surface of the moon. Still, to some men, she was a fetish.

The hefty whore kneeled on the floor in front of the bed. A small man, who couldn't have weighed over 130 pounds, lay on his back with his legs over his head. Bonnie's fat face was buried in his ass. As she tossed his salad, her fat jiggled with every aggressive lick of his turd cutter. The man was folded in half with his pecker pointed at his face. With a feverish pace, he stroked his dick.

Cee clicked off just as he blasted a load in his eyes.

Wandering The Doll House from above, Cee looked in on the more mundane offerings of the club. Girls gave lap dances to men and women. Lines of cocaine were snorted from bare asses. Not-so-discreet hand jobs were given in private booths. Tits—some beautiful, some hideous—were suckled and nibbled. All of it was part of the machine. With each spurt of cum or snail trail left on a pair of Chinos, the wheel spun. And with the wheel came money. Lots of money.

The girls were a commodity, livestock meant to sell and sometimes butcher. If a girl wasn't pulling her weight, there were ways of dealing with her. A certain group of clients had very *peculiar* tastes in fetishes. Tastes that would make most shy away. But to Cee, everything had a price. She liked to remind them of such, letting them know they meant nothing to her.

Cee found what she was looking for: Porsche's oxygen tank. It was tucked behind the bar, which would not work. The girls would never see it there, and Cee wanted to make a point. To play a little game. Cee picked up her radio and called Marty.

"Yeah?" he asked. The thumping of house music could be heard in the distance through the earpiece. He was still close to the strip joint.

"Go back into The Doll House and move that tank. I want it to be a little more visible," Cee said. She clicked through the cameras, finding her man.

Marty had his finger pressed to his earpiece as he entered the club. Men and women moved for him like schools of fish evading a shark. He walked behind the bar and grabbed the tank.

"Stick it by the stage," Cee said. "But keep it in the shadows. I want the lights to bring it to life when they hit it. It'll be a pleasant surprise for the girls."

Marty obeyed.

Some girls, those not being fingered or jerking a cock, noticed the oxygen tank in Marty's hand. A look of shock burst onto their faces like an unexpected cumshot. They were pros, and like an errant load, removed the surprise from their faces. They surely knew their co-worker wasn't coming back, that Porsche had been summoned to the chambers of the boss, the woman they all called The Black Widow, and would never return.

More patrons filtered in through the front door of the club, men and women looking to drown their sorrows in flesh. But Lilly walked in with a man that stood out to Cee.

He was of average height with a crop of red hair. His face had a sallow look of desperation, that of a broke newbie to the casino. Cee had seen them daily, their eyes wide from the perversions under the stone roof. But there was something else that caught her eye. Across the man's face and bleeding onto his neck was a port-wine birthmark. Cee had to do a double take to ensure his throat wasn't slashed.

The pair walked by the stage where a one-eyed dancer gyrated to house music. Her small tits shook as she squirmed and writhed, simulating sex with no one. Lilly's gaze drifted toward the stage as the lights flashed, pausing on the discarded air tank. It was only for a moment, but enough to get a smile out of Cee.

Cee grabbed another cigarette, lighting it as her dark eyes followed the mysterious man. He and Lilly moved through the club, stopping at the bar.

Cee watched with a sneer. While the other girls were shaking their tits and asses, Lilly was at the bar, still clothed. It did at least look like she had the remnants of spunk in her hair, from whom Cee didn't know. A blow job wasn't worth much, especially after giving a cut to the house, so if Lilly was going to earn her keep, she'd need to do better than that. And from the looks of it, she would not be earning much with the birthmarked man.

The two of them sat at the bar, eyeing each other up as if they were long-lost lovers, not a degenerate and a stripper with a load in her hair.

Cee reached into her desk and took out a bottle of bourbon and a glass. She generously filled it and sipped. A cigarette followed, mingling smoke with the booze on her tongue. Cee clicked the microphone icon. It was another aspect of her voyeuristic endeavors, although not nearly as secret as the cameras in the rooms. The speaker under the monitor crackled to life.

"It's my, ma. She's in a bit of trouble right now," the man with the birthmark said.

"What kinda trouble?" Lilly asked.

"Well, let's just say if I don't leave this place in the next couple days with at least six figures, something really bad is gonna happen to her."

Lilly grew quiet.

He banged his fist on the bar. "How did this all get so fucked up?!"

When his eyes returned to Lilly, there was a despondent look on her face.

"How'd your mom get wrapped up in it?" Lilly asked.

"It's a long story."

"Shit, all I've got is time."

"My ex, Brittany, a few years back she was in a bad way—we were in a bad way. It was our dependence on heroin that started everything. Things started to go downhill and kinda snowballed from there. Anyway, long story short, I saw her do something terrible. Something that disturbed me in a way that I can't forget. When I saw that side of her, it made me question everything. Then she ran away..."

He stopped talking and pulled the lime out of his drink, sucked on it for a moment, and tossed it onto the bar. A grimace twisted his face, but Cee didn't think it was from the citrus fruit. It was the look of sadness, of grief, one she'd seen repeatedly, often in the mirror.

"There are times when that can be for the best," Lilly reasoned. "If ya put a pair of firecrackers together, sometimes the pop's too loud."

He looked down.

"It would've been fine if she'd just left—that's what I was hopin' for. But she took our daughter with her."

Cee perked up. She pulled her cigarette from the ashtray. It was almost out, so she grabbed another and lit it with the dying light from the other.

"Shit, how long has she been gone?" Lilly asked.

"Little under a year now. I just tried to forget about that part of my life for a while. You see, Brittany was hookin' the whole time she was with me, and—even outside of her job—she wasn't exactly the faithful type. After she left, I tried to convince myself that my daughter, Dessi, wasn't *my* daughter. I put enough powder up my nose to where I actually started to believe it. Then I took a bunch more to help me forget what it was I'd convinced myself of. I eventually forgot everything…but you can only forget for so long. It wasn't until after I got clean that I realized it."

Lilly looked at him with sorrow in her eyes as he unwound the tragic tale layer by layer. "Realized what?"

"That I never knew what guilt was. And then it just happened. One morning, I woke up and I just had to see her. Even if I wasn't sure she was mine, and even though I had no clue where the fuck they were, I had to know."

"But I don't get it. How'd you end up here? Oh, fuck, do you think she brought Dessi here?" Lilly asked.

"No, it wasn't that—thank God. I didn't have the first clue about how to track them down, so I hired a PI. Problem is, that cocksucker's expensive. The kind of money he wanted to continue the search wasn't the kind of scratch I just have layin' under the mattress."

Lilly leaned in, enamored.

"So, what'd you do?"

"The type of people I work for are dangerous. I'd seen the kinds of things they did to people and it wasn't anything I ever wanted to see again. I was a bookie—I organized and took bets, but they also gave me the bets to lay down with other bookmakers. But I noticed my boss was making the same shitty parlays every week. Impossible bets if you knew anything about football…or so I thought. The scam worked smoothly for a few months—instead of placing the bets, I kept the money and rolled it over to my PI so he could keep looking for Britt and Dessi. Until last Sunday."

He picked up the sweating glass in front of him and sipped.

"What happened Sunday?"

"The impossible bet hit. They would've won big—and I mean *big*—if I'd laid the money down like I was supposed to. Now, I'm in the fuckin' hole, deeper than deep. Now, it's all or nothing for me."

Lilly reached out and placed her hand over his blood-stained palm.

"How much money do you have?" Lilly asked.

"Nothing," he grumbled.

She turned his hand over slightly and looked down at the freshly cauterized 'S' burn.

"I see. We have more in common than I thought."

"What do you mean?"

"I mean we both got dealt shit hands." She smiled.

"How'd you end up here?"

Lilly looked like she wanted to tell him but brushed off the question. "That's a story for another night, love. We'll definitely need a *stiff* drink for that one. Let's just focus on one problem at a time, okay?"

He nodded and stared at Lilly, seemingly enamored by her. But his lips twitched, like he had something he was holding back. He picked his moment and spoke.

"You know anything about The Black Widow?" he asked.

Cee couldn't help but smile when a look of discomfort

washed over Lilly's face. The whore peeked back at the stage, looking at Porsche's discarded oxygen tank. This time Cee laughed, blowing a cloud of smoke from her mouth.

"What is it?" he asked.

"I'm familiar with her, too familiar," Lilly said.

"I been told it's best to stay clear of her."

"You been told right."

He took another sip of his drink. "Why does everybody call her that?"

"Because she's fatal. Like a spider sucks life out of its prey, she sucks the life out of the people in this place."

"Shit," he said.

"She was never put in charge of this place—she took charge. Actually," Lilly shook her head, "I could probably learn a thing or two from her. I guess taking freedom's the only way to truly have it."

"What do you mean?"

Lilly looked around with a conspirator's glare. No one of importance was within earshot, but Lilly had no idea Cee was listening. If she did, she would've shut her mouth. "The way I heard it, when she was a little girl, her daddy lost her here on a bet. And the fella that ended up winnin' her, he was the previous owner—the creator—of Shadows."

"Cunt, you have no idea the shit I had to endure," Cee said to the empty room. "No fucking idea how much of a monster he truly was."

"And what happened to him?" he asked.

"You should've seen him already, or at least what's left of him. His skin's pinned up in a glass box at the entrance."

"She did that to 'em?"

"That and a whole lot more. I haven't seen it myself or anything, but I know some girls who have."

"Seen what?"

"She kept his cock and balls, like a trophy, on her desk."

"Christ."

"She thinks cuz she had it hard and went through some things that everyone else deserves to take it up the ass along with her." Lilly began to cry as she gazed at the oxygen tank. "She's gettin' revenge on the wrong people and it ain't right."

He rubbed her back. "Jeeze, I'm sorry. Sounds like you've been through hell."

"How fucking sweet." Cee sneered.

"It wasn't just me," she corrected.

"She's probably all fucked up from what her daddy done to her," he said. "Now she's just mad at the world. Few things in life hurt worse than abandonment."

Lilly snapped sideways. "Don't try and fuckin' justify her actions—you didn't see what I saw, okay?"

"I'm—I didn't mean nothing by it. I'm sorry. I ain't saying it's right. I just try to look at both sides of the coin sometimes."

"Yeah, well, both sides are black. It's all death and darkness. Trust me, I been through my fair share of it, but never even considered the unspeakable things she's done."

"I believe you, I'm just—"

"Listen, I like you, Red," Lilly said. "I wanna see you stay alive and find your little girl. Maybe we should just talk about that instead."

Red, what a clever fucking name, Cee thought.

"Fair enough," Red replied. "But I just want you to know—hey, look at me, please."

Lilly turned to him.

"I'm on your side, okay?" he whispered.

Lilly nodded and seemed calmed by his statement.

"You're about the only normal person I've met in this shithole. I'd be a dumb fuck not to be grateful that you're even talkin' to me."

"You—you think I'm normal?"

"Better than normal." Red smiled. "You're the cream of the crop."

"You know, you ain't so bad yourself." She took another swig of her drink. "So, you said you've got a six-figure problem, right?"

"No wonder he's here," Cee said. Some bettors came to Shadows for the thrill of it or to watch people fall to the deepest lows. Others came because they had nowhere else they could go. Their fates outside of the casino were worse than anything Cee could conjure up, and she could get downright nasty. After hearing Red's sob story, Cee had a better perspective of the man.

Red sighed. "Right."

"Well, there's only one bet in this place that can haul in that much. But it's a risky bet—the riskiest. I don't think I have to tell you what's at stake."

"What's the bet?" Red asked.

"That's the thing, it's kind of a mystery—"

"Oh, Red, I hope you find out," Cee said

"Hey, *puta,* you got two minutes," Day Day said. "Better move that fuckin' ass quick."

The Colombian club manager was decked out in an all-white suit and shiny black shoes. He removed the lollipop from his mouth and licked his lips, his quick tongue tagging the wispy mustache.

"You spend too much fuckin' time running your mouth when you should be poppin' that pussy. Then you wonder why you don't make shit. You keep your head in the wrong place and eventually it'll get knocked off those pretty little shoulders."

Day Day's eyes shifted from Lilly to Red. He squinted at him and held his arms out. "The fuck you looking at? Got something to say, *pelirrojo malparido?"*

Red opened his mouth like he wanted to say something, but Lilly squeezed his hand. "Ouch."

Lilly leaned into him and whispered.

Cee strained her ears, but the microphone couldn't pick up the low chatter.

"That new *puta* Star is in the casino for the magic show tonight," Day Day said. "She's had an eye on the buffet since she walked in. Keep her fuckin' nose clean until show-time, the boss has big plans for her. Understood?"

The magic show, Cee thought. For a moment it had slipped her mind. Star, a local junkie, had been purchased just for this one-time show. Cee doled out a hefty amount of money for the woman and needed her ready for her stage debut.

"Where is she?" Lilly asked.

"She should be in the locker room." Day Day turned. He shuffled the candy around his mouth, letting it clack against his teeth. "Now get movin'."

Lilly nodded then turned to Red.

"I've gotta start my shift—and apparently, I'm babysitting now too. But it's only a few hours until the show starts. Come and meet me back here later, and we'll figure things out, okay?

Cee had seen and heard enough. She killed the sound. The chair creaked as she leaned back and stared at the dark ceiling. With a hard pull, the cigarette crackled and burned between her lips. Before exhaling, she took another long drink.

He has a daughter?

She didn't know why the thought had permeated her brain. Lots of people who came to Shadows had children, and some liked to bet them. But Red seemed different, at least from most of the standard scum that came to the casino. He was certainly different from her father—much, much different.

But is he?

Was he truly a good man who was down on his luck, or was he a selfish drug addict like her father? There was a good chance his entire story was bullshit. That he was lying to a semi-attractive hooker, looking for a sympathy blowjob. Even that made little sense, as it was probably his cum in Lilly's hair.

Cee finished her drink and put her cigarette in the ashtray to burn out. Her head was swimming from the influx of booze and nicotine. She gazed into the darkness of the ceiling, her mind wandering.

What if her father had tried to save her and not use her?

What if he'd been a loving man instead of a bum who brought his daughter into a world of depravity, taking her to meet bookies and drug dealers?

The 'what-ifs' danced in her mind. The pleasure she'd felt earlier from fucking and killing Porsche was fading away. Cee was drowning, being yanked back to a time in her life she'd like to forget—a time of pain, suffering, and ultimately rebirth.

TEN YEARS EARLIER

ABANDONED

When Cee first started school, she hated it. There was nothing more she looked forward to than coming home and watching TV, especially if her mom had gone food shopping that day.

Those days were the best, when the pantry was full of fruit snacks, cookies, other treats, and all the sweet drinks Cee could chug. There was little to no homework, and the tasks she had were done in a matter of minutes. During the warmer months of the school year, Cee would go down to the park and play with a few of the kids she liked. It was childhood bliss.

And then her mother left. Just like that, poof, she was gone. Not a reason or note. One day, Cee stood outside her school, waiting for her mother to roll up in her old Nissan. But she never came. Cold and alone, Cee waited, bundled in her second-hand coat. She rejected rides from friends and avoided questions from concerned teachers, certain her mother would show.

When the lights came on in the parking lot and the janitors were preparing to leave, Cee knew her mother wasn't coming. The worst thoughts ran through her mind. Her mother's car smashed into a tree. Kidnappers has stolen her away and were doing horrible things that were only real on TV. Or maybe her car broke down? Finally, Mr. Cranston, a janitor who also lived down the street, called her father.

When her dad pulled up in front of the school, his eyes red with tears, Cee knew her mother wasn't coming back.

That was over a year ago, and Cee had changed. Not just with her growth spurt, which had made the twelve-year-old girl sprout up like a weed. It was her new found hatred of her home. She still hated school, but the droning of the day was enough to distract her mind from what horrors awaited back home.

Now when she got home, it wasn't fresh snacks or a new show she looked forward to. Her excitement had been replaced with dread and wonder. What mess had her father gotten himself into?

Cee stopped waiting for her father to pick her up from school. He'd often be late or not show at all. Mr. Cranston would sometimes give her a ride, but she knew the school administration didn't like the idea of a male employee with a twelve-year-old girl in his car. As much as she hated the school bus, Cee had no other option.

The interior smelled like piss. She was in middle school, but the bus carried the elementary school kids as well. Some of them were on the wrong side of potty training, and the pungent odor wafting from the faux leather seats was a constant reminder.

Cee had her head against the window. Her breath was fogging the glass as the world went by in a gray blur. Winter was in full swing. Christmas was over, and it was the first year that "Santa" had forgotten about her. When she came out and saw her tree with nothing underneath, she sprinted back into her room in tears.

Her father joined her but held back the sobbing. He apologized, but the damage was done. It was that morning, just after she'd turned twelve, that Cee learned the bitter truth about adults.

They lie.

Her dad made it up the only way he could: a diner breakfast and a small shopping spree in the local dollar store.

"Is your name really Charity?" someone asked from behind Cee. She snapped out of her daydream, and back to reality.

At first, Cee didn't think they were talking to her. She didn't have many friends, and the ones she had didn't take the piss bus.

"Huh?" she asked, turning in her seat.

Jade looked over. "I asked if your name was really Charity or not. Are you fucking deaf?" Jade laughed, garnering cheers and whoops from the other girls in the area.

"Um, yeah, it is," Cee said.

The girls laughed. "Yeah, that's fitting," Jade said. "My dad said your dad is a fucking bum. Owes half the town money."

Another girl, Maria, laughed. "He even has a loser for a daughter."

More laughs. Each one stung Cee's pride but ignited something else in her: rage. The whole of it—her mother leaving, her father's drinking and gambling, the neglect, these mean girls—it all pushed and pushed, alighting something feral.

"I heard this bitch is so fucking useless that her mama even left," Jade said. "Dumb slut is probably sucking cock right now." The girls laughed.

Cee grabbed a pair of scissors from her bag. The wide eyes of the handles felt good in her hand. She caressed the blades, touching the tip where they came together. Never once had she stabbed someone, but in that instance, she fantasized about what the steel tool would do to the girls' faces.

The bus slowed to a halt. Cee hadn't realized how far they'd gone until the air brakes hissed. It was her stop. Cee licked her chapped lips and let the scissors go. Without looking at the cackling bullies, Cee threw her old backpack over her shoulder and walked off the bus.

DADDY'S ISSUE

Vin was fucked. What else was new?

Nothing in his miserable existence seemed to go his way. From his shitty childhood to marrying a fucking skank, nothing ever worked out for Vincent Sable. Even his daughter, whom he once cherished more than anything, seemed distant. Then again, he could be partially to blame for that. Since his wife had left, things had been pretty shitty.

His gambling and drinking, which were mostly in check, began spiraling out of control. Working at the assembly plant was a good job, but it was boring. The pay was decent, but now that he found himself as the sole income provider for himself and Cee, things were tight. What was once a nice paycheck with a little leftover to splurge, was now just enough to cover the bills.

Vin had always been a gambler. It was something in his nature. He liked to take risks and always had. A few times early in his life, he'd gotten lucky, but most of his bets came back to bite him in the ass. And sometimes tenfold.

His latest endeavor, putting a grand on a fight that was *supposed* to be fixed, was just another of his many follies.

"Look, I have the cash," Vin said into the phone. "Well, most of it." He bit a nail that was already too short. As the pink flesh bled, he sucked it. "But I have something precious to make up the difference." He stopped pacing and listened to the bookie on the other end of the line.

Shadrick Boone was not a man to test. Vin knew what happened to those on the wrong side of the man's ire.

"Shad, I'm telling you, I can cover it," Vin said. He pulled a crumpled pack of cigarettes from his shirt pocket. With the phone pinned to his ear with his shoulder, Vin dug a lighter from his pants. "Yeah, I'm on my way with the money." He put a bent cigarette in his mouth and lit it. "No, no, I'm coming to you. No need to send anyone."

Vin was quiet as Shadrick spoke.

"Trust me," Vin continued, "I know you know where I live. C'mon brotha, we go back, don't we? I'd never burn you. I'm just waiting on my daughter to get home, and then we're on our way."

He had to sit. The pacing and nicotine were making him dizzy. An old clock above the stove ticked slowly. Cee would be home soon. As if he'd summoned her, Vin heard keys jingling outside of the door.

"She's just walking in now." Vin paused and smoked. "Yeah, we're leaving right away," Vin said as Cee walked through the door. "Thank you—" the line was dead.

"Fuck!" Vin yelled, startling his daughter.

Cee looked at him with obvious concern in her eyes. "Rough day?"

Vin held his head in his hands. The smoke formed a halo above him. He took a long drag and crushed the cigarette in an overflowing ashtray. "Drop your shit and let's go."

Cee's face scrunched up. "Go where? I just got home."

She set her backpack on the ground and walked over to the fridge. Cee knew there would be nothing in there, but her habit of checking had yet to die. Just as she'd expected, the refrigerator was nearly empty, with only some old condiments, a few beers, and moldy food. Cee closed the door and grabbed a cup from the counter. She ran the sink until the water was cold and semi-clear.

"Well, we have to go," Vin said. He looked back at the clock, which appeared to be running faster than ever.

"Where are we going? I have a test tomorrow, and I need to study." Cee sipped from her glass.

"The city," Vin said. He patted himself down, making sure he had everything he needed to pay Shadrick. "And I'm already late, so let's fucking go."

"Dad, the city? Really? That's like two hours away, especially with traffic. I can't fail this test, you know that."

Vin didn't, nor did he care about her grades. "Yeah, well, bring your shit. You can study in the car."

Cee dumped the remaining water in the sink and put the cup in the drying rack. There was no dish soap to clean it anyway. "I get carsick," she whined.

Vin was scrambling, looking for his keys. He tossed a stack of overdue bills from the table and found them. A crumpled fast-food bag lay in the mess. It was grease-stained from age-old discarded French Fries. Vin grabbed it and threw it at his daughter, striking her in the chest.

"Here, puke into this."

HOW MANY FINGERS DO YA REALLY NEED?

Shadrick's club wasn't much of a club. The space was more like a hangout spot for his friends and a few players who were brave enough to enter the lion's den.

Vin walked down the basement steps, stopping at the metal door. Rain fell from the dark sky, and Cee pulled her jacket tight. She shivered, but Vin didn't know if she was cold, scared, or a mixture of both. He knew what he was feeling.

"Hey," he said, wrapping an arm around her shoulders. Even at twelve, she was tall, yet lanky. "I just need to see my friend, and then we'll be done, okay? In and out." Vin smiled, but he knew it looked as forced as it felt.

Cee smiled back.

Vin knocked on the door. His knuckles stung from hitting the metal. Sound echoed in the small stairwell as multiple locks were released on the inside.

Terrance, one of Shadrick's hulking bodyguards, stood on the other side of the door.

"That'd better be Vin," Shadrick said from inside.

"Yup, it's me," Vin said, as he and Cee slipped around Terrance. "I'm sorry I'm late, but traffic on the bridge was a bitch."

Shadrick sat on a leather couch in front of four TVs, each

tuned to a different sporting event. Two ledgers sat on the coffee table in front of him, right next to a copious amount of cocaine. A few other men sat at a far table, each watching a small TV. There was a bar cart against the wall, with a fridge next to it. Sitting across from Shadrick on another couch was a man who Vin was familiar with.

Barry was a gambler, but his problems were even worse than Vin's. He'd been losing his entire life and had jumped from city to city, avoiding loan sharks and bookies alike. Barry's credit was shot, and the only way he could make a bet was if he stuck around for the event he was putting money on.

It was a stupid fucking move, especially with someone as ruthless as Shadrick. Barry sipped a watered-down drink. A pile of cigarette butts filled an ashtray in front of him. His horseshoe bald head was slick with sweat, and the hair he had left was long and unkempt. There was a slight stench of onions in the room, and Vin could only guess it was coming from the man's body.

Barry leaned forward and grabbed another cigarette. His bloodshot eyes were focused on one screen in front of him. With trembling fingers, he plucked his last smoke from the pack and lit it.

"Go baby, go baby!" Barry said.

The cigarette bobbed up and down as he stood. A running back on screen was pushing his way past the defense, with the endzone in sight. Time wound down as he stiff-armed a linebacker, creeping closer to the goal line. But the free safety had other ideas, streaking across the turf and leveling the ball carrier. Down he went, and with him, every vestige of hope Barry had.

"Fuck!" Barry yelled, falling onto the couch. He pulled the cigarette from his lips and chugged the last bit of his drink.

The announcers came on the screen as Shadrick looked at the defeated Barry. "Tough break, my dude." Shadrick opened the ledger and located Barry's wager. "Looks like you owe me eight fifty."

Barry licked his lips and looked toward the door.

Terrance stood there, with Vin and Cee nearby.

"Sure, sure, eight fifty," Barry said.

He stood up and began riffling through his pockets. Crumpled wads of cash fell out as he plucked random bills from every spot he had. None of it appeared to be over a twenty. Barry smoothed out what he had, slowly organizing the bills. He kept glancing toward the door, but his feet were still planted. If he thought he was going to reenact what the running back had done to the linebacker on Terrance, he had another thing coming. Besides, the door was locked.

Shadrick leaned forward and snorted a line of coke. He rubbed his nose and threw his head back. "Come on, Barry. Time is fucking money, and I think you're out of both."

Barry paled as if he'd swallowed a lump of hobo shit. "I-I'm a little short." The wet wad of bills was clenched in his fist. "I have four hundred here, and I could go 'cross town to my brother's house and get the rest. Promise." His smile was brown.

Shadrick sucked his teeth. "Now, you know the fucking rules, especially with you." He looked at Terrance. "Grab this fool."

Barry jumped up and rushed toward the door. For a drunk, middle-aged man, he was quite nimble but not nimble enough. Terrance grabbed him around the throat with a massive arm, crushing Barry's neck. He lifted Barry off the ground and walked him back over to Shadrick.

"Put his fucking hand on the table," Shadrick said. He grabbed a pair of channel locks from the end table and opened them, showing Vin the small teeth. "How many fingers do ya really need?"

Vin looked over at Cee, who was watching with a blank stare on her face.

"Please, don't fucking do this!" Barry begged as the tool clamped down on the tip of his pinkie.

Shadrick grinned. "Bitch, you're lucky I'm only taking a finger or two. Try that shit at Shadows and see what happens to you. That motherfucker, Gianni, is a monster. I'm just a businessman."

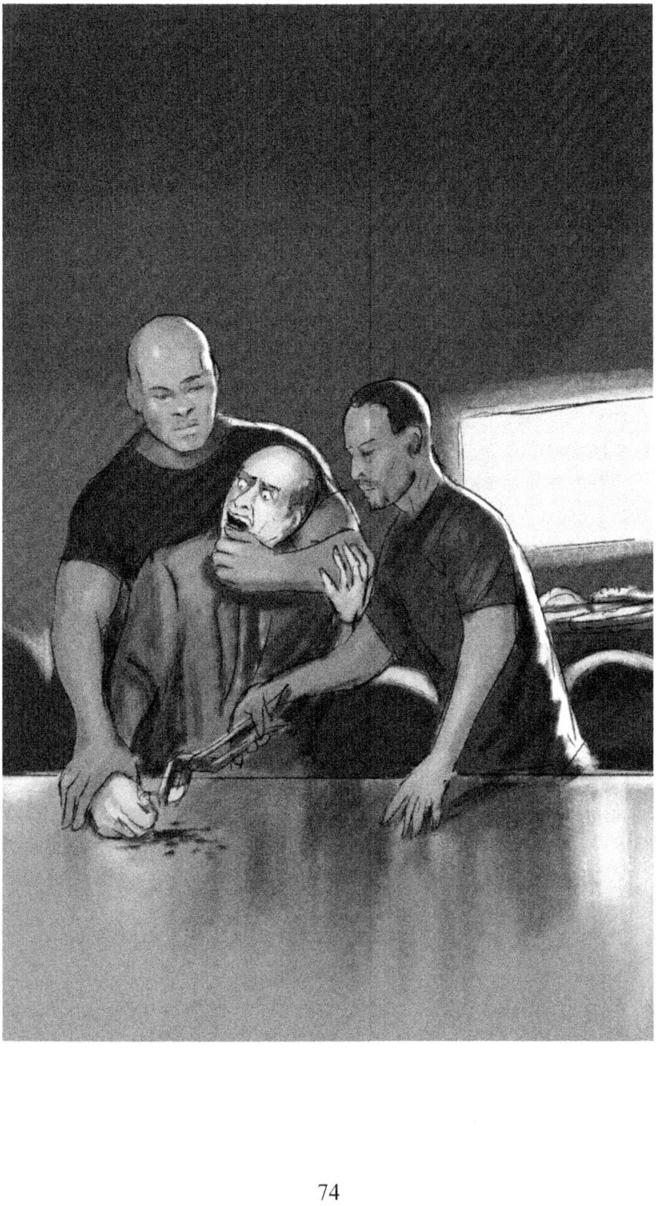

Shadrick clamped down and twisted. Barry's finger snapped like a piece of dry kindling. Tendons cracked and tore as Shadrick spun the tool in a circle. Blood oozed from the ripped flesh as it gave way to the barbaric punishment.

Barry screamed and bit, trying to escape the torment, but Terrance wouldn't budge.

With a final snap and yank, Shadrick ripped Barry's pinkie off. "Ah, that little fucker was hard." He smiled and looked at the mangled digit. "I bet the thumb is gonna be a real bitch." Shadrick snorted another line of cocaine. "Wooo!" he yelled like Ric Flair.

Snot ran down Barry's face, and blood dripped from the shredded meat where his pinkie used to reside.

Shadrick grabbed Barry's thumb with the clamps. "Okay, I think I got it now," he said. This time Shadrick crushed the tip of the finger, squeezing the pink mush of the nailbed out like toothpaste. He tugged on the clamps, extending Barry's thumb and pulling the joints apart. Quickly, Shadrick rotated, snapping the thumb. Flesh ripped like fabric and the bone splintered.

"Come on, you motherfucker." Shadrick grunted. Sweat broke out on his face as he worked on separating Barry's thumb from his hand. Finally, it came off. "There we go. That was fun, right?"

Terrance released Barry, who fell to the ground. He clenched his ruined hand to his chest, weeping.

"Here," Shadrick said, tossing the fingers at the crying man, "you can have them back. But I still want my fucking money. Tomorrow." He pointed the tool at Barry. "Or I'm taking your cock next." Shadrick dropped the channel locks and sat down on the couch. His nimble fingers began rolling a joint from a pile of weed. "Vin, I'm sorry. I forgot you were there."

Vin's throat clicked as he cleared it. He prayed his voice didn't crack. "Yeah, no worries," he said.

Terrance picked Barry off the ground and threw him out into the pouring rain.

"And who is this lovely young lady?" Shadrick asked. Coke residue clung to his nose hairs as he smiled. His drug-addled eyes scanned Cee up and down. "Sorry you had to see that, but you look like a big girl. I'm sure you're *very* mature." He stuck his tongue out and licked the rolled joint.

Vin took a deep breath and glanced at his daughter. He saw her hug herself tightly at the older man's gaze. Her face had a look of fear on it, but Vin didn't know if it was from the violent display or lewd insinuations.

"My daughter," Vin said, with a bit more attitude than intended. The door slammed behind him as Terrance stood at his back.

"Hey, I'm just asking," Shadrick said. He sparked up the joint, filling the room with the skunky smell. "You said you brought something valuable to trade, so I wasn't sure what you'd meant." Shadrick licked his lips before putting the joint in his mouth and winked at Cee.

Vin reached into his pocket and pulled out a ring. It shimmered in the light from the TVs. "I meant this." He took a step forward, holding it.

"Hey, you never know," Shadrick said, taking the ring. "At Shadows, people trade all kinds of things, even each other." He examined the ring. "Not bad. It'll knock five hundred from your tab." Shadrick threw the ring back at Vin.

"What?" Vin shouted. "That thing is worth a few G's easy. It's my mother's wedding ring."

Shadrick shrugged. "Yeah, and your fucking point? It ain't worth that much to me. To me, it's worth about five hundred, but if you keep running your mouth, the price is gonna go down."

"Fuck," Vin muttered. He played with the ring, running his fingers over the stone. He'd done that as a boy, spinning the ring on his mother's finger. It was soothing to him as a kid, but now it only gave him anxiety.

"I'll tell ya what," Shadrick said. "How about Terrance takes little Cee over to the bar and makes her a nice Shirley Temple. And then you and I can talk like adults."

Cee looked at her father with big doe eyes. Vin felt like a piece of shit for bringing her into this life.

"Go ahead. It's fine," Vin said.

"Follow me, sweetheart," Terrance said. He had a few drops of blood on his shirt from wrestling with Barry moments earlier.

Shadrick stepped up close to him. He draped an arm over Vin's shoulders and brought his lips close. "I'll tell ya what. You let that pretty little thing suck my cock, and all of your debt will be squashed. Leave her with me for a weekend, and I'll give you 10k in credit."

Vin felt sick. He wished it was for the fact this monster was making such a vile offer, but it was because part of him wanted to take it.

Could I sign my little girl over to these sick fucks for a weekend? She'd be ruined for life, scarred beyond repair, physically and mentally, even by just a blowjob. He couldn't imagine Cee putting a penis in her tiny mouth.

Vin did the first decent thing he'd done in months. He shrugged Shadrick's arm off his shoulders and reached into his pocket. "Here, the other five hundred I owed you, plus the ring." He handed the payment to the bookie.

Shadrick took it and smiled. "Ah, you didn't say no, Vin. You didn't say no." He slapped his palm with the cash. "Terrance, put that drink in a to-go cup for little Miss Cee. They're leaving." Shadrick leaned in closer. "But the offer is always open. Don't go making bets you can't cover. Or someone is gonna take her from you. And there's not a fucking thing you can do about it."

Shadrick looked at Cee as she rejoined her father. "How's the drink, sweetheart?"

Cee sipped the sugary concoction through the straw and gave him a weak thumbs up.

Vin ushered Cee through the icy rain and into the car. He didn't wait for it to warm up before taking off. His mind was racing, thinking about what he'd seen and heard. But one thing kept pushing to the forefront.

Ten grand was a lot of money.

PRESENT DAY

EYE IN THE SKY

Black, red, black, red, life, death, life, death. Cee watched the poker chip spin. It was a blur to the naked eye, but she picked out each color as it twirled. With serpent-like speed, she snatched it out of the air. The chip, now in her palm, was hidden from view.

Marty sat in front of several monitors watching the casino floor.

Cee had her private screens set up in her office and The Red Room, but the main security hub dwarfed both. Screens were stacked upon each other, giving access to dozens of cameras at once.

Alex was her tech geek who watched the monitors, keeping Cee and Marty informed.

Marty's attention drifted away from the screens to his boss and her infamous poker chip. A chip that belonged to a sadist.

Cee slapped the chip onto the back of her left hand, keeping it concealed.

"Wanna guess?" Cee asked. She looked at Marty from the corner of her eye.

The hulking bodyguard shifted, causing his chair to groan under him. The piece of furniture wasn't used to such bulk, but Marty had sent Alex out for a pack of smokes. Not that monitoring the cameras much mattered—people knew better than to cheat at *her* casino.

"Hmm, I'm feeling lucky tonight." Marty crossed his arms in front of his chest. His tailored suit flexed just a little as the big man moved. He pulled his right arm free and put his hand to his chin, rubbing at his stubble. "I'm going with red." Marty nodded. "Yeah, definitely red."

Cee smirked and lifted her hand. The black side faced up—battered and worn, but still black.

"Always bet on black," Cee said. She rolled the chip over her knuckles, letting it dance its way down her hand. Nimble, well-manicured fingers made the chip come alive as she repeated the process over and over. Cee looked over Marty's shoulders at the cameras. "Anything interesting tonight?"

Marty spun the chair around, fully facing the screens. "Not much." He grabbed the mouse and clicked on a few of the monitors, enlarging them.

Cee looked at the players on the floor. The night wasn't too busy yet, but it was still early. Shadows was more of a nightlife casino, and in the wee hours of the morning, the place would be full of shouting and screaming. If she had her way, lots of screaming.

"There, click on that one," Cee ordered, cupping her chip. She pointed to a screen.

Marty moved the mouse and selected a screen over a poker table. He enlarged it, allowing the vantage point to take up the entire side of one monitor.

At first glance, it looked like a normal poker table: a dealer standing in the back wearing a crisp black shirt, players in every seat, cards flying around, and bets in the center.

A bloody, severed pinkie lay among the poker chips in the center of the table. The man whose finger it *was* sat with a handful of bar napkins clutched to his bleeding stump. His face was pale, but his eyes were sharp as he looked at the cards. With his intact hand, he grabbed his cards, gently lifting the edges to see.

Cee couldn't help but think of the man whose fingers she watched get yanked off when she was just a girl. Now, Cee watched another man lose his finger to his gambling addiction. She could almost smell his blood through the screen. Her heart raced. No matter how many times she'd seen death, a good bet was always fun. Money was a dominant medium, but that could be re-earned. Flesh was another story. A person who bets flesh, whether their own or others, is a person with gusto.

The now nine-fingered man had something good; she knew it. His poker face was stoic, but Cee had been at this since she was a teen. She knew every tell or bluff known to man. Just a twitch of an eye or adjustment in the seat was all it took for her to sniff them out.

"He's gonna go all in," she said to Marty.

Marty was watching intently. "I'll take your word for it." He watched and waited. Marty knew what an 'all-in' bet entailed at Shadows.

"Turn the mic on," Cee said.

Marty clicked the icon on the screen. The speakers in the room came to life with the dull sound of the casino floor.

Cee leaned closer. The poker chip was dancing over her knuckles again to the rhythm of her beating heart. She watched the bleeding man, willing him to say the words. She needed him to.

The man licked his dry lips. He left his cards face down and picked up a watery drink. His hand didn't shake, but his lips trembled when he put it to his mouth. In a gulp, he drained the glass, grimaced, and set it down.

"All in," the man said.

The light of the monitor illuminated Cee's smile as the poker chip stopped in her grasp.

Marty stared at Cee. More and more, she'd craved violence and death. He knew it was part of the job, but he didn't necessarily need it the way Cee seemed to.

The gasps of the other players could be heard through the speaker. None of them were new to Shadows, but anytime someone went 'all-in' it was a big deal.

The dealer, Singh, looked at the man. Singh was all business and had been with the casino for years. This wasn't his first 'all-in,' and after a while, they no longer seemed to faze him. If only he'd seen the aftermath of a lost 'all-in'. Then he might not have been so calm.

"Sir, company policy dictates that I remind you of the consequences of your bet," Singh said. "That if yo—"

"Fuck your policy. I know what I'm doing." The man said. The bar napkins had fallen away from his mangled stump, which was weeping blood onto his pants. "I'm all fucking in." With no chips left in front of him, everyone knew what losing the bet meant: death, and not a pleasant one, either.

Cee watched the rest of the table check and recheck their cards. They all looked at the bleeding man. His façade of calm had waned, now replaced with a look of insanity. To bet one's life on a card game required a bit of craziness.

Around the table, players folded, tossing their cards into the center. Except for one. This man, whose skin was chalk white, stared at the injured bettor. He didn't check his cards again, just stared.

Cee watched, the poker chip tight in her palm.

"What's the rate on the finger?" Mr. White asked.

Singh looked at the pinky. "A pinkie is ten thousand, sir."

Mr. White grabbed at his chips, of which he had plenty. "And the house covers the 'all in,' right?"

Singh nodded. "Yes, sir."

"Right," Mr. White said, tossing a stack of chips in the center. A few of them bounced off the severed digit, landing with the rest. "I call." He looked at the wounded man.

Sweat poured down the man's face and neck. His color had drained, but a smirk formed on his cracked lips. Gently, he flipped his cards over.

"Full fucking house, and not that stupid fucking show, either. A real full house!" Three kings and two aces stared up at the camera above.

"Good hand," Marty said. He watched the action with Cee at his side.

"Yeah, it's good, but beatable. Our other guest hasn't revealed his hand yet. We may still cash in soon."

Mr. White looked at the cards in front of the man. He nodded and pushed his hand, unshown, into the center of the table. "Good hand. No point in embarrassing myself," he said.

"Fuck," Cee muttered.

She watched the table congratulate the wounded man as he raked in the chips. Painfully, she watched Singh issue him an 'all in' voucher, which she knew she'd be paying out shortly.

Marty went to click the mic off. "Eh, can't win 'em all." A scream shot from the speakers, and they both perked up in response.

"What the fuck was that?" Cee asked. It hadn't come from the poker table, but the mics were sensitive enough to pick up sound throughout the floor. She scanned the other monitors, trying to find the source of the pained scream. "There." She pointed to a roulette wheel.

Marty clicked and moved, reducing the poker screen to normal and grabbing the one with the roulette wheel.

Another man was in the process of cutting his ocular nerve, severing his eyeball from his body.

"Oh, now this is promising," Cee said. Her perfect teeth glowed in the monitor's light. The door opened, and Alex walked in.

"What did I miss?" he asked.

Marty took the cigarettes from the man and stood up. "We had an 'all in' that won, but now the roulette wheel just took a lively turn." He slapped the cigarettes on his palm before peeling away the cellophane. Marty's earpiece crackled to life.

"Hey Marty, we have a good one on roulette, in case Alex didn't see it," Saul said over the radio.

Marty reached for the volume knob on his radio and

lowered it. "Fucking Saul loves to scream in this thing," he muttered. "I'm gonna kick his balls in if he does that shit again." He pressed the mic button on his shirt and spoke. "Yeah, the boss picked it up."

Cee watched the screen, half listening to Marty talk with another pit boss. "Marty, give me a smoke." Cee held out her hand, not taking her eyes off the monitor.

Marty opened his pack and took out two cigarettes. He handed one to Cee and waited.

The filter sat between her lips, and she knew Marty was waiting to light it for her. He knew his place. Yet, she couldn't peel her eyes away from the screen. The desperation of the one-eyed man was breathtaking.

For as many years as she'd run Shadows, she couldn't help but love that look of desperation. It was almost as good as them begging for their lives when they went into The Red Room. Roulette didn't have many big winners like poker, at least not with a bet of flesh. She had a feeling The Red Room was going to be busy shortly. Goosebumps rose on her skin when she thought about the racks of shiny instruments.

Cee turned toward Marty, the cigarette cushioned between her lips. As she'd expected, he'd been waiting with a lighter in hand. He lit it and pushed the flame to the tip of her smoke. The tobacco and paper crackled as she inhaled. A cloud of blue smoke rose above her head.

Marty lit his own.

"Let's head down," she said, taking another drag. Cee took her poker chip and touched her neck. A locket resembling a pocket watch rested against her skin. She popped it open and slid the poker chip inside, closing it up with a slight click. "I have a feeling I'm going to want to watch this one." She turned to Alex and said, "Call the croupier and tell him to wait for me."

"Yes, ma'am," Alex said. He reached for a long microphone and selected the right frequency. "Roulette 6, stand by on that spin."

The croupier was holding the eyeball in a gloved hand. He snapped his head up to the camera and adjusted his earpiece, listening to the message.

"The Boss is coming to you," Alex said into the mic.

Cee smiled as she watched the color bleed from the croupier's face.

TABLE 6

The private elevator moved quietly on well-greased rails.

"We're coming down now," Marty said into his radio. He put his cigarette into his mouth and checked the equipment concealed by his suit jacket. It wasn't much but hadn't failed him yet. His gun—a Glock 23 chambered in .40 caliber—was holstered on his right hip. He drew it, checked to ensure the batteries on his red dot sight hadn't died, and made sure there was a round in the chamber.

There was. There always was.

He re-holstered the gun and patted the two spare magazines on his left hip and the expandable baton next to them. His knife never left his pocket, but he touched it all the same. It was there, razor sharp and folded up in his expensive pants.

Since becoming the head of security for Shadows, he hadn't much use for his tools. His crew was the real muscle these days, and he had some of the best. The pit bosses were good, but most of them were pussies. They talked a big game, but with The Red Room shit, they were fucking soft. And since Cee had taken over Shadows, The Red Room had been busy. Busier than Marty had expected.

Her ascent to power was one of the bloodiest days Marty

had ever seen, and he'd served three tours overseas. He figured with Cee at the helm, The Red Room wouldn't see as much action.

Many men fell for Cee's looks, but they didn't know about the monster lurking in the three-thousand-dollar dress. She made warlords look like Boy Scouts with some of the shit she'd done. Just the death of Gianni was enough to give Marty goosebumps.

The elevator stopped, and the doors slid open. Marty's team stood waiting.

His two most loyal members—Manx and Rachel—looked like sentinels with their arms crossed over their belt buckles, faces stern.

Cee took a final drag of her cigarette and put it out in an ashtray by the elevator doors. Marty did the same.

"Ma'am," both Manx and Rachel said, giving slight nods to Cee as she walked by in a cloud of smoke and perfume.

"Evening," Cee replied with a grin on her face. "We're heading out to the floor if you'd care to join us." She didn't wait for a reply, and it wasn't a request.

Manx and Rachel fell in next to her, one on each side, with Marty taking the rear.

Demarious Manksell, aka 'Manx' still walked with the cocksure gait he had back on the block. He and Marty served together for a tour, both saving the other's ass more times than either could count. Manx was ruthless and had a 'no fucks given' attitude, often running headlong into gunfire to kill the enemy. He was awarded many medals for valor, but when he was discharged, he found out medals didn't pay for shit. But killing did, and that paid well.

He slipped back into his old life in Baltimore, running with the same crew he'd been with since he was a boy. The only difference was he had bodies when he returned… lots of bodies. Everyone gave him a wide berth, even some of his boys. Everyone knew if he showed up, someone could die. Loyalty was everything to Manx, and when his boys set him up in an ambush, he killed them all. While on the run from the cops and other hitters in the city, Marty called him with a job opportunity. The rest is history—bloody history.

Rachel Schinner pushed her earpiece deeper, crushing it past her cauliflower ear. Her early life as a semi-pro fighter had left her scarred and damaged but gave her invaluable life lessons. The main one: don't trust anyone. The cage was her domain, where she left her opponents crying and bloody on the stained canvas.

Marty knew that for Rachel, there was nothing like the feeling of her fists or elbows crushing bone and cartilage. The pay was never great, but more than sufficient to support her. It was good enough, and it let her succumb to her first love: hurting others. Until she became the one on the receiving end.

Her promoter was shady, but it was all part of the game. The day he walked in and told her she'd be throwing a fight, things changed. That wasn't her; she wasn't a loser. And certainly not a loser to some bitch who didn't deserve it. But she played along and took her beating, vowing it would never happen again. When Marty walked into her dressing room and looked her nude and battered body up and down, she knew her life would never be the same.

Marty followed the trio onto the gambling floor, scanning the tables as he stalked.

The stone walls of the former mine, where Shadows hid from the world, played havoc with acoustics. Marty's trained ears easily followed the sobbing of the maimed man.

Cee moved by the tables, passing scenes of controlled chaos. Wheels spun, lights flashed and people wept as they lost their life savings in an instant. The other screams of pain were ever-present. But one overruled the rest.

"Alex, do you still have eyes on roulette 6?" Marty asked into his radio.

"Yup, still watching," Alex replied. "The poor sap is crying like a baby with a handkerchief pressed against his face. But the croupier isn't spinning yet. He's just smirking with the eyeball in his hand. A real sicko, if you ask me."

Well, I didn't fucking ask you, so don't worry about it. Marty thought. "Copy, we're almost there."

Cee turned past a game where a player was pulling his molars out with pliers. The man set the teeth, roots and all in front of him, waiting for the dealer to send the cards his way.

Rachel glanced over her shoulder at Marty. "He'll be Red Room material soon, I'm guessing."

Marty agreed but didn't speak, just nodded.

Rachel snapped forward her stare leaving the man with the bloody mouth.

A low sobbing could be heard over the din. Cee seemed to home in on the weeping like a shark to blood. The wheel of roulette 6 sat awaiting its true master.

A small group of onlookers—high rollers, mostly—gathered around the table. Some of them gave her a nod of respect. Others refused to make eye contact with the woman many referred to as The Black Widow. One man scurried away into the crowd.

Rachel and Manx spread out, watching the onlookers. They'd seen worse than a severed eye and would probably do worse in the next few hours. Cee's safety was their number one priority. Any slight to her was unacceptable.

Marty clung to his boss, becoming her shadow as his muscle watched the crowd. No one was stupid enough to attempt an attack on Cee, but desperation drove people to commit wild acts. Acts that would leave their lives forfeit in the worst ways possible.

One of their regulars—a guy decked out in a cowboy hat—tipped its wide brim toward Cee. She ignored him.

The croupier looked up at his boss. The eyeball rolled in his gloved hand.

Cee smiled at the bloody tears running down the bettor's face. "Give it a spin."

The croupier nodded, and with an expert flick of his wrist, he tossed the eyeball into the wheel.

BLACK, WHITE, AND RED ALL OVER

The wet eyeball slid around the rushing wheel. A thin coating of ocular slime and blood left behind a snail trail along the polished granite. Cee watched it with girlish glee, waiting for the eyeball to land in a slot, fixing the bettor's fate.

The bet marker was set on red, meaning the bettor had many outs. A near 50/50 chance of life and riches, or a death worse than anything imaginable. The eyeball swirled and spun, thudding wetly as it skipped along.

A crowd of onlookers watched anxiously, every eye locked on the severed globe. Cee scanned their faces—most ripe with disgust, some with morbid fascination, but one with a look of curiosity.

Red.

It was the same man she'd spied on earlier. Cee still felt the remnants of the daydream that had plagued her mind. The one in which she watched her father's first dilemma—deciding not to bet her away for a gambling debt. It was the first time she'd seen real violence, when Barry had two of his fingers torn off.

The memory was burned into her young psyche. It had done something to her, changed the chemistry of her brain.

As a twelve-year-old, she had been terrified, but deep down she'd liked it. There was something primal about the power Shadrick had over the other man and her father. That one person could have such power felt forbidden.

Almost like the first time she'd masturbated. It'd felt so good, yet dirty all at once. When her orgasm had abated, she'd cried, thinking she'd done something wrong. Until the next night, when she'd done it again with the same results. Pushing the thoughts of shame from her mind, Cee accepted her pleasure and didn't look back.

Violence was the same as sex for her. It felt wrong at first, but it became her love, beating out cumming. There were few things better than a wonderful orgasm, as proven by her tryst with Porsche, but the feeling of holding someone's life in your hands was ten-fold. Watching them beg when you knew horrid things were on the horizon was the equivalent of a good lay. And when the first cut was made…

The man with the port-wine birthmark on his face, aptly known as Red, watched the severed eyeball roll around the roulette wheel.

The crowd gasped as the eyeball slowed. Each bounce was less and less. The wetness diminishing, becoming sticky as it slid from one slot to the next.

Red, black, red, black. Cee watched with bated breath. The Red Room was calling to her. The eyeball slowed. At last, it stopped.

Black.

A bloodcurdling howl of despair rang out from the wounded man's mouth.

"No, please," he moaned. His legs turned to mush. Tumbling forward, the one-eyed man braced himself against the table.

The bloody rag fell out of the crimson maw where his eye used to reside. Tears of despair and blood stained the felt of the table.

"I guess you should've bet on black," Cee said. "Take him to The Red Room."

It was something she'd been waiting to say all night. The Red Room was her sanctuary. Killing Porsche earlier had been fun, but that wasn't the primary goal. That was strictly to get Cee to cum, even though she probably would've killed the woman anyway. If she'd survived, Cee wouldn't have cared so long as she came first.

"With pleasure," Manx said as he and Rachel moved in.

The one-eyed man attempted to flee but Manx slammed his fist dead into his nose. The punch shattered the bone and distorted cartilage. Blood and snot from the one-eyed man's nose mixed with the gore running from his empty eye socket.

Before he hit the floor, Rachel stepped in and hooked him under his armpits, using her years of fighting to brace his weight.

"Show's over," Cee said, smacking her palms against each other. "Time is money, so get those bets in, and enjoy the night."

Cee turned and followed her crew as they dragged the wounded man towards The Red Room. But something was tugging at her. *Red.* She stopped and turned back to the crowd, seeking Red with her eyes.

"Oh, and don't forget, the buffet is open. I encourage you all to do whatever it takes." She looked at all of them, but stopped her gaze when it found the port-wine stained face of Red. Never had she taken an interest in a bettor, but something about him and his story dug at her. It was insidious, finding its way into her mind.

Guilt. Guilt for what happened to my father. No, fuck him. He deserved the fate he was given. Another word lit up in her brain: redemption. What if Red was noble and not a piece of shit like her father? Did he and his daughter deserve a shot at redemption? An opportunity she'd never had?

Before she could stop herself, Cee blurted,

"Hey, Red."

The shock on Red's face was obvious.

His mouth fell open slightly, and he flinched at the sound of his name.

He cleared his throat. "Ah, yes, Ma'am."

"How far are you willing to go?" Cee asked.

Red licked his lips and fidgeted. "I'm—uh—I'm not exactly sure what you mean."

Oh, you know what I mean. Don't play fucking dumb with me.

She pointed at the one-eyed man. "I mean exactly what I said." Red couldn't help but look at the crying man being led away from the main floor. "Would you be willing to go that far for Dessi?" He winced at the sound of his daughter's name. "Do you want it enough to pull your own fucking eye out of your head—or worse?"

What kind of father are you, Red?

"I suppose you don't have to answer just yet," Cee continued. "But I only ask because you need to be prepared to go the distance if you ever want to have a chance at seeing her again. The road to leave this place is bumpy and littered with bodies. So, start thinking about it." She could see the struggle on his face. As if he were thinking about every mistake up until this point.

"I'd do whatever I needed in order to find her," Red replied firmly.

"We'll see about that." Cee turned her back to Red, Marty at her side. When they were out of the crowd, she leaned in to him and said, "I need a smoke."

Marty pulled his cigarettes from his pocket, offering one to his boss. Cee took it and leaned in for a light. She needed the nicotine to calm her nerves and steady her hands.

The Red Room was calling to her, and she couldn't wait.

THE PATH TO DESTRUCTION

Clayton thought the pain in his hand when they'd branded the 'S' on his palm was the worst thing he'd ever felt. Then, the agony of extracting his eyeball made the burn almost seem like a tickle in comparison. Even his shattered nose, which throbbed and poured blood, was nothing compared to the eyeball. The hurt was severe enough, but the phantom feeling was the worst. His brain couldn't process why it was only seeing half. Why there was a deep burning where the gory gap now lived.

Clayton tried to regain his feet, but the two goons were moving too fast. It didn't matter, anyway. He knew his fate was sealed. He had one last chance, a trade that might save his life.

His life had been full of shitty decisions. The last one, the one that landed him with one eye and being dragged to his death, had been his worst. Clayton liked whores. It was a vice he'd had since his teen years. The only issue was that he liked to get a little rough. Most girls were fine with that, but only under strict rules. Clayton wasn't a man that followed the rules.

After throwing a beating on a whore in a dingy hotel room, Clayton found himself looking down the barrel of a gun. Her pimp wasn't a man to be fucked with, and Clayton had just knocked out four of his best girl's teeth. The thought of trading his daughter to squash the debt had crossed his mind. But if Clayton was in deep with the pimp, he'd might as well go all in. With his last bit of cash (which he was saving for a threesome) he threw his daughter in the trunk of his old Caddy, and headed to Shadows.

The casino was a rush of chimes and lights. Shouts of victory and screams of loss. His remaining eye took in the macabre games as they pulled him deeper.

A woman stood topless at a gaming table, her left nipple being severed with a razor. Butter-yellow fat peeked out of her veiny breast, taking the place of her missing nub of flesh. With bloody, shaky hands, she put the nipple on the table.

Her face was a rictus grin of insanity. Snot and cocaine residue ran down her nose as she began cutting the other nipple off. With both bits of flesh on the felt, she smiled at the dealer, awaiting her next card.

Clayton's head swooned. The blood loss and pain were setting in. A trail of crimson followed them through the casino. A set of double doors loomed ahead. The goons didn't even slow down, using his battered head to open them.

The luxury of the casino disappeared like a magic trick from Calypso the Cunning's show. Gone were the games and lights, replaced with an old tunnel from the days when the mine was still active. The walls were roughhewn and damp. Water glistened and trickled, leaving puddles on the floor. Banks of fluorescent lights lit the tunnel.

Clayton's shoes dragged on the stone floor, leaving patent leather streaks. The tunnel continued into the darkness, but the trio stopped. A red door was cut into the rock wall. The condensation on the dark paint looked like weeping blood.

The bitch from the floor—the hot one in the black dress, who kindly advised him to bet on black—walked in front of them. Another goon shadowed her. He reached into his suit pocket and produced a key, which he handed to the lady in black.

She unlocked the door and pushed it open.

"Shall we?" she asked.

The room was dark, but Clayton smelled death wafting from the gloom. The woman stepped forward and turned on the lights.

Clayton screamed.

THE RED ROOM

The man's screams were music to Cee's ears. Showing the condemned The Red Room was one of her favorite parts of the night. That first glimpse of the rest of their life, the place they'd die in and die horribly. It was special every single time.

The Red Room—her room—stood unoccupied and smelled like spilled blood. The iron odor was like heaven to her, a welcoming aroma. The showpiece of the room, a lethal injection table, was stained brown. Splotches of old blood, shredded viscera, and shit, marred the leather.

Against one wall was a metal table. It had an industrial look as if it belonged in a garage, not a casino. Tools of all shapes and sizes shone in the fluorescent lighting. Cee's small desk sat against the other wall. Gianni's genitals floated under the glow of the surveillance monitors.

Cee hoped the condemned saw the grisly trophy. Fear was just as sweet as pain, something she'd learned from her predecessor.

As much as Cee hated Gianni, his method and torment molded her into the ruthless businesswoman she was.

Cee wasn't sure if that was something she should be grateful for. With every cut of the blade or ignored cry for mercy, she became more and more like her evil predecessor.

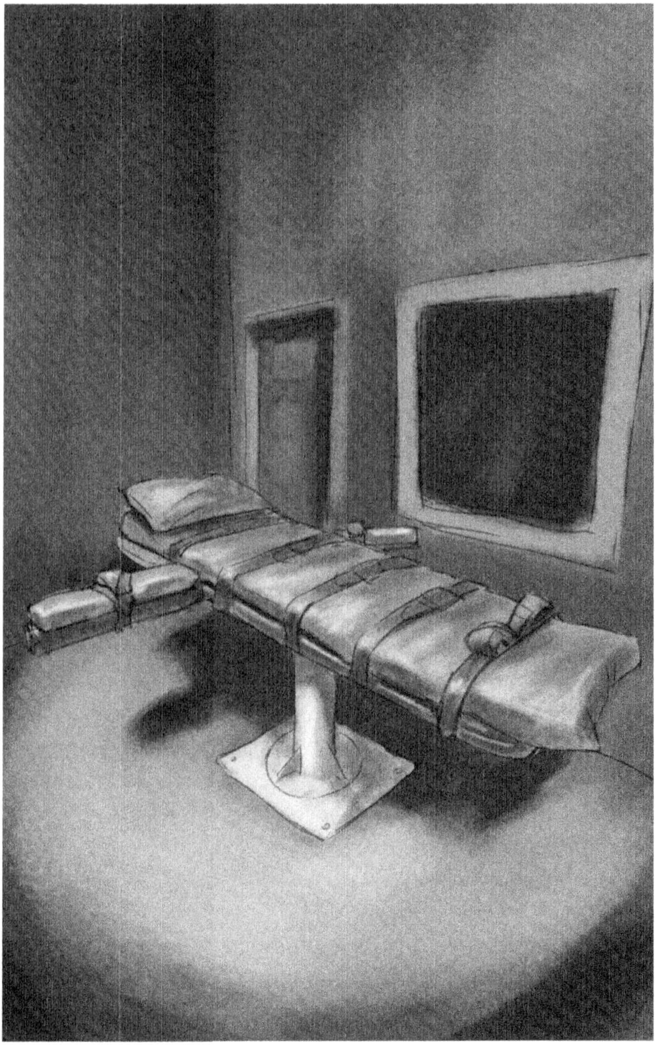

"No, please, fucking no!" the man screamed.

"Strap him down," Marty ordered.

Manx and Rachel dragged the condemned deeper into the room. Marty closed the door behind them. The pair wrestled with him, but his will to live was strong. He wasn't much to look at, but he gave them a tough time.

"Get on the fucking table!" Manx growled. He dodged an elbow as the man flailed.

"No, please. I'll trade you, please!"

"Fucking cocksucker," Rachel said. Her grip was waning on the man's bony arm.

Marty had enough. He moved in and grabbed three of the man's fingers. With a flick of his wrist and a loud pop, he broke them.

"Ah! My fucking fingers!" the man shrieked.

Shards of white poked out of his skin. Blood oozed from the torn flesh. As hard as he tried, the man couldn't cradle his destroyed fingers.

"Now, get him on the fucking table," Marty ordered.

The fight had all but drained from the man. Manx pulled, nearly taking him off his feet. He and Rachel slammed the man on the table. Within moments, he was secured.

Sweaty and embarrassed, Manx and Rachel backed away.

Cee gave her two thugs a look, but the job was done. She stood in front of the condemned and looked at his sweaty, pale face. He wept like a baby, his empty eye socket crying crimson.

"Pl—please." His pleas were intensifying. "I can make a trade, please. You have to believe me. Take someone else. I have an offering, I swear it!"

Cee heard him but paid no mind.

"Strip him," she ordered.

Marty didn't hesitate. He grabbed a pair of surgical shears from the table and began cutting the man's clothing, starting at the bottom of his pants. The blades sliced through the fabric, revealing the man's shriveled cock. A thatch of dark pubic hair hid most of it in its darkness. A small squirt of piss dribbled out, wetting his bush.

"Sick fuck," Marty muttered. He continued to cut until the man was nude.

The man's sunken chest vibrated with every nervous heartbeat. He shuddered in his nudity as the air conditioner turned on.

"There, now I can see what I'm working with," Cee said. She opened a drawer under the table and removed a leather apron and a white Halloween mask. "Unzip me, please." She turned around with her back facing the other three.

Marty took a step forward and partially unzipped his boss's dress.

"Thank you," Cee said.

She reached back, grabbed the zipper, and pulled it down to her ass. Cee slid the dress from her shoulders and let it fall to the floor. She stood nude, her backside the only thing on display to her staff. The nudity didn't bother her but getting her dress stained would.

The night was young, and she already had her first guest in The Red Room. Hopefully, he would not be the last. Cee put the apron on, covering her breasts and vagina. She pulled the white mask over her face, breathing the scent of cheap plastic. Looking like a deranged porcelain doll, Cee's fingers played over the array of tools on the table. She caressed each of them lovingly, feeling the lives each had ended, wondering which one would end this sad sack's existence.

"Listen, listen," he spat. "I know how it works, right? A life for a life. I fucked up, I know that, but I'm a good guy. Honest." He craned his neck, trying to see what Cee was grabbing. "I have a life I can give you. A young one… a fresh one. She'd be perfect. Y-y-you could use her for whatever you want. She'll do it. I fucking promise." The man's lone eye was trying to stay locked on Cee.

She lifted a rubber mallet. She loved it. The heft, the force behind the head, the weight—it was her favorite. To start with, at least.

"I don't want some washed-up skank you call a wife," Cee said. She touched the mallet to the man's left kneecap.

He writhed under the coolness of the rubber.

"No, no, not washed up. Young, and willing. Yeah, she'll do whatever the fuck you want. Trust me, I've seen it."

Cee had listened to the man long enough, but something wasn't sitting right. A part of her just had to know. She glowered at him through the mask.

"And who might this be?" she asked. Her voice was distorted by the plastic.

"Thank you. Thank for hearing me out." He cried. "My daughter. My fucking daughter. I have her, and she's yours. Do whatever with her, just let me go."

Cee lifted the mask. "Your daughter, you say?"

The man was nodding so hard that the pooled blood in his empty eye socket spilled out.

"Yes, fucking yes. That's what I was trying to tell you. I have her." He gulped, and his Adam's apple bobbed and clicked. "Well, not here, but close by. In my car. She's tied up in the trunk. Blue Caddy, parked in spot number 8. Go up and grab her; she's all yours. Just free me, and we can go get her together."

Cee's face was blank. The mallet swayed at her side. She placed it back on the table and stood silent for a moment. With her well-manicured fingers, she stroked the other tools.

"Well, that's certainly convenient," she whispered. "You just so happen to have your daughter, knowing you may lose big."

"Yup," he beamed. "Ol' Clayton isn't so fucking dumb after all. I know I can trade her for my life. It's happened before, right?"

Cee didn't speak, but her hand found a tool: tin snips.

Clayton looked down as Cee's left hand grabbed his pathetic cock and balls. He tried to pull away, but the straps on the table were snug.

The snips trimmed off a few long pubic hairs before biting into the root of his penis.

"Fuck!" he wailed.

Cee squeezed. The sensation of steel cutting flesh never got old for her. She yanked, and the severed lump of dick meat came off in a mess of hair and blood.

Clayton screamed. He thrashed on the table. Blood and piss from his severed urethra sprayed wildly.

Cee threw his genitals into the trash with a thud.

"Motherfucker," she said.

Cee faced away from the dying man. Blood ran freely down the crack of his ass and overflowed from the table. She wanted to hurt him, make him pay for what he'd offered. The tools called to her. One in particular called loudest: the ice pick.

Cee yanked it off the wall, remembering how it had been used to paralyze her father. It was just another reminder of a life lost.

"Hold his head," she ordered.

Manx swooped in and grabbed Clayton's thrashing head.

"I don't want your daughter," she said. "I want you. I want your pain and your suffering, but I don't want your last vision to be of me. The last thing you'll see before you die is darkness. Do you hear me, Clayton?"

Clayton tried to buck Manx from his head, but the bodyguard held tight. Cee placed the tip of the icepick at the bottom of Clayton's remaining eye. The pressure and pain stopped his flailing, knowing the slightest movement could pierce his eyeball.

Cee slowly pushed on the handle of the icepick. The tip of the tool slid through the bottom of Clayton's eyelid. A tiny burgundy tear fell as she pushed harder, feeling the lovely pop of the eye giving way to the icepick.

A pitiful whine escaped Clayton's throat, and he seized. That didn't stop Cee. Harder, yet just as slowly, she pushed the tool, skewering his lens and hitting the ridge of his ocular bone. The icepick passed through Clayton's eye and entered his brain. His seizures increased, and he vomited.

Cee stopped and left the tool where it was. He would certainly die from his injuries, but she wanted it to take a while. She wanted him scared in the darkness, just like his daughter.

Cee yanked the mask off and wiped her hands on a towel. She untied the apron and quickly replaced it with her dress.

Marty stepped next to her. "You want us to finish him?"

"Let him bleed," Cee said, walking from the room.

EIGHT YEARS AGO

TWO ON ONE

Cee had stopped taking the bus. Now that she was fourteen, she felt safer walking to and from school. She didn't think there was anything much worse that could happen to her on the trek than could happen on the bus, especially since the fight with Jade and Maria.

Cee had always been tall, but she was rail thin. That was until she'd turned thirteen. Puberty hit her like a ton of bricks, and for once in her life, things worked out in her favor. Rather than have her skin plagued with a dreaded combination of acne and dry skin, Cee's skin smoothed out. Her hair took on a luster that rivaled models in shampoo commercials. And the minuscule amounts of fat she held found its way to her chest and rump.

Cee was turning into a woman, and the changes garnered some attention. She was shy, knowing the boys ogled her, a few of them sporting obvious erections. What sickened her even more than her horny classmates were the glares of male teachers, men who were old enough to be her father or grandfather, in some instances, looked at her teen body with lust in their eyes. Cee had taken to wearing loose clothing or covering her chest with her books when walking past them.

Most of the other girls had begun their path down puberty lane, but not so many of them were as lucky as she was. Jade and Maria had it rougher.

Jade's skin revolted against the rush of hormones, speckling her face with acne. And it wasn't just a pimple here and there but a field of red sores. Mounds of white heads and valleys of dry craters. Her hair even took a hit, drying out and becoming brittle. The daily use of a straight iron didn't help, and it continued to look like shit.

Maria was bitten by the acne bug as well, but not as bad as her friend. Instead, every bit of baby fat Maria carried around, doubled. She wouldn't have cared if most of it went to her tits, but it flooded her gut, giving her the belly of a truck driver. And for her, none of it went to her chest or ass, leaving both areas woefully flat.

Winter break was just around the corner. Kids were filled with joy at the prospect of the holidays and time off from school. The thought of presents, good food, and fun in the snow was something that most kids looked forward to yearly. But Cee wasn't most kids.

Christmas in the Sable household had been less than bountiful over the last few years. Her father had forgotten Christmas the year her mother had left, and last year's 'gifts' were from the dollar store, after Cee had to remind her father about the holiday at the last minute.

Cee was daydreaming, trying to do anything to keep her mind from wandering back to what she'd do during the break. Her father was rarely around, and when he was, he was either drunk or asleep.

Food was another questionable commodity. At school, she could eat for free thanks to government assistance. But at home, she didn't have the luxury or guarantee of a hot meal. Most of her meals would come from a can or the freezer, if her father hadn't gambled or sniffed all his money away.

Cee's father thought he was keeping her in the dark about his growing cocaine addiction, but she wasn't stupid.

He'd thrown her headfirst into his secret life, and she'd seen things no child should ever have had to witness. The day she watched Shadrick tear the fingers from Barry's hand, she'd ceased being a little girl. Gone were the fairies and unicorns, replaced with loan sharks, drug dealers, whores, and pimps, all of whom had been to their apartment.

The fight with Maria and Jade had been brutal. The bus was warm, a little too warm for Cee's liking. She slid into her seat like she'd always done, but before sitting down, took off her jacket.

She didn't realize she'd caught the attention of Jose, and almost every other boy on the bus. Jade had been twirling her hair, talking with Jose. He appeared to not be paying attention to her, rather he was staring at Cee.

Cee noticed his lustful gaze locked on her chest and crossed her arms.

"So, I told that bitch…," Jade stopped, noticing Jose's attention wasn't on her anymore. She locked eyes with Cee, who Jose was staring at. "Puta," Jade grumbled.

Cee ignored the insult, but noticed as Jade looked over to Maria before turning her gaze away. Jade stood and left Jose, jumping into the seat next to her friend.

Cee watched the two girls talk, but their whispers were too low to hear. The bus rolled to a stop, and Cee stood to put her coat back on. This move again garnered looks and chatter from everyone on the bus. Cee stepped into the blustery cold, wrapping herself tightly in her coat. She hadn't realized Jade and Maria had gotten off, too.

"Hey, bitch!" Jade yelled.

As the bus took off, Cee turned and took a punch square in the face. She'd never seen stars before and always thought it was bullshit. Now that she'd been hit for the first time, she knew it was true. Cee stumbled back, her left eye throbbing, and tripped.

She landed hard on the cold pavement, sending a shockwave up her tailbone. She scrambled to get back up.

"You think you can just show your titties off and not pay

the fucking price?" Jade stepped forward and kicked Cee in the crotch, knocking her back down.

"Yeah, you fucking slut," Maria said. She kicked Cee, hitting her across the ribs.

Cee gasped and tried to scurry away. She had to get to her feet so she could fight back or run. Either was better than getting the shit stomped out of her.

"I heard you sucked Mr. Michum's dick after class the other day," Jade said, circling Cee. She stepped on Cee's fingers, pinning them to the ground.

Cee shrieked. "Leave me alone, you fucking bitch!" Painfully, she pulled her hand out from underneath Jade's shoe and grabbed her ankle. Lunging forward, Cee yanked Jade's foot and thrust her shoulder into the girl's midsection.

Jade, mid-laugh, wasn't expecting the attack. She fell backward, smashing her elbow on the ground.

"Oh, you're fucking dead!" Jade said. She reached into her pocket and pulled out a thin box cutter. "I'm gonna carve that pretty little face. Ain't no boys gonna wanna fuck you."

Cee stood, prepared to fight, but something had shifted. Jade's face was red. She was hurt but doing her best to not show it. Her bloody elbow peeked out from her torn sweatshirt. Maria, winded from the short conflict, looked like she was losing steam. The blade in her friend's hand caused her to pause and didn't appear to be a part of their plan.

Cee shrugged her bookbag off and put her fists up. She knew she would get cut, but her height and reach would help equalize Jade's weapon. Cee could see it in Maria's eyes that she didn't want to go any further. She probably didn't want to be involved in the first place, but saying no to Jade was never a good idea.

Jade lunged forward, the tip of the blade leading the way. It was a weak thrust, lacking confidence. The stiff jab Cee delivered was far from that. Sharp and accurate, Cee's fist caught Jade on the tip of the nose. Blood ran from the girl's face, amplified by the cold, dry air.

"You're fucking dead," Jade growled, wiping away the blood. She looked at Maria, who had yet to reengage with Cee. "Get her, you fat bitch!" Jade snapped at Maria.

Maria had her wind back, but the gusto was gone. The two girls stalked in, ready to rip Cee apart.

A car horn blared. "Hey, cut the fucking shit!" a passing motorist yelled.

With Jade and Maria distracted, Cee took the opportunity to grab her bag and run.

"That's it, run, bitch!" Jade yelled. "Enjoy Christmas. It's the last fucking one you'll ever have."

ROCKS AND POWDER

Two weeks had passed since the incident with Jade and Maria. Cee had been walking to school every day, deciding it was a much better option than having to worry about getting jumped. It added some time to her day, but she cared little. Getting home wasn't a break from the depressing life she'd been cast into.

Winter was in full swing. The holidays had come and gone, leaving behind sparse gifts. It also brought with it the gray, miserable cold. Gone were the cheery holiday lights and festivities, replaced by the chill steel of the sky, which fought to keep the sun hidden from view. Bitter cold and snowstorms covered the area. The beauty of the white blanket was short-lived. The salt trucks and plows turned most of the snow into mush. Even the bare trees held little snow.

A trail ran through the woods behind her school. It was a common route used by kids to walk home or just to fool around on. An icy stream that fed a much larger river ran alongside the path. The trail was wide in most parts, but narrowed as it began going uphill. Higher it climbed above the stream, which ran swift and cold below.

The wind blew through the trees, gathering some of the

chill from the stream and carrying it to Cee. She hugged herself against the breeze. The trail was desolate, the subzero temperature driving most would-be walkers to instead take the bus or a ride from their parents. Neither was an option for Cee.

Cee wasn't particularly scared of the two girls, but fighting every day or getting cut wasn't something she wanted to deal with. She didn't fear them, but part of Cee feared herself.

When she hit Jade and saw the blood rush from her nose, something shifted in Cee. Violence wasn't new to her, thanks to her father. The night she witnessed Barry's fingers being torn off, she went home and touched herself. She didn't know why it aroused her, but it did.

After hitting Jade, something just changed in Cee. During the fight, she was too adrenalized to be scared. It was human emotion, especially for the psyche of a fourteen-year-old girl. But when she'd gone home, there was something different in her. The pain she'd felt from being hit and the soothing throb of her sore knuckles ignited something in her that was relaxing and relieving. She'd never had a better night's sleep than she did thinking about hurting the girls.

But it didn't stop there. Dreams of violence and murder flooded her brain. Visions of death replaced anything cheery. In her dreams, the blood flowed, and the weak begged. Things she'd seen on the news—mass shootings, genocide, rape, murder—swarmed her mind. What should've left her with a feeling of dread instead left her with happiness and ambition. And that alone caused her concern.

"I can't believe that faggot suspended us," a voice said, cutting through the cold air.

Cee froze, not wanting to crunch the icy leaves. She knew that voice. *Maria.*

"I know, right," Jade replied. "I think he's a fucking pedo, but he fucks little boys. A full fucking week for smoking a cig? And we were outside, being respectful."

At the mention of a cigarette, Cee could smell the smoke in the air. It appeared the teacher in question hadn't taken the cigarettes from Jade and Maria.

"My dad is gonna beat my ass," Jade said.

Cee inched closer, stepping carefully. As much as she hated them, Cee's curiosity pulled her in. Around a sharp bend, the girls came into view. Both stood on a large outcropping overlooking the stream. The white water was rushing, drowning out any sound Cee made.

Maria looked at her friend but didn't respond. Even Cee knew that Jade came from an abusive family. Her father had been in prison more than once and was constantly on parole. That didn't stop him from hitting the bars almost every night then using his family as punching bags. Jade's older brother, Julio, had left the day he turned eighteen, never looking back. But he had trade skills and money, two things Jade lacked desperately.

"I-I can take the blame for you," Maria said. "I'll go home with you and explain everything to your parents. Maybe your mother will understand and put in a good word for you."

Jade took another drag from her cigarette and shook her head. "Nah, my mom gets it worse than me. At least he doesn't rape me like he does her. Our walls are thin."

Cee watched the interaction between the girls. Her spying was voyeuristic and made her feel dirty. And while it excited her, it also made her feel something else: anger. There were two of the biggest cunts—tormentors to everyone—having a heart-to-heart, when they got their rocks off by hurting others. Cee was not one to forgive and forget.

Keeping her eyes on the girls, Cee bent down and pried a frozen rock from the ground. It wasn't very large, but it fit in Cee's palm perfectly. Coldness seeped into her flesh, but her heart was already frozen.

Cee moved down the trail, staring at the backs of the girls. Her heart thumped, and her brain begged her to think this through. What was she going to do, kill both of them in cold blood? She'd end up in prison for sure. No one would want to hear any self-defense argument when she bludgeoned them with a rock when their backs were turned. Cee didn't care. Just thinking about hurting them, seeing their blood, made her slick with lust.

The stream rushed below. It wasn't far beneath the trail, sitting maybe twenty feet to the rocky shoreline. It babbled, echoing up to the girls above.

Cee stalked closer, not knowing when they'd finish their smokes and turn. If they caught her, she'd have no excuse. What could she say when they saw her sneaking up with a rock in her hand? Nothing. It would be fight or flight at that moment.

The girls smoked, apparently oblivious to Cee lurking just steps behind them.

Jade flicked her cigarette down the embankment, where the icy stream took it away. "Come on, I'd better get home and prepare myself for when my pops gets off work."

As Jade turned, Cee swung, aiming at her nose. The amount of blood she'd drawn from a fist the last time she connected with it had been a lot, so she figured a rock would do nicely. She was right. The cold chunk of stone twisted the girl's nose sideways and shattered her top teeth. Gore shone brightly against Jade's skin as she stumbled back, losing her balance.

Maria stared, stunned, watching her friend blindly grope for something to stop her from falling down the embankment. She jerked away from Jade's flailing hand.

Cee didn't waste a moment. She swung the rock at Maria's head. The bloodied stone caught the girl under her right ear, breaking her jaw at the connection point.

Maria staggered. Her hand shot up, and a look of fear came over her when she felt the broken bone. Cee planted her left foot on the unsure ground and kicked, hitting Maria in the crotch.

Maria staggered back and turned just in time to see the rocks below as she fell.

Cee's heart was racing. She was cold, hot, warm, angry, happy, and alive. Her head snapped around, looking for anyone else on the trail. No one. Not even a squirrel to witness her crimes. The bloody stone felt great in her hand, but she had to get rid of it. She threw it over the embankment and into the rushing water.

A moan rose from below. Cautiously, Cee looked over the edge at what she'd done.

Maria was dead, of that there was no doubt. The girl had swan-dived into the rocks. Her legs went over her head, snapping her back in half at the waist. Even from high up, Cee could see Maria's bloody, dead eyes.

Jade was still very much alive. Something Cee was ready to change.

Carefully, Cee found a trail down the embankment. Using the trees to support her and cautious foot placement, Cee made it down to the stream, where she could witness her handiwork up close.

Jade was a mess. She lay on her back, gasping for air. Blood filled her mouth, and she spat, trying to get a breath. The bone of her left shin was jagged, exposed to the light. The torn flesh bled, soaking her pants.

Jade's eyes pled for help, but her words were only bloody croaks. Primal fear washed over her, the realization apparently dawning that Cee would offer her none.

"Not so fucking high and mighty now, are you?" Cee asked as she pried a large rock from the frozen shoreline. With any luck, the cops would label this an accident. There was nothing to link her to the girls, and she'd tossed the initial stone into the water.

The rock Cee lifted was large, just about the size of her head—a perfectly fitting size.

Jade began to cry and hyperventilate as Cee hoisted the rock high, blocking out the sun. Without another word Cee slammed the rock into Jade's face. A death rattle came from the bully's ruined mouth. Jade's jaw hung at a jaunty angle, and her fractured skull exposed a sizable amount of brain matter.

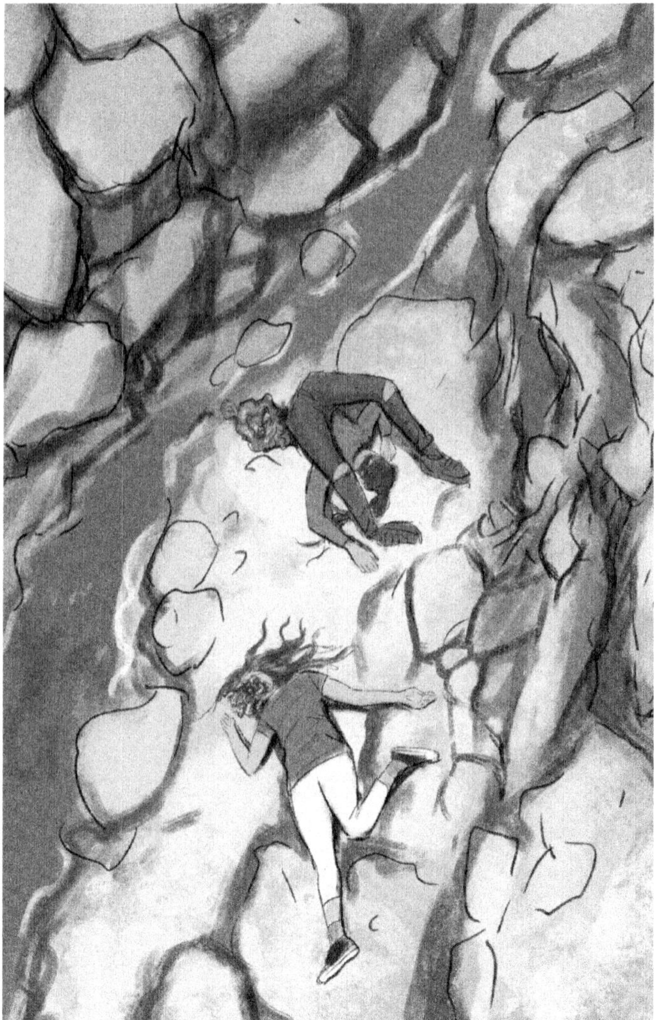

Cee stared at the dead girls like works of art. She couldn't help it. She wanted to take a picture, something to have and hold for the rest of her life. Something she could look back upon and smile. They might rule this an accident, but the cops would come sniffing for anyone who'd had issues with the girls. Cee wasn't stupid, even as a teenager.

She climbed back up the embankment, carefully checking herself for blood splatter. Satisfied, Cee grabbed her bookbag and walked the rest of the way home.

HOME

Vin grabbed a handful of clothes and stuffed them into a garbage bag. Frantically, he ripped the drawer from the dresser, upending it into the bag. Most of the clothes fell onto the ground, but he didn't have time to stop.

The phone rang again, and he could feel the anger seething through the rattle.

"Shit, Shadrick," Vin mumbled.

Vin ignored it, but the call felt like another tick off the time clock. He leaned over his dresser and snorted a generous pile of cocaine, which he'd purchased with money he'd stolen from the bookie. Vin's eyes watered and he could taste the potent narcotic in the back of his throat. He rubbed at his raw nostrils and snorted harder, ensuring the drug made it into his system.

Right when the phone stopped ringing it started up again.

"Fuck! He won't leave me alone!"

The clock had officially started. Since Vin wasn't about to answer, he knew it wouldn't be long until Shadrick or one of his hired hands paid him a visit.

Vin looked around his sparse room, trying to figure out what was worth stuffing into the car. He was out of time. With the garbage bag in one hand and the coke in the other, he darted back into the kitchen.

Keys rattled in the door. His eyes went wide.

There's no fucking way Shad made it here that quickly!

The coked-out paranoia was eating away at him. Vin dropped his bag and gently set the drugs down on the dirty table. He ripped a knife from the butcher's block and stood behind the door, preparing to kill at least one of them. If he could take out Shadrick, the world would be a better place.

The door swung open, and a head of black hair was the first thing he saw. Vin thrust with the knife, intending on sticking it into Shad's throat, but the man was much shorter than he'd remembered.

Cee!

His mind flashed a warning.

Vin stopped the thrust into the side of his daughter's neck at the last moment.

"Cee." Vin looked at the time on the stove. He didn't even realize how late she was. "Where the fuck have you been?" Vin put some concern into his voice, but he knew that once he was packed, he was leaving, with or without her. It hadn't been a conscious decision, but his self-preservation was number one.

"Dad, what's going on?" Cee looked at the disheveled kitchen. Cabinets stood open and bare.

Vin slipped the knife behind his belt like a pirate. He ripped a garbage bag from the black roll on the table and pushed it into his daughter's chest. Vin slammed the door behind her and threw the locks.

"Did you see anyone outside?" he asked. Vin's nostrils were white and caked with cocaine residue. He took Cee's shoulders and gave her a shake. "Cee, did you fucking see anyone? Remember that guy, Shad? We met him a few years ago when I traded off Grandma's ring. Was he out there?"

He read the confusion on Cee's face and shook her again, this time harder. "Answer me!" he yelled. His daughter recoiled.

"No, no one was out there," she said. "Where are we going?"

Vin let her go and checked the time. It had been almost five minutes since the phone started ringing.

"Fuck," he said. "I don't know, but we're leaving now, so get all your shit."

***

Cee was bewildered. Her dinky apartment wasn't a luxury house or high-rise, but it was home. She was even looking forward to school, being able to feign sadness about the death of her two classmates while secretly relishing the memory. But now things had changed once again.

Vin lifted the dwindling plate of cocaine from the table and snorted the rest. He licked any bit of residue that remained and washed it down with a warm beer.

"Fucking move your ass!" he screamed.

With tears in her eyes, Cee dashed away from him. Within moments, she returned with her belongings in a black garbage bag then stuffed them into the trunk of their shitty car.

With a chirp of bald tires, and her coked-out father behind the wheel, Cee left her life behind, heading into her uncertain future.

PRESENT DAY

THE BEST PLACE FOR A LOAD

The music thumped like a racing heartbeat. Even in the locker room, it could be felt through the walls. The girls of The Doll House had a better chance of escaping Shadows than they did the sound of the music. Still, the small locker room was a bit of a reprieve.

Juicy sat on a chair and unbuckled her heels. The tall shoes came off, exposing her cramped toes.

"Fuck me, that feels good," she said, rubbing at her feet. "I'd give my left titty for a real deal foot rub."

Juicy removed her blonde wig, revealing her natural, kinky hair in a net. Next were her dentures, which left behind a line of drool dangling from her mouth. What was originally a punishment had become her signature. A lot of johns came to see Juicy for her classic 'gummer' jobs.

When Juicy had first come to Shadows, she had been known as Shanice. Shanice heard of the underground casino and the millions of dollars that passed through it every day. She could deal cards and make drinks, so she thought she'd be a lock to land a job in the casino. But, Shanice also had another gift: a sleight of hand.

Ever since she'd been young, Shanice had nimble fingers. When she needed something, she didn't ask her mama;

she went and snatched it. On the few occasions her hands weren't quick enough, she ended up in some trouble, but nothing too bad. Until she wandered into Shadows.

Hired as a bartender who wore low-cut shirts and tight pants, the men couldn't help shelling out tips for the thick black girl. Shanice would talk them out of their hard-earned money, often swiping a little extra if she could. That wasn't the problem, even though she didn't know if the casino had caught on. Her problem was that she enjoyed dice, especially Sic Bo.

Sic Bo is a dice game that many gamblers aren't familiar with. It only uses 3 dice and some luck, making a perfect game for the streets. Shanice grew up hustling the local players when she'd swap loaded dice for the real ones. She was smart, only winning a few rolls here and there, but when she won, she won big time.

Shanice thought she would have the same luck at Shadows. After her first winning streak, she played it safe and called it quits. She didn't make it past the entrance of the room before two pit bosses grabbed her. Shanice almost pissed her pants when they brought her into a backroom where the owner of the casino, that cruel bitch Cee, sat waiting.

Shanice got to test her luck, rolling to see how many teeth she'd lose. It was Sic Bo rules, with three *legit* dice. Nine was her number and that day, Nine teeth were smashed out of her mouth.

"You don't work for me anymore," Cee told her as Shanice lay on the floor in a pool of blood and shattered teeth. "I own you now. Tomorrow, bring that juicy ass to The Doll House and meet Day Day."

That had seemed like ages ago, but Shanice still remembered the pain and sound of her teeth breaking. She gave her dentures a quick cleaning and popped them back into her mouth.

"Girl, one of these fools would probably pay to rub them dogs," Melinda said.

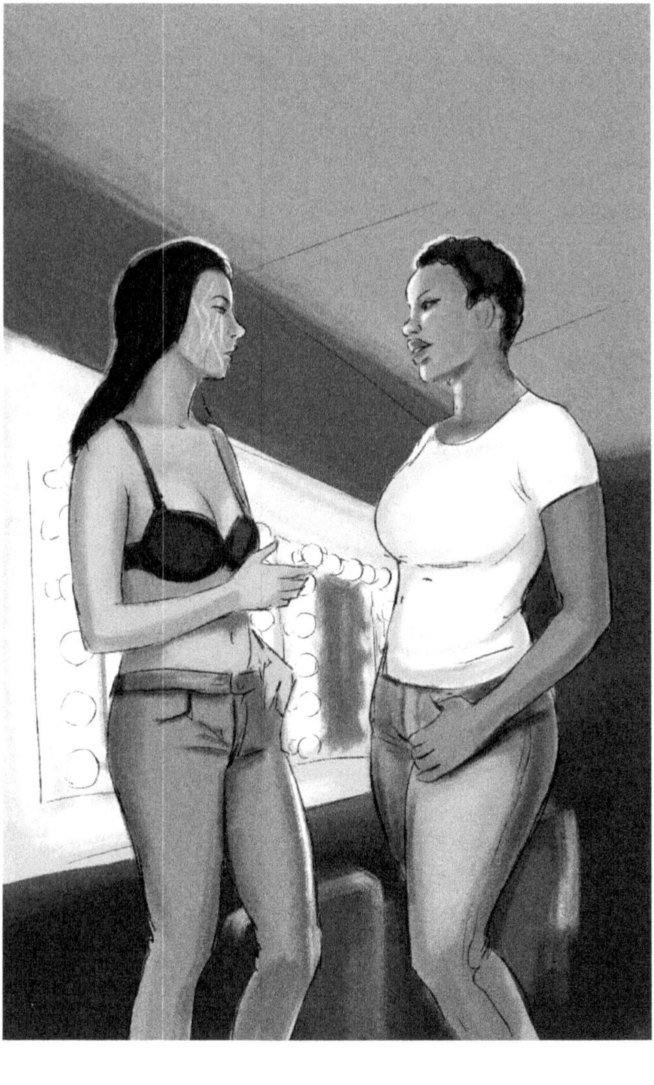

Melinda pulled her fake eyelashes off and set them on the locker room's makeup table. Giant hoop earrings dangled as she expertly used her fake nails to remove them. "Some of these sickos like to fuck feet." Melinda snapped her gum and grabbed a makeup wipe from a pack. She began scrubbing at her face like she was trying to remove her skin. It was the only way she could get the multiple layers of foundation out of the crisscross pattern of scars.

Melinda was a simple gambler. She liked straightforward games like slots, roulette, war, and her favorite, cut. Cut was the easiest of the games, with each player randomly cutting the deck and showing which card they pulled. Depending on the rules, the high card almost always won.

But, as she quickly learned after losing all of her money and having the trademark 'S' branded into her palm, nothing was easy in the casino. The first cut to her face was one of the worst feelings she'd ever experienced. By the end, her once smooth skin was flayed and gushing blood.

Her opponents didn't fare much better, each of them losing flesh and blood. Melinda had healed, but the itch to gamble hadn't. Finally, she'd been able to save a bit of cash, which she fully expected to blow with Juicy in the next few hours.

"I can't stand when they nut on my feet, but it's better than my face," Melinda said. "But nothing beats a good back shot, or a few thick ropes on my tits." She grabbed her chest and squeezed.

Lilly walked in looking at Melinda groping her breasts. Traces of dried semen were in Lilly's hair.

"Speaking of cum dumpsters," Juicy said. She picked her hair into a small afro.

Lilly looked at her. "What?" She turned to the mirror. "Jesus Christ." She pulled a makeup wipe from Melinda's pack. "How the fuck did no one tell me I had a load in my hair still?"

Melinda laughed as she rubbed the rest of the makeup from her face. Her scars stood out white against her pink skin. "You mean to tell me you didn't know you had nut on you? Damn girl, you are a slut. And who the fuck was that weirdo you were blowing? Fucking guy wearing a purple suit, lookin' like the Joker or some shit."

Lilly blushed, but there was nothing to be ashamed of. Each of them had done reprehensible things and would again. The plum suited man was far from the worst guy she'd blown.

"He certainly was a joker," Lilly mumbled just loud enough for Juicy to hear.

"Hey, why don't you come out with us tonight?" Melinda said. She put her hair in a tight ponytail and stripped off her shirt. "Nothing crazy, just a few drinks, maybe some blow, and possibly a semi-decent lay." She looked up and sighed. "Fucking a guy of our choice. Oh, what a dream."

Lilly didn't respond, seemingly lost in thought.

"You hearin' me?" Melinda persisted.

Turning her way, Lilly bore a subtle smirk.

"Girl, why you look so happy?" Juicy asked. "What isn't you tellin' us?"

"I think I might've met someone," Lilly said still trying to wipe the cum out of her hair.

"That much we can see," Melinda said glaring at the congealed nut. "Must've been packin' somethin' special to get you all worked up like this."

"No, it's not about that," Lilly said. "This guy's different. We talk, and like, he listens to what I say, and I listen to what he says but not in a john kinda way. And he's here for noble reasons: to save his mother and find his daughter."

Juicy glared at Lilly. "Sounds like a crock of shit. Baby, ain't no man walkin' into this place that's worth your time."

"I think you might be wrong about that," Lilly replied.

Juicy raised her eyebrows. "Say that same shit once you been here as long as I have."

Melinda glanced back at Lilly. "No need to argue about such things. Either way, Lilly, you should come with us. You don't gotta gamble."

"You need to get out a little," Juicy said. "Focus on somethin' else besides those silly ideas. She put on a lace bra, which was a size too small, and pulled a snug white top over it. The outline of her nipples were visible through the fabric. "Let us do the gambling, and maybe you'll bump into your little prince charming again." Juicy squeezed her thick ass into a pair of jeans that looked painted on.

Lilly, now devoid of random cum, tossed the wipe in the garbage. "I couldn't even if I wanted to."

Juicy shrugged, and Melinda's brow furrowed. "Why not?" Melinda asked.

Lilly tilted her head toward the club. "There's a new girl here. Apparently, she's going to be a part of the magic show tonight," Lilly said.

Melinda applied the lightest amount of powder to her face. It wouldn't cover the scars but would at least even her skin tone. "And where is this mystery girl?"

Lilly scrunched her face. She rolled her eyes back in thought. "She went to take a piss, but she should've been back by now."

The door to the room flew open. Carly barged in. Her scarred face was red and shiny.

"Lirry, yur gurl," she said as clearly as a person with no lips could say.

"What, what girl? The girl for the magic show?" Lilly shrieked. She grabbed the one-armed whore and shook her.

"Yeh, she'd dead," Carly said. "In da battroom. Ober-dose, I think."

Lilly went pale, pushing the woman out of the way and running.

Akari was almost struck with the door as Lilly burst from the room. She moved her wheelchair out of the way just in time to not get run over by the fleeing woman.

"What's going on with her?" Akari wheeled into the room and closed the door behind her.

"Apparently the girl she was supposed to be watching

just OD'd in the bathroom," Melinda said. "Day Day isn't gonna like that."

"Fuck Day Day," Akari said, a look of concern on her face. "I'd worry more about The Black Widow, if I were Lilly. The fucking bitch she is."

"Shhh," Carly said, putting a finger to her mouth. "She'th gonna hea you."

Akari sighed. "Probably, but I don't fucking care anymore." She looked down at the stumps of her legs. "Lilly is one of the good ones. Always has been. Hell, she helped me after," Akari looked at Carly, but lowered her voice, "Cee, took my legs." She rolled over to a mirror and touched up her makeup. "I'd hate to see anything happen to her. But, whatever. We're all fucked, aren't we?"

Juicy looked at the legless woman. "Damn, bitch, you're killing my vibe." That got a smile from Akari, even if it was strained. "Okay," she said to Melinda as she applied lip gloss. "Enough of this sad shit. Let's go gamble."

BOX OF HORROR

Shadows was always busy, but the employees knew when it was nighttime. The crowds changed, almost like the tide of the ocean. It didn't matter whether day or night, bettors would filter in to lose their life savings or lose their lives. It was a place where time didn't matter.

Juicy and Melinda were on the second shift at The Doll House, so they knew when their night ended, the real night-life was just beginning.

They left behind the pulsing sounds of the strip club, but their battered ear drums still played the house music in their brains.

"So, where do you want to hit first?" Melinda asked. Even with her scarred face, men still looked at her. She wasn't as busty as Juicy, but her chest was more than full enough to garner a catcall and double take. The amount of makeup she had to wear in the club was too much, but Day Day insisted. That was unless they had a specific john with a scar fetish.

A lot of the other girls bore horrific scarring as well, but most of theirs was throughout their bodies. Some johns didn't want a girl whose tits were scarred or partially missing. They just wanted a pretty face that was lined with deep cuts to dump their load on. It was another reason she wore fake lashes. Men liked to see their cum hanging from the falsies, and it kept the stinging load out of her eyes.

Juicy eyed up a group of young men, obviously first-timers, shouting with joy at a roulette wheel. They were drunk and hadn't realized the few pit bosses paying attention to them. If they didn't get their asses beaten, maybe Juicy would find them later. She didn't mind a gangbang from time to time.

"Mama needs to play some dice," Juicy said, blowing a kiss at one of the young men. He greeted her back by putting two fingers to his mouth like a 'V' and flicking his tongue.

"Charming," Melinda said.

A dull blast echoed from the walls and ceiling.

The young pussy licker jumped at the sound. His tongue shot back into his mouth and he seemed to sober up when he looked toward one of the smoking slot machines.

"Oh shit," Juicy said, picking up her pace. "Someone hit the big one."

Melinda followed suit.

All the girls knew the games had real consequences in the casino, but except for those who had found themselves enslaved due to losing a game, many of them hadn't witnessed much. Most of the girls wouldn't venture into the other parts of the casino after their shifts. They were content with staying out of trouble and saving the meager amount of money they were paid.

A small crowd had gathered around the remains of the slot machine. The machines were all surrounded with explosion-proof glass, making them look like an art exhibit. These were far from modern art but vessels of death. Just like at a regular casino, a bettor could hit it big in the slots. But unlike a traditional machine, the bettor could land on something not so desirable, resulting in the machine exploding.

Melinda and Juicy pushed and shoved, getting closer to the carnage. Gore splattered the inside of the clear box.

Teeth, bone, organ meat, and what appeared to be a breast implant, clung to the glass.

"Oh shit!" Melinda said, pointing. "Look at the clothes."

Juicy pushed an older woman out of her way and peered through a crack in the crowd.

Tattered pieces of a plum-colored suit, some of it still holding pieces of meat in its fibers, were strewn about inside the glass box.

Juicy laughed. "Isn't that the guy? The dude who nutted in Lilly's hair?"

Melinda chuckled. "I think so. Dumb fuck he was." The crowd was still gathering as casino staff converged on the mangled meat. "Let's go hit the buffet before we game. I need a little pick me up, and some blow would hit nice right now."

Juicy nodded. "Girl, you read my mind."

UNDERGROUND ALLEY

With their noses full of dust and drinks in hand, Juicy and Melinda made their way past the drug buffet and open bar before reaching the water fountain. They couldn't help but notice a very distinct man slumping on one of the wooden benches within the annex near the entrance.

"I seen a lotta strange ones in here, but that's different," Juicy said.

A man with a blackened eye, bloody hand, and massive port wine birthmark enveloping the side of his neck and face sat twitching. His eyes were closed, but his lids shuddered. His face was caked in dust.

"What the fuck is that thing on the side of his face?" Melinda asked, pointing at the port wine stain. "Looks like he got some super-herpes or suttin'."

"Girl, I don't know," Juicy said sipping her drink. "All I know is I wanna hit the tables."

Just beside the massive stone waterfall, the women passed a sign that outlined the primary sections of the casino. It read:

The Doll House.

The Main Floor.

The Theater.

Mystery Parlay.

Juicy and Melinda took the path to The Main Floor and made their way past the primary games to a small section at the rear of the casino. A black sign with the words 'Underground Alley' glowed eerily above a set of double doors.

While The Main Floor of Shadows was full of popular games such as poker, slots, roulette, and blackjack, the two women didn't concern themselves with them. After a long shift of dancing, fucking, and sucking, they couldn't be bothered with too much strategy, especially with games they didn't care for. Not to mention, many of those games were full with would-be players waiting and watching for someone to bust or lose too much blood.

As the doors to Underground Alley opened, Juicy and Melinda descended the steps into darkness. When they came out at the bottom, a series of lesser played and somewhat offbeat games faced them. Keno, Sic Bo, cut, three-card monte, pai gow poker, and other not-so-popular games were packed in the small area. A few of the tables had bettors, but others were nearly empty. Cigarette smoke created a haze, clinging to the ceiling.

Melinda upended her drink. She chewed on the ice cubes and rubbed her nose with the back of her hand, snorting any residual cocaine.

"Hey," Melinda said, grabbing the flabby arm of an aging cocktail waitress, "get me another gin and club. Heavy on the lime and the gin."

The waitress looked at the hand wrapped around her meaty bicep and shrugged it away. "Coming right up."

Juicy didn't want to miss the opportunity to get a fresh drink and downed hers. "Henny and Coke." She placed the cup on the already crowded tray.

The waitress walked away, grumbling.

"Fucking bitch," Melinda said. Then, snapping back to her friend, "Okay, let's make some money."

***

Melinda moved over to the Cut table. Even though the game resulted in horrific scarring, she couldn't help but listen to the call of it. If the table was empty, she'd play against the house, but if another player was present, they could opt to play against each other. The house would simply control the cards, ensuring that no one was cheating.

One other player sat there. He looked to be in his early 70s, balding, but his comb-over screamed of a guy who didn't want to give up. The stack of chips in front of him proved he didn't have to bet flesh, yet he wasn't with the normal bettors. An ashtray and a glass of bourbon sat in front of him. A pack of Marlboro Reds and an engraved Zippo rested on the felt.

Melinda followed his gaze as it slithered over her body. He licked his lips when he looked at her tits. There was no revulsion in his gaze when he noticed her scars. Melinda wasn't stupid. She knew how to play a man like a fiddle. And she was Charlie fucking Daniels.

The cocktail waitress returned with Melinda and Juicy's drinks. "Thanks, hun," Melinda said. There was a slight slur already. She tossed a $1 chip onto the tray. The waitress rolled her eyes and walked away, heading to Juicy, who was in her glory playing Sic Bo.

Melinda stuck out her tongue, licking the tip of the straw in a drunken, yet seductive manner. She didn't think the older smoker would be much of a lay. He wasn't ripped, but under the slightly loose skin, she could see muscle tone. His denim shirt was tucked in and only the slightest bit of a belly pushed against the blue fabric.

"Chet," he said, extending a hand to her. A jade ring adorned his right ring finger.

Melinda switched her drink to her left hand. Her palm was damp from the glass, but Chet didn't seem to mind. "Melinda," she cooed.

Chet gave a little laugh and grabbed his cigarettes. He popped a cowboy killer in his mouth and lit it. He squinted and exhaled through his nose.

"That's quite the lighter," Melinda said, admiring his Zippo.

Chet turned it over in his hand, looking at the insignia. "Oh yeah, this bad boy has been with me for decades." He put it to his lips and kissed it. "This was my good luck charm in 'Nam. Can't believe this place charges us to bring our trinkets in here. Bloodsuckers just can't get enough money, I guess. But I just wouldn't feel like a winner without it." He looked back at the design. "Company insignia engraved on her, but mine might be the only one left."

Melinda drank. "And where are the rest of them?"

Darkness washed over Chet's face, and his steel-blue eyes went gray. "Dead and buried, along with the men who carried them."

The seductive smile Melinda had on her face melted away like cotton candy in hot water. "Oh, I'm sorry to hear that."

Chet waved her away and picked up his glass. He sipped the amber liquid and took a healthy drag from his smoke. "Eh, water under the bridge." Chet looked at the dealer, who was watching and waiting. "Say, do wanna play the house or each other?"

Melinda put a few stacks of chips, mostly $1 and $5 denominations, on the felt. "Let's take *their* money, and then maybe me and you can make things interesting?"

The hint of sex in her voice snapped Chet out of his PTSD memories. He smiled at her, letting the smoke slither out from between his yellowed teeth. "Now that sounds like a great idea."

BOTTOM'S UP

Juicy's drink was going down smoothly. The waitress must've told the bartender to make it strong because it was almost all Hennessy with just a splash of Coke. Juicy looked at the Sic Bo board in front of her. The combinations of dice were numerous, but in her former life, she always seemed on point with her picks. Even though the game was random, Juicy had a knack for it, especially if she was using her loaded dice.

That was a mistake she'd never make again. She sucked at her dentures as a reminder of the day Cee knocked her teeth out for cheating and made her a sex slave to the casino.

It had been rough to get used to, but Juicy was resilient. She knew when she was beaten and when to fight. And the things she'd seen and heard in the deep casino led her to believe she'd made the right decision. She was grateful The Black Widow only took a few teeth and not her life.

The dice rolled again. Juicy missed her main bet but hit on two smaller ones. Her stack of chips was dwindling quickly, and the last thing she wanted to do was play with the 'S' branded on her palm.

Again, she stacked chips on the board, knowing her bet would hit. It didn't.

"Fucking bullshit," she said, a little louder than she should've. The alcohol and cocaine were getting to her. Juicy looked up at the black dome over the table. It was doubtful anyone was watching a Sic Bo table, but it was better to be safe than sorry. She mouthed *sorry* and made one last bet.

Melinda had a nice stack of chips in front of her. She was chatting it up with an old guy, who could've been her grandfather. They'd seen men like him constantly at The Doll House, old widowers hopped up on dick pills and bourbon looking to bust a nut or pop their heart. Either way, they were getting a release.

Juicy sucked at her drink as the dice rolled and landed. All losers. Nothing of hers hit, and just like that, she was out of money. She rolled one of her lips into her mouth and bit. It wasn't hard enough to draw blood but more than enough to keep from yelling. Juicy pushed the chair back and stepped away from the table. With a final slurp, she finished her drink. The booze was getting to her already and she turned to see the waitress standing there.

The older woman had a smile on her face and a fresh drink for Juicy. This one looked even lighter and was almost all alcohol.

Juicy's first sip confirmed her suspicions.

If I didn't know any better, I'd say this old bitch is trying to get me drunk. Maybe she's a dyke with a hankering for a black girl.

Sic Bo was not the game to play with flesh. There were too many ways to lose and not enough ways to keep your body intact. But three-card monte was another story. Not the perverted, Maxi pad version near the entrance of the casino, but with real cards.

A lonely dealer sat watching the rest of the tables. He was clean-cut with a Clark Kent haircut and not a trace of stubble. If Juicy hadn't seen him blink, she would've been convinced he was a robot.

"Can I interest you in a game?" he said with a voice that was just too smooth. For such a good-looking guy, Juicy was surprised they had him hidden away in the obscure room.

Juicy leaned in, showing her ample tits to the young man. "Baby, you can interest me in a lot." She pushed her tongue against the inside of her cheek, mimicking fellatio.

The young dealer smiled and shuffled the cards. "And what are we betting with this evening?" he asked, noticing Juicy hadn't laid down any chips.

"This," she held up her hand, showing the brand of the casino. "And these." She set her drink down and pulled her shirt low, exposing the top of her dark areolas. Juicy leaned in and looked at his nametag. "So, Bryce, you ever fuck a black girl? Split some black oak?"

Bryce's all-American cheeks turned an embarrassed shade of pink. "Ah, no. I can't say that I have."

"Play your cards right, and I'll show you why they call me Juicy." She blew him a kiss with her shimmering lips. "Now, deal the cards, baby."

"Of course," he said. Bryce flipped three cards face up. "Are you familiar with the rules? And would you like to bet shots to start, I assume?"

The cards landed face up and read:

Black jack.

Red nine.

Black three.

The player picked which card they wanted to follow before the dealer flipped them face down.

"I know the rules and yes, shots please," Juicy said. She finished the rest of her drink and pointed to the red nine. "I hope that's not the only nine I'm getting tonight."

The seductive insinuation that Bryce had a nine-inch cock was lost on the young man.

"Ready?" he asked, flipping the cards over.

"Do me, baby," Juicy said.

The cards danced. Juicy followed them with ease. Even with her vision blurred, she could keep track of her nine. Bryce stopped and Juicy tapped on the back of a card with a lacquered nail.

Bryce smiled and flipped it over, revealing her card.

"Yeah, baby," Juicy said. She drank from her cup and winced at the burn of alcohol. Bryce put a small stack of chips in front of Juicy. "Double or nothing," Juicy said, pushing the stack toward the center.

Bryce flipped the cards face-down again, and his nimble hands went to work. This time, he moved them like a man possessed. Juicy didn't know if the alcohol had finally caught up with her in full or if the dealer was fucking with her. After a few seconds, he stopped.

She was certain she had the right card. Again, Juicy tapped on one, but this time the jack stared at her. "Fuck," she said, as Bryce swept her chips away.

Bryce flipped and shuffled, and again, Juicy was wrong.

"Eat my fucking ass," she said.

Juicy looked at her cup, glad she had some booze left. Her gag reflex was strong but she didn't know what foul shit she'd have to shoot down.

Bryce reached under the table and pulled out a shot glass. It, like everything else, was marked with a red 'S' on one side and a black 'S on the other. Next, he removed a pitcher containing a murky liquid.

"Garbage water," Bryce said, as he filled her glass to the brim. "Fresh pressed only a few hours ago by the trash compactor." Bits of filth floated in the putrid shot. The sickly-sweet, pungent stink of rot was already testing her resolve. But she wasn't a fucking quitter.

"Gimme that shit," she said, grabbing the glass and throwing back the fetid drink. It burned, but not like alcohol, rather like the rancid taste of decay. The little chunky bits clung to her tongue, some wedging themselves between her gums and dentures. Juicy covered her mouth with the back of her hand, stifling a burp, but didn't vomit.

"Again," she said, putting the glass down.

Bryce smiled and nodded. His all-American charm was drifting away. What Juicy had found sexy only moments earlier now seemed downright creepy. He was too perfect and was enjoying watching her suffer. The cards flew, and Juicy picked.

Wrong again.

Juicy sipped from her drink, hoping the alcohol would kill whatever bacteria was in her mouth. The waitress hadn't been back, so she had to make it last.

Another pitcher was placed on the table. This contained a brownish liquid, but with nothing floating in it.

"The piss of our resident, Dirty Ricky," Bryce said as he poured a shot.

Juicy had been a prostitute long enough to have her share of golden showers. She'd taken down a little gulp here and there. Never a full shot, but a drunken john or two had pissed in her mouth. Like a pro, Juicy tossed the ammonia-smelling shot back.

"Gotta do better than that," she said.

Bryce smiled and moved the cards. But just as he got moving, his shuffle was interrupted by a scream.

A LITTLE OFF THE TOP

Melinda couldn't believe her luck. She'd won almost every hand against the house, and she and Chet had each amassed healthy stacks of chips. The liquor made her warm and horny, and the more she stared at her tablemate, the more she knew they were going to fuck.

Melinda leaned closer to Chet, breathing in his scent of cigarettes and old man cologne. She rested a hand on his inner thigh, running her nails up toward his bulge.

"Say, why don't we do something a little more fun than cut cards?" she asked. "How about you take me somewhere quiet and split me open?" She opened her legs as if Chet didn't get the hint.

He smirked and picked up his drink. "Why don't we play for it?" Chet sipped, grimaced, and chugged back the rest. "We've been beating his ass all night. Let's take a run at each other. No money, only flesh."

Melinda smiled. "Oh, daddy, that sounds good."

"Head?" Chet asked.

Melinda stuck out her tongue. "Oh baby, I'm sure that tongue of yours would do wonders to my pussy. And even if I lose, my punishment is putting this thick cock in my mouth?" She squeezed his growing erection. "Sounds like a win-win."

Chet smiled as Melinda pulled back into her chair. "Ladies first," he said, gesturing to the shuffled deck.

Melinda grabbed the deck and cut it, revealing the seven of spades.

"Oh darn," she said, but with a smile. "I can taste that cock already."

Chet grinned and cut the deck, showing a ten of hearts.

"Looks like you win," Melinda said. Again, she leaned in toward him, both hands on his thighs. "Do you want me to suck you off right here? Give everyone a show while you drain your heavy nuts down my throat?"

Chet touched her face with a rough finger, then grabbed her hair.

Melinda shrieked as he pulled her head back, making her eyes snap open. "Ow, what the fuck?" she yelled, reaching for his hand. "Let go of me."

"Do you know why the Viet Cong killed my entire squad?" With his free hand, he picked up his lighter. "This." He held it in front of her face. "This emblem was their fucking boogeyman. Men, women, children—it didn't matter. We killed what we saw. And you know what? We fucking loved it." He was grinning, yellow teeth slick with saliva. "We'd take their fucking scalps, all of them. If we were lucky, we'd catch one or two alive, usually the kids, and cut them fresh. They were our trophies, our poker chips. Many nights, we'd sit in the jungle betting scalps. Killing was our business, and we were fucking good at it." Chet looked at the dealer, who was less than impressed. "A blade, my good man."

The dealer dropped a box cutter on the felt. Chet grabbed it and exposed the edge.

"No, please!" Melinda screamed. Tears ran down her face, ruining the light makeup she'd put on. "I'll do whatever you want."

"I know," Chet said and began cutting. The blade sliced through her forehead with ease, marring the skull. Chet pulled as he cut, separating flesh from bone. It tore and ripped like fabric, only drowned out by the sound of Melinda's screams. "The gooks screamed the same way. I guess language has nothing to do with pain."

Blood ran down Melinda's face as she clawed at Chet's hands. The old man had a steel-like grip on her scalp, pulling still. Her wet skull was exposed, pink and glistening. Melinda's fake nails snapped off as she gouged furrows in Chet's hands.

"Cunt," he growled. With a flick of the wrist, Chet changed the angle of the blade and slashed Melinda's face. The tip of the razor slid through her eye, laying it open. Ocular fluid and gore mixed with the steady wave of blood already rushing down her cheeks. Melinda grabbed her ruined eye, cupping it as if that would keep the pain from setting in.

Chet clutched the flap of scalp that was hanging from her head and kept cutting. Moments later, her skin came off in his fist. Strands of hair and torn meat dangled from his grip, dripping onto her chest.

"Looks like I win," Chet said, admiring his grisly trophy.

Finally, freed from the madman, Melinda jumped from the chair and ran. Her bloody skull reflected the light of the casino as she fled.

***

Chet looked at the dealer, who almost seemed bored. "How much is this worth for a bet?"

The dealer huffed and took back the bloody knife. "Sir, you can only bet with your flesh, not others."

Chet laughed and laid the scalp on the seat where Melinda once sat. He picked up his cigarettes and lit one. "I know. I'm just messing with you. This is my trophy." He tossed some chips in the middle. "Shall we keep playing?"

SHOULD HAVE CALLED IT

Juicy felt a pang of guilt as she watched Melinda run away screaming. It was all part of the casino, and they both knew coming out could lead to some dangerous shit. Juicy was getting close to calling it a night, but it was hard for her. She knew her luck was bound to change and hated the fact that she'd go back to her bunk with no money and a belly full of sick shit.

"Is there any way to up the ante? Maybe a bigger shot or something?" she asked.

Bryce nodded at her and smirked. "So, you want the big shot, do you?"

Juicy watched the crowd part for her injured friend. After the disappearance of Porsche and Melinda's fucked up face, Juicy should've known better than to tempt fate. But she wasn't a quitter.

"Yeah, let's do the big shots, and then I'm done. Win or lose, this is it for me."

"As you wish," Bryce said. He removed the shot glass and reached under the table. What he came out with left Juicy speechless.

A metal tray held three hypodermic needles and three unlabeled vials.

"Whoa, whoa, what the fuck is that for?" Juicy asked. Her dark skin glistened at the sight of the needles.

Bryce began filling the hypodermics each with a different chemical contained in the mystery vials. "These are the big shots," he said, flicking one of them to push the air bubble free.

"Oh, hell no," she said. "I didn't agree to this. I wanted bigger glasses, not fucking needles," Juicy said. She stood. "I never seen any shit like this before."

Bryce smirked. "Well, here in Underground Alley management is always looking to keep things interesting. You can only do the same old thing so many times."

Juicy's eyes peeled wide. "Yeah, I think I'm done for the night."

Bryce looked at her and raised an eyebrow. "I don't think so. You made the bet, and I've already prepped the game. You have no choice. You're playing."

"You can kiss my black ass," Juicy said. She stumbled a bit from the alcohol, but she was not sticking around one second longer.

"I wouldn't do that if I were you," Bryce said. He pointed at the camera above them. "If you refuse to play, you're stealing from the casino. And I think you know what the penalty for that is. Trust me, this game is nothing compared to what will happen if you walk away." He leaned in close to her. "I've heard things. Fucked up things that she does to people." He didn't realize Juicy was also an 'employee' of the casino. "The owner—the one they call The Black Widow—you don't want to cross her."

Juicy was on the verge of tears, but she knew he was right. The woman had spared her once and that was a blessing. There was no way she'd survive a second time.

"Listen, it's a two in three chance of survival. I loaded two of the needles with nothing but saline. But the third," Bryce waved his hands over the hypos like he was in an infomercial, "is full of some nasty shit. A special cocktail just for this place."

Juicy's mind raced. There had to be a way out of it, a way to cheat the game. She tugged at the bottom of her shirt, exposing more of her ample cleavage.

"Listen, Bryce. I work here too. I'm stuck in The Doll House, so I know how shit goes down. If you just tell me which one is the poison, I'll throat that cock of yours every day. Just come find me, day or night, and I'll suck you off so good your fucking ears will ring. Or you can fuck me. I take it in the ass, titty fuck… Whatever shit you're into, I'll do it." Juicy noticed the swelling in Bryce's crotch. It wasn't quite nine inches, but it looked plenty big for her.

Bryce blushed. "While that does sound enticing, I can't. Even if I wanted to, I wouldn't be able to help you. The bottles came to me unlabeled, so I couldn't be tempted to help the bettor. Not that I would; that would be suicide."

Juicy didn't believe him. "Okay, let's fucking do this then." She wished she had some more blow to take the edge off or maybe get her hyped to possibly end her life.

Bryce pushed the tray forward, each needle full. "Make your choice and pick a spot."

Juicy's hand hovered over the tray. Her eyes flashed back and forth between the needles. Going on instinct, Juicy grabbed a hypo, hesitated for a second, and plunged it into her bicep.

"Do it," Bryce ordered.

Juicy pushed the plunger, flooding her body with a mysterious substance. She didn't know what to expect or how long it would take for the poison, if she'd chosen wrong, to take effect. After two heartbeats, Juicy found out.

It was as if she'd swallowed a bag of cotton balls. Her throat closed tight, sealing it off. Panic set in as Juicy ripped the needle from her arm and clawed at her throat. Her vision blurred, but she could see enough to feel hatred toward the playful sneer on Bryce's face. Juicy hacked, yet couldn't find the air. Her lungs felt full of liquid and each cough seemed to bring more forth. She spewed a wad of tan phlegm onto the table but still couldn't breathe.

Juicy's vision worsened, as she wept blood. Another hack coursed through her body, again bringing phlegm a nasty shade of brown.

Falling to the ground, Juicy's mouth was open and flapping as she fought for just one breath. The desire to fill her lungs with air distracted her from the fact that blood was leaking from every orifice in her body. Burgundy slop ran from Juicy's vagina as her body dissolved from the inside out. Her fertile uterus became nothing but sludge, more reminiscent of strawberry jam, as it poured from her slit. Blue jeans turned a horrid shade of crimson.

Juicy tore at her throat. Her fake nails were long gone. The stubs she had filed down opened her neck for just one breath. Foamy, pink vomit spewed from her mouth and nose. Her body convulsed, and her bloody eyes rolled back into her head. Within moments, she was still. The only movement was the flood of ichor that continued to flow from her corpse.

EIFFEL TOWER

Lilly pushed people as she ran toward the bathroom.

"Get the fuck out of my way!" she yelled, shoving another john. His drink sloshed all over the floor, and he yelled something unintelligible at her. The other girls looked at Lilly, some glaring.

Most of the girls got along with Lilly just fine. They were all in it together, stuck working in The Doll House. Each of them had their methods of survival, and Lilly was no different. Yet to some of them, she was. Lilly was there for the money and another important reason: she had nothing else. The greatest risk she'd taken before that night was when she'd run away from home.

Lilly didn't believe her mother when she told her that if she walked out the door, she could never return. A few months on the streets, one bad assault, and multiple rape attempts was more than enough for the teenage girl. When Lilly went back home, she found it empty. The windows were boarded or smashed, and a pile of bills sat on the cracked stoop.

From there Lilly drifted from flophouse to flophouse, selling herself for a roof over her head or food in her belly. After a few weeks of hitchhiking, Lilly found herself in yet again another city.

Some of the girls spoke about an underground casino and the horrors contained inside.

With nothing but her name, Lilly ignored the warnings, thinking the girls were stuck up. They were local whores, ones who never had to fight for a meal or spend nights on the street. Even if half of what they said about the casino was true, Lilly could deal with it.

Shadows offered a place to stay, food, drugs, and a regular schedule. She didn't have to suck cock or get fucked in truck stops anymore. At Shadows, she could be in a room with a bed.

Through one of the local pimps, Lilly was introduced to Day Day, the manager of the girls at the casino. Lilly was in awe when she first entered Shadows. But when she saw another girl get sliced open on the dance floor, Lilly knew things were different. Under the flashing lights and ringing of bells came screams. Beneath the tons of stone overhead, Lilly longed for the sky and the uncertain safety of the streets.

Lilly was no longer much of a gambler, but she took a major gamble when she let the junkie, Star, out of her sight. Lilly kicked open the bathroom door.

She didn't want to give the two perverts who were fucking the corpse of the junkie credit, but she did. The men, both high and drunk out of their minds, had the dead girl bent over a garbage can. She was nude, and tinged blue. One guy stood by her face, holding her head at an unnatural angle as he fucked her mouth. The second guy, with his pants around his ankles, was behind her, giving her pussy all that he had.

A pungent smell of shit wafted through the air, and Lilly realized the girl had lost control of her bowels when she'd died. Wet feces plopped to the ground with every aggressive fuck from the guy at the back.

Two other degenerates stood off to the side, playing with their flaccid cocks in hopes they'd be next. A third guy groped a dangling tit with one hand and jerked off with the other. He stared at nothing, as if no one else was in the room. Before Lilly could make a sound, the third man increased his pace, jerking his cock like he was trying to pull it off.

"Gah!" he shrieked, and shot a rope of cum onto the dead girl's back and the stomach of the guy fucking her mouth.

"Hey, man, that's not cool," Mouth Fucker said, his hairy gut wet with sweat and foreign spunk.

Lilly's brain and mouth finally caught up with her eyes, and she screamed. "Get the fuck out! All of you!"

The five of them froze as if realizing for the first time they had a small audience that gathered in the bathroom.

Lilly rushed them, swinging. Her first punch hit the guy who was fucking the dead girl's pussy. Not realizing his pants were still around his ankles, he stumbled backward and fell.

"Hey, what the fuck?" he asked, lying on his back.

Lilly wished she were wearing spikes, but the low heels she had on would do just fine. She stepped forward and stomped, crushing his droopy sack against the tile floor.

"Ah!" he screamed.

With Lilly distracted and their gangbang partner injured, the other perverts skittered out, desperately trying to put their dicks away.

She wanted to keep going. Lilly wanted to hurt him. Tears stung her eyes as she looked at the violated corpse of the junkie. It wasn't hard to figure out what happened, especially with the hair tie still wrapped tight around the dead girl's arm. She'd lived with enough users to know an addict when she saw one.

Lilly cried. She cried, but she didn't know why. Was it for the life lost in the bathroom? This poor girl was brought in as entertainment for the night, only to find herself dead and violated in a filthy bathroom, a scene Lilly had seen before, living on the streets. Or did she cry for herself, knowing it was her responsibility to keep this girl safe? It could've been the totality of everything, the hell that was Shadows and the devil that kept them all in check.

It was the same pain and finality as the day she returned home with her tail between her legs to find her mother gone. She knew now, and then, times were about to get rough.

"Ay yo, what the fuck is going on in here?" Day Day asked as he pushed through the small crowd. He put a hand to his nose. "Oh fuck. It smells like shit." He looked at the carnage then at Lilly and grabbed her. "Tell me that's not the girl? Tell me that ain't the bitch whose showtime is in an hour."

Lilly just looked at him with her mouth agape and tears in her eyes. "I… ah, I'm—"

Her plea was cut off with a slap in the face. "Spit it the fuck out," Day Day said. The injured john clutched his ruined balls as he walked by them. Day Day gave him a swift kick in the bare ass with his designer shoes just on principle.

Snot ran down Lilly's face. "Yes, that's her." Lilly looked at the dead girl, who'd fallen off the garbage can and lay face up, staring at nothing.

"Fuck." Day Day let Lilly go. He clenched and unclenched his fist but didn't strike again. "Out, get the fuck out!"

Lilly listened and slipped out past the crowd. She wished she could burrow into the wall and disappear, but in Shadows there was no hiding.

THE LOWEST EARNER

Cee pushed the flashback out of her mind, snapping back to the present. It was long ago, but one of the most important days of her life. Watching Jade and Maria die and feeling no remorse might have been excusable. They'd tormented her for years, and they'd finally received justice. But that Cee *enjoyed* killing them, watching them suffer and die, was another thing.

From that day, she knew she was a changed woman. Something deep inside her had awoken. The pleasure she'd felt from hurting and killing was second to none. Only when she could combine sex was it any better. But death came before orgasms in her world. A world shaped by two men: her father and Gianni.

Cee sat in her high-backed chair. It groaned as she leaned, but she needed a breather after The Red Room. Often, she'd find herself too worked up after a kill, seeking another one too soon. If there were a lot of careless bettors, that wouldn't be an issue, but if there weren't, she'd look to force one. It was bad for business, trying to rig anything. But lately, Cee had a hard time resisting her urges. Every day she felt herself slipping, and it was noticed. Marty wouldn't challenge her, but she'd seen his stares of disapproval at some of her decisions. His quips or comments about Gianni didn't go unnoticed.

Gianni was a reckless man, thinking himself always to be in charge. Cee wasn't reckless, at least in her mind. Her eyes wandered to the screen showing The Red Room.

Gianni's severed manhood was a case in point of how careless he was. His were preserved, unlike Clayton's pathetic pecker, which had been discarded like trash.

Marty sat in a leather chair near to her, reading a day-old newspaper. He thumbed through it, stopping to scan the obituaries. He sat up and closed the newspaper then adjusted the volume on his radio. "Yeah, go ahead." He put a finger to his earpiece, pushing it deeper. "No shit." Cee looked at him with concern and excitement in her eyes.

"I'll tell her," Marty said. Pointing at the monitors, he stood and walked over to Cee's desk. "Some crazy fuck just entered The Mystery Parlay. Apparently, he's been making the rounds all night." He paused and listened to whomever was on the other side of the radio. "Before he went into The Mystery Parlay he put a note on some guy who was passed out."

Cee perked up. "Perfect. He sounds like the ideal player for our little parlay."

The Mystery Parlay was one of the best things Gianni created in Shadows. It was the ultimate gamble for those desperate enough, containing three rooms of risk. Like everything in Shadows, the consequences were severe, but the payout was unlike anything else. No other game in the casino could make you as rich as The Mystery Parlay, but there was no 'breaking even' in there. It was all or nothing, and the 'nothing' was death.

Cee clicked on the keyboard, showing the first room of the parlay. A bald man stood with his head down, defeated. The wheel he'd just spun was stopped on *saw off your arm.* His chest rose and fell, and he looked up toward the camera.

Cee clicked the microphone icon as the man spoke.

"This can't be the end!" he yelled. Cee turned the volume down as his shrill voice was distorted. "I don't fucking lose!"

His time was running out. "Fuck!" The man grabbed a hacksaw and placed the teeth of it in the crook of his elbow.

Cee stared with anticipation, waiting for the first cut. The blade hissed across his flesh, opening his pale skin.

"Mmmm," he grunted. The blood was flowing but not pouring. Not yet, at least. Time was ticking away. "Ahh!" He pistoned his arm back and forth, burying the blade deeper, ushering forth more crimson.

The sound of tearing played over the speakers as his flesh parted beneath the saw. Then, the sound changed. A loud rasp whined through the room as the metal teeth found bone.

A rictus grin of insanity was etched on the face of the bald man. Sweat poured down his pale skin, mixing with blood as it dropped to the floor. The fingers on his ruined arm, one of which was adorned with a garish ring, were immobile, as tendons and nerves were severed. His arm hung slack but was still attached by strands of meat.

Time was running out. Cee found an icon on her screen that would allow her to release the poison gas, killing the man. Her finger hovered over the button as his time ticked away.

Lowering his mutilated arm to the ground, the bald man stepped on his ruined hand. He stood tall, pulling the arm in attempt to rip the last bits of flesh keeping him from the next spin of the wheel. Blood spurted from the jagged wound he'd inflicted, coating the floor. As time ticked closer to zero, the arm came off.

The bald man fell to his ass, just as time expired. "There! Are you fucking happy?" He struggled to his knees and reached out for his mutilated arm. With shaking fingers, he tried to pry the blue-gemmed ring from his severed hand. Blood rushed from his stump. The dexterity in his remaining hand was waning as he struggled to get the ring free. "My… my good luck charm." It was the last thing he said as he collapsed.

"Oh well," Cee said. The timer for the man's next spin of the wheel ticked down to '0'.

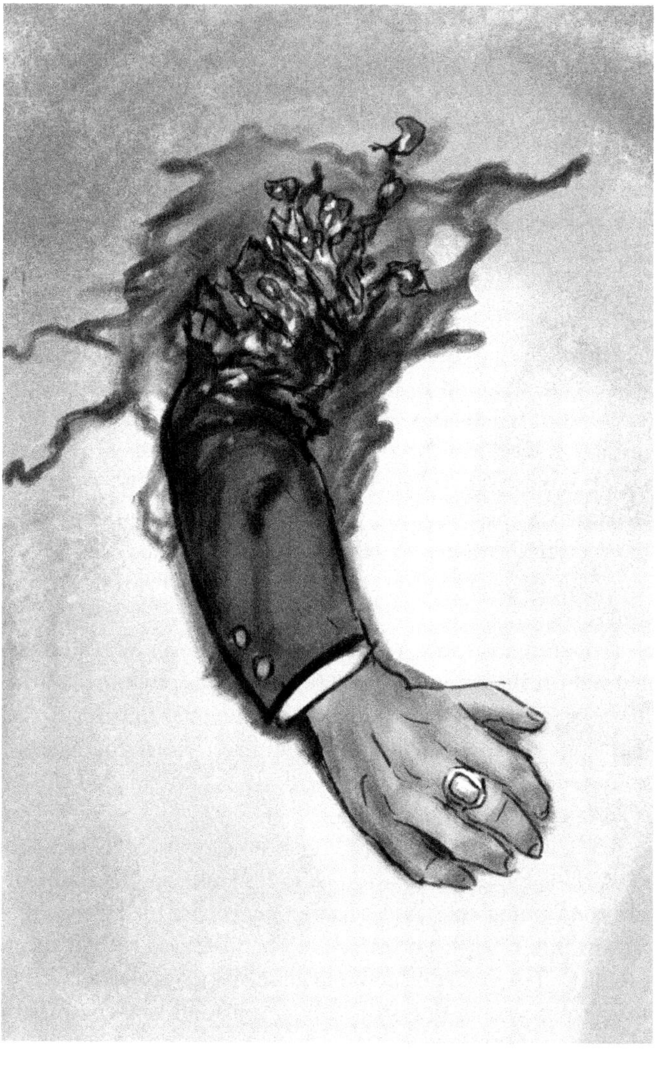

With a touch of her mouse, Cee filled the man's room with deadly Zyklon-B gas.

Blood continued to ooze from the mangled stump of his arm as his breath slowed to a halt.

"Give that a few minutes to work its magic and then call a clean-up crew," Cee said.

Marty reached down and changed the channel on his radio. He spoke into the mic, giving the order to those who would dispose of the man's body. He stood and wandered around listening to the chatter on his radio.

Cee watched him but noticed a shift in his demeanor. Marty pressed the earpiece deeper as if struggling to hear.

"What is it?" Cee asked.

"I can barely hear you. Call me in the boss's office," Marty said. He shook his head. The phone rang and Marty snatched it before it rang twice. "Day Day, what the fuck is going on?" Marty listened, his face growing more and more aggravated. "Hold on! I'm going to put you on speaker. Okay, tell the boss what you just told me."

Cee leaned forward in her chair.

"Ah, heya, boss," Day Day said. "So, the girl you brought in for the magic show, she had herself a good time at the buffet. A little too good."

"Spit it out," Cee demanded.

"Well, she took a little too much H. She's dead, boss."

Cee licked her lips and took a deep breath. "You mean to tell me that the girl we brought in specifically for Calypso's act, one of the biggest acts we've ever seen, is dead? Is that what you're fucking telling me?"

"Um, yeah," Day Day said. "I had a girl assigned to watch her, but she didn't." He spoke with a little more gusto, realizing he could pin the death on someone else. "You know how busy it gets running the club, so I took one of my lowest earners and made her into a babysitter. And let's just say, the bitch fucked up." Day Day had a glimmer of hope in his voice, finding a common enemy. "I would've beat the shit out of her myself, but I know the girls are yours, boss."

Cee's thoughts went again to the severed cock and balls floating in the jar in The Red Room. She wished they were Day Day's. "And which one of the skanks did you put in charge of her?"

"Lilly," Day Day blurted, all too excited. "She was supposed to be watching her, but somehow the girl ended up with her face in some dope. They found her dead in the bathroom a short time later."

"Lilly, huh?" Cee said. She smiled and nodded. "Okay, don't let her out of your sight. Tell her she's done well. Tell her that after tonight, she's going to be a big star."

Cee hung up.

"I can send Manx down to grab her," Marty said, with his radio already in hand.

"Do that. Lilly doesn't like to gamble or play my games. That's fine. Let's see how she performs on the big stage."

Marty grabbed the radio and spoke. "Manx, come in."

"Go ahead, Marty," Manx said. The sound of casino games rang in the background.

"Head over to The Doll House," Marty said. "Day Day is going to have a girl waiting for you. Her name is Lilly, and she's needed for the magic show, ASAP."

"Consider it done."

Marty clipped the radio back onto his belt.

Cee stood and adjusted her necklace, finding a thrill in her proximity to the scarred poker chip kept within it. "I supposed we'd better get to The Theater. Wouldn't want to miss the show now."

GRAB AND GO

A neon pink sign flashed The Doll House above the entrance to the club. Manx stood outside; he'd seen enough freaks in his time overseas and in the hood to last a lifetime. A woman came walking out in a pink leather dress and fishnet stockings. Her face was caked with garish makeup, which did little to hide the pockmarks on her skin.

Manx looked to Day Day, who bobbed his head in the direction of the girl.

"Lilly, I assume," Manx said, approaching her.

"Yeah, that's me," she said. "So, what's this all about?"

Manx gently grabbed her by the arm. "Just come with me." He ushered her away from the club, through the annex, and past a large sign with an arrow that read: The Theater.

Lilly was getting visibly nervous. Her breathing was picking up, and she was chewing her bottom lip. "Why can't I know what's goin' on?"

Manx exhaled. "The main act in the magic show had to cancel, and the boss needed a fill-in. Day Day said you were one of the best, so he sent you."

Lilly tilted her head and huffed. "I figured as much. And if by cancel, you mean died, then yes, she canceled. So, what do I have to do?"

Manx looked at her and stopped. "Well, first, you need to wash the dried cum out of your hair. Then you get to star in the magic show. What that entails, I don't know, nor do I care."

Lilly blushed and put her hand on the side of her head—the semi-dry load clumped her hair together. The makeup wipe must not have worked as well as she thought. She scurried away, finding the nearest lady's room.

She emerged moments later, the side of her head slightly damp. "Better?"

"I guess," Manx said. "Now, let's get going before the boss has both of our asses."

The pair walked around a side entrance to The Theater and into the backstage area of the magic show.

"Oh my God, are you the new talent?" a flamboyant stage manager wearing a shirt two sizes too small and way too much cologne shrieked.

Manx pushed Lilly forward. "Knock 'em dead."

"Ah, yeah, I guess," Lilly said.

The stage manager started eyeing her up. His gaze wandered to her hair and stopped.

"What's in your hair?" he asked.

"I had some… someone spilled a drink on me, so I washed it."

The stage manager reached out and touched her wet hair. His fingers stuck together with the tacky residue of semen. He licked his fingers. "Spunk? Why do you have spunk in your hair?" He wiped the remaining semen on his skinny jeans. "Forget it. I don't want to fucking know. Just follow me, and we'll get you dressed and cleaned up."

THE SHOW MUST GO ON

Cee took a seat on the balcony above the audience. The Theater wasn't very large but spacious enough for Shadows' intimate shows. It was a packed crowd, with only a few seats remaining. Calypso the Cunning and his assistant, Dead Betty, were one of the hottest acts around. It had been sheer luck that Cee'd been able to snag them for a performance. They were mere weeks away from becoming a permanent fixture in Vegas. Their act was amazing, all too perfect for a place like Shadows.

The curtains were closed and the projector displayed the image of Calypso's signature mask—horned with spirals for eyes. A dull murmur rose from the anxious audience as the lights dimmed and corny music played. The crowd quieted down and the curtains opened.

Marty handed Cee a cigarette and lit it for her.

"Have you ever seen these guys before?" she asked.

Marty extinguished the flame and drew on his own cigarette. "No, can't say that I have." He clicked his radio off, she assumed to enjoy the show uninterrupted. His staff knew where he was and were more than capable of handling just about anything, so she granted him the time off.

Cee grinned. "Perfect. You're in for a treat."

Calypso and Dead Betty came running out onto the stage to the sound of applause. Dead Betty's grim grin beamed back at the audience. Her skull-face mask was every bit as unsettling as Calypso's devil mask.

"It's fun and with an acceptable amount of gore." Cee put her cigarette into her mouth. "Dead Betty dies," she raised her fingers using air quotes, "in every act. Only to come back again. The front row or two will get a little bit of fake blood on them from time to time, completing the effect."

Marty grunted. "Huh, pretty cheap, if you ask me." He smoked. "With the amount of death under this roof, why bother faking it?"

Cee shrugged. "I suppose sometimes it's just nice to use your imagination."

The first illusion began. Calypso rolled out a realistic guillotine in front of the audience. Dead Betty was silent as she was led to the execution machine. Her skull-face morphed into a worried grin when her neck was set beneath the heavy blade.

With a magician's flourish, Calypso stepped off to the side. He grabbed the pull rope and yanked.

The blade fell, biting through flesh and landing with a thump. Dead Betty's head rolled off, landing in a basket. A fan of blood sprayed from the stump of her neck, misting the crowd. The audience gasped and shrieked, but Calypso didn't seem nervous.

He pulled another string, which released a black curtain over the guillotine. With a few waves of his magic hands, the curtain fell completely, landing on the floor to reveal a very intact and alive Dead Betty. The crowd cheered and hollered, clapping for the miracle of theater.

"Impressive," Marty said. He put his cigarette out in an ashtray nearby.

"You haven't seen nothing yet," Cee said. She smoked hers to the filter before stubbing it out.

The show went on, each trick more and more gore-filled and death-defying. Cee watched Dead Betty be fed into a wood chipper, turning her into a human slurry, from which she was miraculously resurrected, only to then be wrapped in wire and electrocuted until her skin blistered and eyes burst. Finally, she was drowned in a dunk tank, covered in heavy chains, until the bubbles stopped rising. Each time, the skull-faced assistant came back as good as new.

But during the series of magical feats, Cee's focus drifted momentarily to a familiar face—an unmistakable one.

The man with the red birthmark.

As she stared down from the balcony, she spotted him in the back of The Theater. Even in the low light, she could make out Red's glaring port-wine birthmark.

But it wasn't just her who had noticed him, he'd returned the favor. Red was staring up, looking at her as if she were a demon.

As Red's limbs tweaked about, Cee saw the signs of intoxication. She let out a long sigh.

Looks like he went back to his old ways.

She wasn't surprised when he nodded out in his chair. He looked like he'd spent some quality time at the buffet. Could she blame him? After all, she was the one who suggested he and the others at the roulette table drop by.

Red's weakness was one she was all too familiar with. In some ways she believed the man harbored the same personality traits as her father. Yet when she first laid eyes upon him via the cameras inside The Doll House, he seemed to be trying to do everything for his daughter that her own father never did for her.

Such a disappointment.

She couldn't bear to look at him any longer. She would deal with the emotions he stirred up at a later time.

Cee's gaze returned to Calypso as he walked off stage and returned with a microphone.

"Thank you, Shadows," he said.

The room applauded him, with a few shrill whistles piercing the air.

"We have a special treat for you—a Shadows exclusive." He pointed off stage. "So please, give a big round of applause for The Lovely Lilly!"

Lilly had exchanged the pink dress for a red and black sequin leotard. The white high heels she normally wore for work remained on her feet. Her breasts were practically spilling out and the front rode up her crotch. She walked out to a fiery ovation and took Calypso's hand. The magician spun her around, letting the crowd get a glimpse of her entire body.

Dead Betty stepped off stage and came back wheeling forward a high, wooden table. It was tall, just high enough that Calypso could walk under if he hunched. Dead Betty grabbed a step stool from behind the curtain and approached the table.

"Now, this is a very dangerous trick, so the splash zone folks in the front row had better be prepared," Calypso said.

They laughed, some nervously.

Lilly looked like she was going to be sick as she was led to the step stool. It shook under her weight as she climbed. The table was comprised of rough plywood with metal shackles where her feet and hands would rest.

"While Dead Betty gets The Lovely Lilly hooked up, I just want to thank this awesome crowd, our lovely hostess, and to remind all of you our residency in Las Vegas begins in the next couple of months."

The crowd clapped out of politeness. They didn't care, they just wanted to see the finale.

Calypso looked over his shoulder and got a thumbs up from Dead Betty. "Alrighty folks, are you ready for the grand finale?" This announcement garnered real cheers and applause. "So am I, so am I."

Dead Betty had returned the stool behind the curtain, exchanging it for a massive chainsaw. The crowd oohed and ahed as Dead Betty lugged the big piece of power equipment out on stage.

"Thank you, my dear," Calypso said, taking the tool from her.

He checked it and touched the teeth. Calypso yelped, feigning injury from the sharp blade. With a firm tug, he started the chainsaw. It roared to life with a sputter of blue smoke. He revved it, drowning out the sound of the crowd, then held it in front of his face. The blade spun like a blur as the motor screamed. Lilly was also screaming, but no one could hear that.

Calypso crouched down and went underneath the table. He raised the chainsaw up and touched it to the edge of the platform. Chunks of wood and sawdust flew. The engine whined at the resistance of the material. Calypso looked up, pushing the blade deeper, seemingly not knowing where Lilly's body started. He'd find out soon enough.

Cee was enamored, watching as the blade crept closer and closer to the woman's flesh. It was only inches away and the entire crowd held their breath. The look of fear on Lilly's face was priceless and Cee leaned forward in her chair, waiting.

Then, it happened.

Lilly's scream cut through the air, even louder than the chainsaw, which was bogging down in her flesh. The toothed blade found the crease of her sex like it was planned, chewing up her left labia as it tangled in the chain. The leotard shed sequins with every rotation of the blade. Lilly's vagina hemorrhaged blood, which rained down on the masked magician.

Calypso didn't flinch; he was a professional. He adjusted the blade, rocking it as it met the resistance of Lilly's pelvis. The motor bogged down as it encountered dense bone, but Calypso kept the trigger pinned, letting the blades eat.

"Did you know the first chainsaw was invented to aid in childbirth?" Cee asked.

Marty looked at her, confused. "You're fucking with me, right?"

Cee laughed. "Look it up later. Fucking barbarians." She turned her attention back to the show.

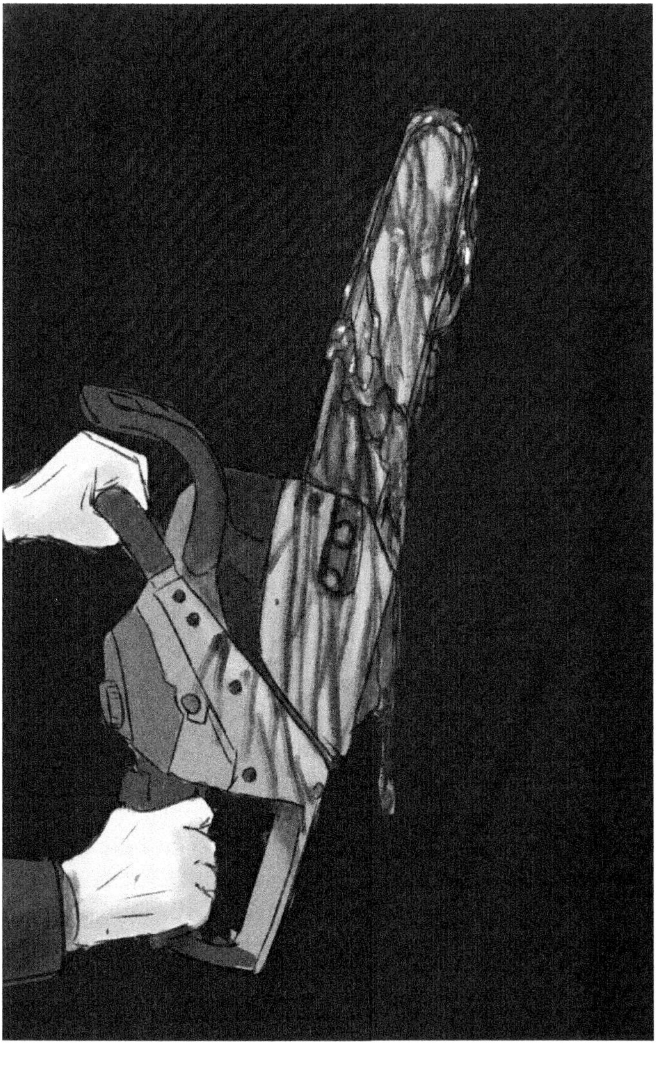

Lilly's face was the color of fresh milk, with splatters from the rain of gore. The tool was so deep inside her that it looked like she was birthing a blood-slicked chainsaw blade from her birth canal.

Calypso pushed harder, driving the saw through the bone. It lurched forward and began destroying Lilly's bladder and intestines. Piss, shit, and blood rained down on the masked magician as he continued the path of destruction. Lilly's stomach was next. Chunks of partially digested food and potent stomach acid flew from the whirring blades, landing in the crowd.

Cee laughed as a fat woman in the front row vomited after a chunk of filth hit her in the face.

The saw kept moving, but Lilly had stopped.

Her ribs cracked and splintered, leaving shards of white sticking up at odd angles. The leotard split, and Lilly's breasts were exposed—the last bit of shame in her fateful life. The mounds of flesh tremored as they were permanently separated by the chainsaw.

Lilly's throat split like an overcooked hotdog as the blade chewed through it. Her cavity-filled teeth flew like white and red confetti, thrown by the high-revving chain.

Calypso pushed and pushed. The saw ate into Lilly's skull and the table was collapsing. With a last thrust, it finished the job, leaving Lilly carved in two and dropping the table onto the magician.

Cee had a childlike grin on her face as Calypso dug himself out of the puddles of gore and wood chips.

"Tada," he yelled.

Calypso was winded and breathing heavy, but he held the chainsaw—which was now off—above his head.

The crowd sat silent, stunned at the display of depravity and violence.

Cee rose and clapped. It was slow at first, echoing through the theater. She relived the performance over and over, each glimpse causing her hands to move faster and faster. All the eyes in the room turned to her, looking up at the deranged woman in the balcony.

Whispers spread through the crowd. A hushed murmur of "The Black Widow" spread like a virus. More clapping echoed hers, each attendee too shocked by the violence but too afraid to go against Cee. Soon, the entire audience was on their feet screaming, whistling, and clapping.

"Damn, that was pretty realistic," Marty said. He was slowly clapping along with the crowd.

Cee looked at him almost like he was dumb. "Marty, that was fucking real. Surprise." Cee smiled at the startled look on his face. "Oh what, did you expect a bunny from a hat or a never-ending scarf from a mouth?"

Marty could only stare. He licked his lips and spoke. "Damn, did she really deserve that?" He shook his head as the crowd continued to cheer.

Cee slowed her applause with a look of confusion on her face. "Huh? Of course, she did. That bitch nearly ruined the show by letting Star get into the buffet." Her voice rose, putting Marty on the defensive.

"Okay, okay," Marty said. "I just mean, that was kinda harsh, but you're right."

Marty looked away from her but didn't miss the last glance he'd given her. It was one she'd seen before, although it was years in the past. The way he looked at her was the way he'd looked at Gianni as he began his descent.

Cee looked down as Lilly's demolished corpse was carted off stage, leaving a variety of entrails behind.

BETTER DAYS

Cee unlocked her office door and looked at Marty. "Just give me a few minutes. It's been a hell of a day, and I need to rest my eyes."

Marty nodded. "Okay. If you need me, just call."

She smiled and it was one of the few genuine things she had done that day. "I will." She leaned in and kissed him on the cheek. He smelled of aftershave and sweat, like her father after a day of work, long before their life took a turn for the worse.

Marty accepted the peck on the cheek. "Let me go check on the others. I'll come get you if anything happens."

"Thank you." Cee disappeared into the office and closed the door behind her.

The room was large, but the lack of windows always bothered her. Being underground had its perks, but it could be downright depressing.

Cee sat in her high-backed chair and opened a desk drawer. She rifled through various papers, pulling free a yellow envelope and setting it on her desk. She licked her lips and noticed her foul breath. Without thinking, she opened the envelope and dumped the contents out. A solitary picture fell.

It landed face down. Cee grabbed it with shaking fingers and turned it over. It was her and her father during happier times. The memories of him faded day by day, but in the recess of her mind, this one would live forever.

She was only seven, maybe eight in the photo. Life had been great, at least to her juvenile brain, but she knew now that her parents already had issues. But not her and Daddy. No way, they were best friends still. The picture was snapped by a stranger after one of her softball games. They'd won, but at that age, most games were for fun.

Cee was missing a front tooth and the other one was growing crooked already. She had the biggest grin, flashing that mouth that would soon need thousands of dollars' worth of orthodontics. Her daddy looked happy—not fake happy, like in the later pictures with her mother, but truly happy. He had his arm around her bony shoulders and a proud smile on his face.

Just that evening she'd come face-to-face with two very different fathers: Clayton and Red. Each of them had characteristics of Vin, just at different stages of his life. Cee wondered about their children, and how they'd turn out from the experiences they were forced into thanks to their dads.

Cee was shaped by violence and the world she was pushed into by Vin. Often, she thought about how her life would've turned out if her father had been a better man, if her mother had stuck around and they stayed a happy family. Or, even if her father wasn't a victim of addiction, either drugs or gambling.

And now, with Red fighting his way through Shadows, Cee wondered about the life he was trying to provide for his missing child. Would she come through on the other side as a productive member of society, or would she succumb to the life in which she'd been submerged?

When Cee took over Shadows, she had an idea of how she wanted to run the place. Brutality was still a necessity, but it wouldn't be unwarranted. The last thing she wanted was to turn into a monster like Gianni.

After the magic show and seeing the look in Marty's eyes, she knew she was on a slippery slope. It was a path she'd been on her entire life, thanks to her dad.

Cee's eyes stung.

The trip down memory lane was tough, especially with her father. She still loved and missed him, but what he'd done to her was unforgivable. Using her as a pawn—a fucking bet to cover his gambling—was inexcusable. It was the worst part of him, but the little girl deep inside of her still remembered the good.

An errant tear ran down her face. She brushed it away with the back of her hand, but more continued to fall. Cee leaned back in her chair, resting her head. She was tired—not just physically, but mentally. She closed her eyes, understanding that as sleep came for her, so would the nightmares.

A NEW POINT OF INTEREST

Marty walked the floor, checking in with the pit bosses and other members of security. It had been a normal day at Shadows with the house filling its coffers. Bets of flesh were made around the casino and the jeers or cheers could be heard over the din of the machines.

"Hey, Marty," a watery voice called out.

Marty looked around at the sound of his name, his eyes landing on J.B., a croupier at one of the craps tables.

"Fuck," Marty muttered.

He hated J.B., as did almost everyone else. The man was a slob; his fat body was unwashed, and his skin was ripe with blackheads. His smile was rotten and dark, full of plaque the color of pond scum. The worst thing about J.B. was his stench. Marty always thought he smelled like a dirty cunt, with a mixed aroma of piss and low tide.

"What?" Marty asked.

"Dirty Ricky needs more chow. He took a real nice steamer earlier, so he needs to reload." J.B. smiled.

Dirty Ricky growled and yipped like a stray dog.

Marty looked at the curtained area where the deranged man was kept in a cage. He wrinkled his nose. "I'll see what I can do."

Someone grabbed Marty's shoulder from behind. He spun, ready to start swinging, but stopped when he realized it was Manx.

"Jesus, I almost fucking knocked you out."

Manx grinned with a facial expression that jokingly said 'try it'. "Someone is about to hit the third stage of the mystery parlay, and he's doing well. He might win the thing."

"Shit," Marty muttered. He walked closer to the annex alongside Manx. "Why didn't you call me on the radio?"

"We've been trying to, but you weren't answering."

Marty checked his radio. It was still off from the magic show.

"Fuck me," he said. Without another word, he started off toward the parlay. "I need to get Cee." He spun and headed toward the elevators.

"What do you want me to do?" Manx asked.

Marty stepped into the elevator and swiped his badge. "Go find Rachel. Have her prep the kennels, and you need to be ready and waiting if he hits that parlay." The doors closed, and he headed up to get Cee.

THE THIRD BET

The lock on her door rattled, snapping Cee out of her uncomfortable slumber. Her hair was in her mouth, and she pushed it away. She looked around, confused, not knowing what time it was. No clocks: one of Gianni's rules that she'd stuck with.

"Hey, Cee," Marty said. He poked his head into the dim room.

"Yeah," she said, standing up. She smoothed her dress, which didn't need smoothing.

"We've got another smart guy who decided to have a run at the mystery parlay."

Cee raised her eyebrows. "Wow, two in one day. That's rare."

Marty nodded. "Thing is, this guy already reached the third stage."

"Motherfucker," she grumbled.

She must've missed the call. "Let's go down to the main camera room." She left the desk area and headed toward him. "Is Alex still on?"

"I believe so."

"Good, let him know I'm on my way. I want to watch. It looks like The Red Room might be seeing more action soon."

"Sure thing," Marty said. He keyed up his radio. "Alex, copy."

Cee felt like she was in a fog. Her brain was cloudy and seemingly filled with holes. She wasn't the biggest fan of cocaine, but she considered taking a trip to the buffet before heading to the camera room. No, she was a professional, not a psycho like Gianni.

Marty talked to the camera operator as he held the door open for Cee. She glided into the hallway with Marty in tow.

The pair moved with a purpose, arriving at the camera room.

"He's at the last room," Alex said. He moved out of the way so the others could see.

Cee gasped. It was the man with the port-wine stain on his face and neck—Red.

"You know him?" Marty asked.

"Yes… Well, no. I saw him a few times earlier, but I can't seem to get him out of my head." Her mind snapped back to her voyeuristic session she'd had earlier, watching Red and Lilly in The Doll House.

Marty grabbed the mouse in front of Alex and zoomed in. "He looks pretty banged up." He wasn't kidding.

The first two parlays hadn't been kind to the red-headed man. His hands were leaking blood from two drill holes in his palms. He was also missing a finger and bleeding profusely from his foot. Disgusting sludge coated the front of his shirt from the storm he had to weather along the way. And yet, he persevered. He was a fighter, Cee knew that, but how far was he willing to go? The third and final parlay was one few people made it past.

Cee looked around the room.

"I already sent Manx and Rachel down there, just in case he doesn't quite finish this one."

Cee nodded and brought her attention back to the screen. The third and final parlay was beginning.

Red went tumbling into the room. The suicide king—a staple character of the parlays—stood waiting, ready to guide Red to his next challenge. Red stuffed his damaged hands under his armpits, as if the warmth would help ease the pain of the twin drill holes. He winced and almost jumped when Gianni's voice rang out.

"Degno di nota," the recorded voice of the former owner, said through the speakers.

"Remind me to update this thing," Cee said. She didn't mind keeping the old man's skin and genitals around, but hearing his voice brought back memories she didn't care to continuously relive.

Red shuffled forward on his knees, watching the screen with the visage of Gianni on it.

"Impressive. Not many people have the will or sheer luck to make it this far. You're almost there." On screen, Gianni lit a cigar.

Cee felt as if she could smell the sweet smoke and cologne of her former boss and captor.

"It was during the first two parts of the parlay where the odds really aren't in your favor, but once you make it here… all that changes. This final bet is fifty-fifty, well, at least it starts out that way. You may have a chance to sway them in your favor."

Fifty-fifty. A flip of a coin. Cee's hand touched the locket around her neck. It comforted her just knowing it was there. She released it and felt the coolness of the metal against her flesh. Her blood raced, making her flush. Her head felt as if it were in a vice, squeezing with every word Gianni spoke. Usually she wasn't nervous—she wasn't the one in the parlay—but this time felt different.

She didn't know if it was some connection to the doomed man or what, but it was something she rarely experienced. Watching closely, the anticipation was killing her.

The suicide king pulled a rope hanging near the corner of the room. Thick black curtains in front of Red parted, and his eyes widened.

The wide-open space revealed a small dog track. The area was lit up and ready. Stadium seating surrounded the four-lane track. Each lane ran quite a distance, until merging into one. When the competitors made it to the single lane, that's when things really got interesting.

Gianni's image looked grainy through the camera but his speech was clear. "While dog tracks may be a dwindling form of gambling across the country, here at Shadows, the tradition remains alive and well. There are no protestors to fret over our rules, there are no lawsuits in the underground. I would even go as far as to say we've *enhanced* the races. As you can see, the track is ready for use, so let's get to the last part of your bet."

Cee couldn't help but marvel at Gianni's madness. As evil as his games had been, the things he'd done before she cut him out of the picture, the way he'd seamlessly married violence and gambling— all were truly feats that would never be replicated.

What kind of madman builds a dog track underground?

The suicide king pulled a second rope. Another set of curtains—these to the right side of the room—parted. With his job complete, the suicide king walked out, locking the door behind him.

Red peered through the curtains.

Cee didn't have to look; she already knew what horrors awaited the doomed man. She smiled.

Even though she was stressed, this was her favorite part of the parlay, one she'd helped design with Gianni. Sometimes victims became monsters, and she was a monster all right.

The curtains revealed a room containing four dog kennels. Cee didn't look at them. She watched Red. She wanted to see his face when he realized what was in those cages.

His nostrils flared and his eyes narrowed when the realization hit him.

Children.

The smile on her face was wide, but part of her couldn't help but feel a twinge of guilt. She couldn't narrow it down, but a feeling was burrowing in the back of her mind. Did she feel sorry for the wretches sentenced to death, knowing that could've been her if her father had bet her when she was little? Or did she feel for the man about to go through the worst time of his life, possibly ending it?

Cee pushed the insidious thought from her forebrain and watched the performance. Her mouth was dry, and her heart thumped. It was time.

The kennels each contained a young child. As bets themselves, the kids had lived the life of the casino, but hadn't been nearly as lucky as the woman who controlled their existence. In Shadows, luck was everything, as Red was about to learn.

Two boys and two girls—between seven and twelve years old—stood in their underwear, shivering. They each wore bags over their heads. For some of them, this was their first race, but they knew. The children all talked. They saw the mangled bodies and heard the screams.

The curtains, which were intentionally slow to open, finally stopped, revealing the final part of the parlay.

A joker statue stood with its arms extended, holding a silver platter. The pump shotgun was dark, like a snake in the water, sitting atop the shimmering tray. Next to it were four shotgun shells.

"Choose wisely, my friend," Marty said, hunched beside Cee watching the parlay play out.

"Is there a wise decision to be made?" Cee asked. She turned her head slightly to look at her bodyguard.

Marty snorted. "Yeah, stay the fuck home."

Cee nodded. "Ah, but greed makes the world run. Man is his own worst enemy. Every person walks into that room thinking they're the hero. That they will slay the dragon in the end and save the day. But you can't win the hearts of everyone."

She swallowed hard, her mind thinking about the torment of her life and where she ended up. Cee didn't consider herself a hero—far from it. She wasn't a hero, she was a monster, one that stopped relying on luck and started making her own.

Red stared at the joker statue. To the side of the macabre figure was a stand with two buttons atop it—one red, one black.

Gianni's olive oil voice spoke again. "It's a simple choice really—red or black. While you may just see four children on the cusp of teenage delinquency locked in the cages before you, I see something different. I see two jacks and two queens. I see the key to your dreams. These pups will all be competing against each other. The first to make it to the end of the track wins. You just have to pick the winner. So, what's the catch, you ask?"

As much as Cee couldn't stand hearing Gianni talk, she loved this part. When they'd designed this particular portion of the parlay, she'd been the one to suggest it. It was so simple, yet downright cruel. Gianni was even impressed. She no longer knew if that was something she should be happy with or upset by.

"I'll reveal that momentarily. Place your bet first by selecting the button of your choice. Once you've made your wager, my final instructional video will play, and then it won't be long before we find out if you're walking out of Shadows, a millionaire."

The sensitive microphones captured the hyperventilating cries of the children. Pleas were made through gags, which Cee knew were jammed into their mouths.

They watched Red's eyes dance back and forth between both buttons. His hands might've been leaking gore from the drill holes and his pinky nub and foot might've oozed too, but that didn't distract him. His bloodshot eyes were focused.

"How the fuck am I supposed to bet when I don't even know what I'm betting on?" A sheen of sweat glistened on his temples, wetting the red hair, making it darker. He lifted his damaged hand and froze before slamming it down on the red button.

Cee's eyes widened. "Betting on himself."

Wet blood shone on the smooth red button, and Red's

eyes snapped back up to the screen.

"Wonderful. Now that the bet is in, I'm sure you're wondering what's next. This parlay is designed not only to test your physical durability, but your mental toughness as well." Video-Gianni took a few puffs of his cigar, letting the cloud of smoke float over his eyes. "The joker holds a shotgun and four shells. While they may all look the same, rest assured, each shotgun shell has the capacity to do a varying degree of damage. One is bird shot, one is buck shot, one is a slug, and one is a blank. You'll fire the four shells from the exact same distance and each shot *must* hit. In essence, you're creating a random handicap. Once all the shells have been fired, the children will remove the bags from their heads, revealing their true colors. If you've bet red, then you'll be hoping that the tiny bodies of the red jack and queen are still operational. If you've bet black, then you're hoping the red jack and queen are as bloody as their designated color. Either way, you'll still have a chance in the race, but some chances are better than others. Should you choose not to fire the shots, then I assure you, what lies ahead for you isn't pleasant. You'd better put that fucking gun in your mouth and hope it kills you, because we'll keep you alive for *weeks*. Maybe months. We'll tear you apart then have the doctors put you back together, so we can do it all over again. Before I go, one final piece of advice. To make the right choice, you need to make the smart choice." Gianni shot him a wink. "Best of luck to you, my friend."

Cee watched Red put a hand in his pocket and remove it quickly. He put his bloody finger up to his nose and snort.

"Ah, it looks like he has a little party favor left over from earlier," Marty said. "Might fuck up his decision making."

He turned to Cee, but she didn't look back at him.

"Do you want me to have Manx on point to collect him afterward?"

Cee nodded, but her focus remained on Red.

Marty stepped away and radioed Manx, giving him the message.

Red rubbed his nose, leaving streaks of gore, and approached the joker. With shaking hands, he picked up the shotgun and opened the breach. Gingerly, he put the first random shell into the chamber and closed the action. The classic sound of the shotgun racking echoed in the camera room. Red picked up the other three shells and loaded them under the gun into the magazine tube.

"Fuck!" Red yelled. He walked to the front of the cages and looked like he was going to vomit. Cee was certain, judging by the coating of filth on his shirt, he'd done plenty of that in the previous parlays. The gun seemed heavy in his hands, and he'd yet to even take aim.

"Do it." Cee growled. She leaned closer to the screen. "Fucking do it, you pussy. Save your daughter, and shoot these little fucks." Part of her wanted to use the intercom and tell him. Call him out for even a slight bit of hesitation. Did he even deserve to win? Life was full of shitty decisions. This was just one of them.

And yet another part of her wanted to stop it all, to let Red out and give him the money and help he needed. A gift that could save the life of his daughter. Something she wished someone would've done for her dad when she was a girl.

Tears ran down his face and for a moment, Cee thought he was about to stick the gun in his mouth and decorate the ceiling with his brains. In the end, that might be the best decision. It was something that had crossed Cee's mind a time or two. The screams in the casino, the nightmares, the life and death decisions she made daily—was it worth it? Was she worthy to play God, like so many others had done, including her predecessor, Gianni?

"I-I can't do it," he wailed. His eyes closed, forcing out more tears. Red wept and his body shuddered as if he was freezing.

"Is he gonna back out?" Marty asked. He re-took his position next to Cee.

"Not sure, but he'd better make a decision soon, or he's not going to like the outcome."

"That's for sure." Marty grunted. He touched his earpiece and listened. "Manx is on point."

Cee nodded. "Perfect."

Red screamed. "No! It's not real."

Cee reached for the microphone, keying up the speaker leading into the parlay. "I asked you before how far you were willing to go."

Red glanced up at the speaker in the room, with a look of confusion, yet recognition on his face. His paranoid mind had him scanning the room as if someone would jump out at him. "What the hell is wrong with you?! They're… they're just kids." Tears ran down his face.

"Why should *they* be protected?" Cee shouted into the mic. "What makes them so fucking special? You know, there's a sad truth to life that only some of us figure out—it's all luck. Like me, I guess these little ones just happened to be unlucky."

"No!" Red screamed.

"Yes! You should just be thankful that because of their sacrifice, you can win. Dessi can win! You said you would do what needed to be done. So, go on then. You're so close. You're close to being who I hoped you'd be. You're almost my hero."

Red closed his eyes as if in deep thought. His hands choked the shotgun like it was a neck, wringing it hard. His eyes snapped open and his hands were a blur.

Blam! Blam! Blam! Blam!

The shotgun roared four times, each shot making Red wince.

"What the fuck?" Marty asked. He leaned closer. "Can he do that?"

"Motherfucker," Cee said with a smirk. "There's nothing in the rules that says he can't."

Marty grunted and looked at the carnage on the screen.

Red had fired all four shells and each of them had struck a child. Except he'd shot the same child—one of the girls—with all four shots. The salvo was brief yet brutal.

The first shell in the big gun was birdshot, peppering the girl's legs with tiny metal dots, which promptly wept blood.

The second shot was buckshot. The cartridge held nine large pellets, each the size of a handgun bullet. His aim was high, taking her in the shoulder. The blast tore through tissue and left her collar bone exposed—looking like a broken twig.

The third shot was the blank, doing no damage. But what it did was give the girl's body time to absorb the shock of the situation. Her frail, injured frame lurched forward, leading with her sack-covered head.

The fourth, and final shot was the slug. The heavy chunk of lead didn't even slow as it entered her skull. A spray of brains, blood, and bone fragments tore through the back, littering the wall with a macabre mess.

Smoke rose from the barrel of the gun. The girl's corpse hit the floor, pissing blood from the multitude of wounds. Her canoed head and exposed brain glistened in the lights.

Cee thought of Jade and Maria, the girls she'd killed when she was only a child herself. She recalled the feeling, the excitement of it all. To take lives and end torment, whether it be hers or theirs, was a power that quickly became an addiction.

"Well, I guess he found a loophole," Marty said.

Cee was watching with a shimmer of admiration on her face. She didn't know if she admired Red's ingenuity, or the fact the girl's life was over in a matter of moments. The girl's life, which had been full of torment even at a young age, was done. If someone had given young Cee that option when things were at their worst, she would've taken it. The final parlay had only seen a few takers in her years and each time three of the four kids were left maimed. A loud bell rang over the speakers and Red jumped, startled at the shrill bleating of the alarm.

On cue, the remaining kids ripped the sacks from their heads, revealing the colored masks on their faces.

The first boy: black jack

The second boy: red jack.

The first girl: black queen.

The second girl: dead red queen.

The doors on their cages opened and the kids took off running. Well, almost all of them. The red queen was still very dead. Blood had pooled under her rapidly cooling corpse.

"And they're off!" Cee yelled over the intercom.

Red rushed to the stadium but remained standing as he watched the race of his life.

For as little food as Cee fed them, the kids had a surprising amount of energy left. It was more food than she got when she was a girl, the empty fridge and bare cupboard of her youth mocking her daily.

Should be fucking grateful.

The three remaining children dropped to all fours and began running like dogs. Cee knew the kids didn't give a fuck about the bettor and winning for him. Winning or losing was a matter of life or death. The winner *may* end up lucky and get a job at The Doll House or dealing on The Main Floor, while the others would get put down like most losing dogs eventually did.

The kids ran alongside one another until they began merging into the single lane portion of the track. Both boys—the jacks—hand fought as they rounded the first corner. The black queen trailed the boys but wasn't far behind. Cee watched the girl from the flickering monitor. She remembered her—another bet like herself. The girl had fight and spirit. Hungry to win, she hung back, letting the boys fight for first.

"Please, God, please, God," Red whispered. His hands were together in prayer, blood leaking from his missing finger and the holes in his palms. He prayed while the fourth child—the red 'dead' queen—lay in a pool of her blood.

Cee watched intently as the boys rounded the last corner, making their way to the home stretch. The black queen was still behind, but to Cee it looked like the girl was holding back. Biding her time for an all-out sprint.

Red cheered as the red jack—his bet—took the lead. "Yes! Go! You're almost there!"

The finish line was fast approaching, and the red jack was still leading. The black jack pumped his arms and legs—his body slick with sweat. He pushed too hard and stumbled.

Marty and Cee both gasped as the black jack sprawled forward, his arms entangling the red jack's legs. With only yards remaining, both boys went tumbling down. A cloud of dirt marked their skid as the black queen narrowly avoided them. The little girl danced around them and crossed the finish line.

Red shuddered and screamed. "Noooo! You fucked it up!" He shook his fists, sending droplets of blood dancing down to the seats below.

The reaction was all too familiar to Cee. She could easily recall her father in such a position many times. But inside, for the first time, she didn't feel anger, she felt sadness. She felt pity.

Marty grabbed his radio. "Manx, come in."

"Go ahead, Marty," Manx replied.

"You're clear to move in." He looked at Cee, even though he knew the answer.

She nodded. "Please escort our guest to The Red Room. We'll meet you down there."

"Copy," Manx said.

Cee looked at the defeated man on the screen. The slump in his shoulders, the tears in his eyes. He was beaten, and his miserable life was in her hands. She could crush him like a bug or open her fist and let him fly away.

Touching the locket around her neck, she thought about the poker chip and redemption in the same breath. Despite the somber feelings stirring inside her, she still wasn't sure how things might play out when she came face-to-face with the man.

On screen, Manx entered the room.

"Let's go," she said to Marty. Cee headed for the exit without waiting for his response.

***

Alex slid back in front of the cameras and closed the monitor for the third parlay. He had the rest of the casino to watch over and knew the penalty for not working.

SO, WE MEET AGAIN

Cee looked around The Red Room. How many people had been brought inside there? How many had *she* brought inside? How many men and women had voided their bladders and bowels on the crucifix table?

Cee looked back at the monitor she'd looked at earlier in the day, the frame remained where Red and Lilly had been sitting. Their seats were now occupied by others, but she thought back to the words he spoke.

As she drifted around the room like a specter, touching the instruments of death, she couldn't help but wonder. What would she use on Red? How would she end his life? Or would she? Cee touched the locket again.

A final bet, perhaps. Something to make my day interesting. A chance that I never had.

She still couldn't get the image of the shock on Marty's face out of her head. Moments ago, when she asked him to step outside, he couldn't have known why. That was fine—he didn't need to. While she didn't know exactly how the exchange between Red and her was going to play out, it wasn't going to be run of the mill. Their situation was different. Despite only knowing the man with the port wine stain for a short time, for better or worse, their situation was personal.

The door opened, and Manx led the condemned inside. From the hallway, Marty glared into the room projecting a mixture of anger and concern. He truly was the closest thing she had to a caring father.

Red was even more disheveled in person.

Next to Manx—the air of professionalism—Red looked even worse. But Cee was the queen, The Black Widow, as many called her. In some ways, she loved the name, but in others, she loathed it. While she enjoyed letting the peasants whisper about her, there was still that voice inside that nagged.

Is this really what she wanted for herself? Were the wicked desires she divulged in something she could live with? Was she okay with her legacy being that of a psychotic tyrant? Had she become Gianni?

The latter thought made her shudder. She shook off the notion and focused on the task in front of her.

"So, there you are," she said. "I had a feeling our paths would cross again." Her voice didn't waver at all. She realized she was still fiddling with her locket.

"Lay down on the table," Manx told Red.

Red stood still, his eyes locked on Cee's. He must've seen something in her coldness—a moment of weakness, perhaps. Red remained standing; the order ignored.

"I think I'd rather stand," Red said.

"Get your ass down now, or I'll break your fuckin' legs and—"

"Manx, it's okay," Cee said, raising a hand to silence him. "Please, wait outside with Marty."

"Are you sure?" he asked. Marty glared at them disapprovingly as he waited outside.

"Yes," she said. "No need to worry, I can take care of this myself."

Manx nodded and moved in close to Red, his nose nearly touching the port wine stain on the man's face. "I'll be just outside, Ma'am, in case you need anything."

Manx left the room in silence, closing the door behind him.

Cee stared at Red. She didn't know if she should admire him or hate him. On the one hand, he was there for a noble reason—to get his daughter back and save his mother. But on the other hand, he'd lost her in the first place and was just now taking her safety into account. A father—a *loving* father—would never let such a thing happen.

"So, I guess that's how you figured me out?" Red asked, pointing at the monitors. "But I don't get it. Why me?"

Cee couldn't help but smile.

"In Shadows, there are always eyes watching and ears listening, even if you don't always see them. You have an interesting face, I suppose that's why you caught my eye initially," Cee said.

Absently, Red touched his birthmark with a bloody hand, smearing it with more crimson.

"Part of me took notice of your nobility, risking life and limb to locate your daughter and save your mother, that kind of thing… speaks to me. But when I saw you nodding off in that theater, I couldn't help but wonder if you were the one that brought the trouble to them," Cee continued.

"I made my mistakes but—"

"Hear me out. You'll get your chance to speak."

He nodded.

"Despite all the violence and depravity inside these walls, do you know what I enjoy most about this place?"

"What's that?"

"The stories. There are hundreds of them scurrying around—more stories than a centipede has legs. Most of them are the same though, predictable reruns. I'd say close to ninety percent are just cases of simple selfishness, nothing more. So that gets quite boring, and after a while, I tend to lose interest. But every once in a while, I run into something that grabs me. A story that I maybe relate to a little more closely than I'd like to admit. I've had a pair like that today—both sides of the chip so to speak."

Cee popped open her locket and pulled out the weathered poker chip. It was red on one side, black on the other, with a bold 'S' in the middle of both sides. Cee rubbed at the clay chip, memories flooding back to her. The day she was reborn in that very room.

"I've dealt with the first side already, and I've been waiting for you ever since. All I have is time in this place, but now and then it drags. Your story got me thinking…"

Daddy, please don't do this to me. Her young voice, still bearing a shred of innocence, screamed in her mind.

The fake remorse in her father's eyes as his daughter was bet away like a stack of shitty chips. She saw through it then and fucking hated him for it. What would her life have been like with a father like the man in front of her? With a man who loved and nurtured his child instead of using them like a game piece in their sick fucking world? Her breath caught, and she cleared her throat. The sting of forming tears made her blink, and she hoped none fell.

"I'd have given anything to have a father like you," she blurted out, almost accidentally. "I know you're not perfect, but just having a chance at life would've…" Cee looked at a circular mirror hanging on the wall.

I could've been anything… a doctor, a teacher, a vet… anything. But no, I deal in chance, black and red, life and death, and I am death.

"That would've meant the fucking world." Her lips quivered. "Who knows what I could've become. I certainly wouldn't have stayed here."

"What happened to you?" Red asked.

The care in his voice seemed genuine, but Cee's job was to spot a fake. Her defenses hardened and she was pissed at herself for even showing a glimmer of weakness.

She was death. She was the be-all, end-all, not some damsel in distress. Those days were long gone and would never return. She'd run Shadows until someone got the balls to try and take her out. And if that was the case, they'd better come with sharp knives and a deep resolve, because hers were always sharp and ready to plunge into flesh. Cee wanted to touch her eyes to ensure no tears broke free, but she didn't.

"This isn't about me. It's about you. And there's only one question left for you to answer." The softness she'd felt moments earlier was gone, petrified back to stone.

Red gulped. His eyes darted around the room, taking in the instruments of torture.

"Are you that piece of shit I saw passed out in the theater and the annex?" she asked. "Or, are you the man looking to track down the daughter he lost and make her life worth living?"

"I'm the—"

"That was a rhetorical question. You answer when you bet. The chip never lies," she explained, rubbing the haggard disk of clay. "It's inevitable. Your truth shall be revealed, and your fate will be decided. Just like mine was."

Cee slid the chip down her thumb and let it rest.

"I don't do this for people, so, consider yourself a lucky man. It's fifty-fifty. If you call the color, I'll get you enough financial support to ensure you can pay off your debts, the PI looking for Dessi, and still have enough left over to start a decent life. A life that you had damn well better not fuck up again."

Red looked at her, swallowed hard and nodded.

Cee couldn't tell if the look in his eyes was genuine—the look of hope. She thought so, and prayed, for his sake, that it was.

"But if you don't call it, well, let's just say you won't be leaving Shadows ever. And whatever becomes of your mother and Dessi will remain an agonizing mystery. Got it?"

Red nodded, but Cee wasn't one to wait. With a flick of her thumb, she sent the chip fluttering through the air. It flipped end over end, Cee staring at it with glee.

Did she have another fly ensnared in her trap of death? She would soon find out, but part of her—the flicker of humanity that cropped up every so often—wanted Red to win. To see him grow and blossom, living a good life with his daughter, a life ripped from her on the flip of a coin.

S

"Call it!" she yelled.

Her eyes were locked on the flipping piece of clay. Red, black, red, black. Life, death, life, death. Closer to her hand, it fell. Red's lips parted. He had a choice to make.

THE GAMBLE

Hello dear reader, at this moment we ask that you locate a coin before continuing on. If you are reading from the limited-edition hardcover of *Through the Eyes of Desperation,* then you should use the special Shadows' casino chip included with your bundle. But if you are reading this in eBook, paperback, or listening to audio, any coin will do.

There are two different potential conclusions to this story, and both are now in *your* hands. Designate each of the heads and tails sides of your coin as either red or black (those using a chip, your sides are already designated). Once you flip the coin/chip and determine what color it has landed on, use the below guide to read the ending that destiny has chosen for you.

THE BLACK ENDING: if your coin landed on black, flip to page 205 and read the black ending.

THE RED ENDING: if your coin landed on red, flip to page 245 and read the red ending.

B
B

THE BLACK ENDING

BLACK

The coin was a blur. Red looked like he was going to puke. Red and black glimmered in his eye, as his fate was about to be decided.

"I said call it!" Cee yelled.

It was do or die. Cee knew what color she would pick, but would Red be smart enough to realize it? Red—the color, that is—had failed the man all night.

His lips pursed, puckering like he was about to kiss the air.

"Black," he finally spurted.

Red looked exhausted, slick with sweat. He held his gorge, but Cee knew the man was on the verge of vomiting.

Serpent-quick, she snatched the coin out of the air and slapped it down on her hand. The black side with a red 'S' in the middle, stared back at them.

Cee looked up at him. She rolled the coin off the back of her hand and into her palm. With deft fingers and years of practice, she slipped the chip back into the locket.

"Smart man," she said.

Red nearly collapsed. He stumbled back, hitting his ass against the execution table.

"Fuck me," he muttered.

Red dug into his pants pocket but stopped.

He shook his head and swallowed the lump in his throat. His blood-caked hand came out empty.

"Never again. Never fucking again." He spoke aloud, but mainly to himself.

Cee walked over to the door and knocked. It opened and she saw Rachel had joined the boys.

Marty poked his head in. His eyes narrowed as he looked at Red, who was still very much alive. It was quite rare for someone to walk out of The Red Room.

"Everything okay?" Marty asked.

Cee smiled at the look on his face. She knew they were surprised; she had quite the reputation.

"Everything is perfect," she said. "Please, my new friend, Red, needs some medical attention. If you could call the doc and have him looked at. I'm sure he'll be transferred to a hospital, but in the meantime have him cleaned up."

"Got it," Marty said. He tapped Manx on the chest. "Go call Dr. Pollard and tell him we're gonna have one coming to him soon." He looked at Rachel. "You, stick with me."

Rachel nodded.

"No," Red blurted. His hands leaked crimson, leaving polka dots on the floor. "I gotta get back to my ma's." He stood up straight but was fighting it. The day's events had taken a toll on the man.

"Okay, let's get that squared away first," Cee said. She pointed at Rachel. "Head to the vault and get some cash. I'll make the call to authorize it."

Rachel nodded and left the room.

Cee turned. "And Marty, take him to the drop. But for the love of fucking God, get him cleaned up a little. He stinks to high Hell. And please get something on those hands."

Marty wrinkled his nose. "Consider it done." He looked at the bloody, disheveled man. "Come on, let's get a move on."

Red took two steps toward the door and stopped. He turned and looked back at Cee. "Thank you. It feels odd thanking the person that put me through all that, but I've come out a better man. I promise."

Cee didn't say anything. She didn't know if she could. Instead, she nodded and watched him walk away.

ONLY THE GOOD DIE YOUNG

Cee and Marty stood in The Red Room. Red, Manx, and Rachel were gone, headed to see Doctor Pollard or one of the few nurses he kept around.

A long sigh escaped Cee's lips as she pulled the chair from under the desk. She looked at the small screen in front of her. The monitor glowed, showing various shots of the casino. Cee put her chin on the heel of her hand and watched as Red was led to Doctor Pollard's office. Her eyes drifted to the jar containing Gianni's severed genitals then back to the screen.

Marty stepped next to her and leaned against the wall. He pulled a pack of cigarettes from his pocket and offered one to Cee.

She took one silently and put it in her mouth.

Marty lit it then his own. They smoked in silence, but Cee could tell Marty had something to say. And she had a feeling she knew what it would be.

"You're thinking about him, aren't you?" Marty asked.

He didn't have to say a name; they both knew who he was talking about.

Cee nodded. "Yeah." She took a drag from her smoke. "I have been for a while now." Her eyes drifted back to the camera, looking at Red. "Ever since he walked into Shadows."

"Well," Marty stubbed his cigarette out in an ashtray, "let's go see him."

Cee looked up at him, shocked by the suggestion. It had crossed her mind, but she didn't know if she'd had it in her. After the events of the day, she knew it was something she needed to do. She nodded, afraid her voice might betray the emotions running through her.

"I'll make the call," Marty said.

***

The smell of filth was pungent. Most of the small infirmary was kept clean and sterile, but where she was headed was the exact opposite. Unwashed flesh, necrosis, and shit was heavy in the air.

Cee knew it would stink, but the level of stench was something she hadn't expected.

"He's in here," Nurse Flynn said. "I just finished scraping the fungus from his feet." She stopped outside a room from which the horrid stench permeated. "Doctor Pollard is just finishing with the stitches on the man that was brought up to us. I can send him over when he's done."

Cee put her hand up. "No, that won't be necessary."

Nurse Flynn offered Cee a slight nod and walked away.

Marty looked at Cee.

Her eyes stung. She didn't know if was from the smell coming from the room or her turbulent emotions.

Marty opened the door.

The smell was nearly a physical thing. What was horrid before became downright putrid as the door swung inward. Cee fought back her gorge and stepped in.

Vinnie Sable lay in a hospital bed. His nude, paralyzed body was covered in sores. Open wounds, each of which were different shades of infection, writhed with maggots. Squirming insects fought to eat what was left of Vinnie's desiccated body. His feet were covered in a nasty fungus, most of which was scraped off.

The day Vin had bet Cee and was paralyzed, Gianni decided his punishment was far from over. Kept alive and tormented, Vin was left in the hands of Doctor Pollard and his nurses. Day in and day out, Vin was left to rot in his own filth. The little bits of his body that still had any kind of feeling were subjected to torment. His teeth were pulled, his face sliced, and his tongue was severed. But, Gianni was sure to leave his eyes and ears (albeit one was missing, but was still able to hear) intact.

Gianni would not only subject Vin to physical torture, but psychological abuse as he showed him what was becoming of his only daughter. Each and every day, Cee became more and more like the cruel casino owner.

The day Cee took over Shadows, Doctor Pollard told her about her father and the state he was in. Thinking the new owner of the casino would show mercy on the man and provide him with proper care, Doctor Pollard was prepared to treat the multitude of wounds. Cee did the exact opposite, vowing to leave her father to rot away to nothing, as bugs and infection ate his body.

Since that day Cee hadn't seen her father. Until then.

Cee sniffled, but it was no longer due to the smell. Warm tears ran down her face, mixing with a thin trail of snot.

Marty handed her a handkerchief.

Vinnie Sable stared at his daughter. The heart monitor he was hooked to began to beep as his pulse quickened.

Cee didn't know if it was out of excitement or fear, but the machine continued to chirp.

"Daddy," Cee croaked.

Vin blinked as tears ran down his face.

Marty stayed by the door as Cee walked closer to the stinking bed.

"I've thought of this moment for years. What I wanted to say to you, to do to you. To tell you I did this, and I'm the reason you're still here, rotting away in rancid shit."

She took a deep breath, ignoring the tang of rot in the air. "I know that deep down you loved me." Cee put her hand out toward Marty.

He stepped forward with a small envelope, handing it to Cee.

She opened it and removed a picture. It was her and Vinnie at her softball game when she was a girl. One of the few happy moments in each of their lives. Lives that were dead and buried like so many unlucky bettors who'd come to Shadows.

Vinnie blinked and a whine came from his throat. His chest hitched as he cried, tears wetting the filthy pillow beneath his bald head.

Cee put the picture on his chest and gently picked up his withered right hand, laying it over the happy memory.

Again, Cee reached back toward Marty. There were no more pictures to hand over, and he knew what she wanted.

Marty unholstered his gun and gave it to his boss.

The gun was heavy in Cee's hand. It was the weight of years of grief and anguish. The stolen innocence at the hands of the man in front of her.

Vin's heart monitor raced. His eyes locked on the black gun in the hands of his daughter. He couldn't speak, but Cee knew he was begging with his gaze.

Cee smiled through the tears. "You know, we have a funny way of showing our love, right dad?" She pointed the gun at Vinnie's head and pulled the trigger.

The sound of the gunshot was deafening in the small room. Vin's face distorted as the bullet tore through his forehead, exiting with a spray of brain.

Cee lowered the gun. Her ears were ringing from the shot. After a moment, she realized the sound wasn't coming from her eardrums but was the tone of the flatline. With the back of her hand, Cee wiped her face.

She handed the gun back to Marty. "Come on, let's see this through."

HOMECOMING

A short time later, Red was in a car with a stack of cash on his lap. Another fat envelope was nestled in the suit jacket he now wore. Both hands wrapped in gauze, the stitches holding them together tender as pulled pork. He was certain some of the bones were broken, but he knew the hospital would take care of that. But first he needed to pay a visit to two of the biggest pieces of shit he'd ever known.

Marty parked the car outside of Red's place. "I'll wait here for you."

"You're not coming in?"

"Nah, this is your fight, not mine. You're a big boy, and anyone that can make the mystery parlay can handle themselves." Marty looked at his watch. "But I wouldn't wait much longer—time is almost up."

Time. What a messed up concept. Red wasn't tired, but he'd been up for over a day straight. Running on adrenaline and drugs would do that for you, but he knew his crash was coming soon. Just one more thing, then he could rest and get properly taken care of.

Red pushed the door open. The place stunk, but it wasn't the smell of death. It was the odor of Buggs.

"Well, looky what the cat dragged in," Dane hissed.

"Patrick!" Mrs. Blanchfield shouted.

She was sitting at the kitchen table with two of the most reprehensible men, but thankfully, she appeared unharmed. Jumping up, Red's mother ran over to her son. Her eyes darted to his bandaged hands but didn't say anything.

"I-I was so scared." She leaned in closer to his ear. "These men told me terrible things, things they were going to do to me, Patrick."

Red backed away and looked at his mother. His eyes stung with tears.

"It's okay, mom. We're good." He snorted. "Hell, we're more than good. I fucking won. I won big time." He looked around her, pushing her slightly out of his way.

"Here," Red said, pulling the overstuffed envelope from his jacket. "It's all there, but by all means, count it."

Dane took it and sucked something from his teeth. He spat on the floor. Buggs, a disheveled and obese gangster with poor hygiene watched his peer as he opened the thick envelope.

"Yeah, it's all there," Dane said, almost disappointed.

Red knew the savagery of the two men. For a moment, he thought it wasn't going to matter. That they might kill them anyway, even after getting paid. What could he do? Nothing really. Marty wasn't coming to save him. In fact, he was leaving in a few minutes, and the rest of Red's money was still in the car.

Dane walked up to Red and smacked him on the forehead with the cash. "You're fucking lucky, my boy."

He looked back at Buggs, who had the baseball bat on his shoulder as if he were in the on-deck circle.

"Buggs was getting ready to hit one out of the park," Dane said.

The two men headed toward the door.

"We'll be seeing you soon, I'm sure," Buggs grumbled.

The door closed, and Red nearly collapsed.

"Patrick!" his mother said, seeing the color drain from her son's face.

Red hugged her, feeling her bones shift under his embrace.

"I'm okay, Ma," he said. Tears glistened in his eyes. "It's all going to be okay." Red's stomach dropped when he heard a loud knock at the door.

He turned, his gorge rising.

In his mind, he saw Buggs and Dane returning to finish the job. He knew two fucking psychos like them wouldn't be happy without a little bloodshed. Red didn't think his body could handle any more abuse.

The door swung open and Marty stood there, a bag of cash in his hand.

For a second time in only seconds, Red thought he was going to pass out.

"I figure you'd want this," Marty said.

Red lurched forward, afraid his legs would betray him. He reached out with a bandaged and shaky hand. "T-thanks," he said. He opened the bag. The bundles of cash stared back at him. He touched them, thumbing through their stacks in awe.

"Where did you get that money?" his mother asked, looking over his shoulder.

Red closed the bag and handed it to her. "It's a long story, Ma, and I'll be happy to tell you, but first, I need to take care of somethin'."

His smile was weak but genuine.

"Yeah, the clock's ticking," Marty said. He tapped his watch with a thick finger.

Red hugged his mother, leaving her standing with a pile of cash. "I love you, Ma." His hand rested on the bag. "I'm going to use this to do the right thing for once. To help you after all them times you helped me. And finally, I'll be able to find her."

Red looked to a picture of himself beside a baby girl in a cradle that sat on the hutch.

Mrs. Blanchfield looked confused, but her old eyes alit with wonder and joy. "Really?"

"Yeah, I've got someone looking for her already, and he's close. But with this," he pointed to the bag, "he'll be able to find her."

Mrs. Blanchfield was crying. It was difficult to get the words out, but she did. "Haven't seen her since I can remember."

Red joined his mother, a steady stream of tears running down his face. "Yes, Ma. She'll be safe now, once and for all."

Marty dropped a heavy hand on Red's shoulder. "Let's go, or I'm leaving you on your own."

Red kissed his mother, tasting her tears. "I'll be home soon, I promise."

THE CALL

Jack Tunney was watching porn on the tube, trying to work up an erection. His poor cock was like a dead snake, but sometimes it would come to life. He stopped fucking whores; he hated wasting money when he usually couldn't get it up anyway. Now and then, he'd spring for some street boner pills that allegedly kept you hard, but he was fresh out.

He was focused on his television screen, which was currently occupied by busty women getting their tits covered in cum. But when the phone by his side rang, it interrupted his stroke.

"Motherfucker," he said. Jack's right hand was slick with lube, so he answered with his left. "Great fucking timing. Hello?"

"Jack, it's Red. Listen, I don't have long, I need to know what the status of the investigation is."

Jack sat up, letting the footrest on his recliner close shut. He shifted the phone to his right ear, holding it with his shoulder. Hastily, he wiped the lube on his pants. His dick was left out, laying limp in his lap.

"I-uh, I'm on it," Jack stammered. "I've been on it."

"Yeah, you been on it for too long already," Red said. "I

shouldn't have to do this, but I need things expedited. There's an extra payment—biggest one yet—in it for you if you can make it happen."

"I'm listening," he said, trying not to act too excited.

"I don't need you to listen, I need you to fuckin' find her."

Oh, someone finally grew a set of fucking balls.

"Well, you know these things can't be rushed, Red. I kick over the wrong rock and *boom,* she's gone forever."

He knew that was bullshit, but he didn't want his cash cow to leave. Jack was like a doctor—healthy people didn't make him money, but sick people did. If he cured Red's ailment, he'd be out of a gig. Still, the thought of a bonus sounded nice.

Jack wasn't sure if he believed the man, but he was willing to hear him out. "I'm sure I can press a little harder, but it'll take some cash to grease certain palms."

What Jack failed to tell Red was that he'd found his daughter weeks ago. Well, he hadn't seen her, but he had it on good authority that her location was pinned down. He might have to crack a skull or two to get some more info, but he was sure he could make it happen.

"Double your rate and a 10k bonus if you find her in two days," Red said.

The porn wasn't doing it for Jack, but the thought of ten grand made his cock twitch. Now that was a bonus worth ending on. "Consider it done, friend."

"Good," Red said. "I'll call you soon."

The line went dead.

Jack looked at the porn still playing on the TV. He actually felt his erection growing. It wasn't much—more like jerking off a roll of cookie dough—but it would do.

After he made a mess on his stomach, he'd make a few phone calls and maybe go pay the girl a visit himself.

ALLEY CAT BLUES

Jack entered the alleyway. It stunk of bum-piss and smoke, but he knew where to look for information. It was dark, but a burning barrel glowed. Shadows of derelicts danced on the wall as they passed a bottle around the circle.

Jack put his hand in his coat pocket, touching the black jack he always carried. The weapon was a family heirloom—a leather tab filled with lead on a small handle—his grandfather had carried it for years as a cop. The brutal tool had cracked a skull or two over the years, and Jack knew its work was far from over.

"Evening, fellas," Jack said as he approached the fire. Three sets of eyes snapped toward him, each one more pitiful than the one before.

"Dah fuck you wan?" a gap-toothed bum mumbled.

He had to have been in his late 60s, if not 70s. A few teeth resided in his mouth, hanging from his gums like drops of brown rot.

"Just looking for a little info, that's all," Jack said. His fist closed around the handle of the black jack. "I'm willing to pay for it." He smiled.

"We don't need no pigs snooping around our shit," another bum said.

The black guy in his mid-40s looked strung out, with yellow eyes that glared with insanity. "In fact, I think youse gonna pay us, anyhow." He pulled a knife from his hoodie pocket.

"Look, put that fucking thing away before I use it to cut your filthy pecker off," Jack said. The black jack was almost out, ready to strike. "I'm not a cop. I'm just a man looking for a girl."

"Heh, aren't we all," the third and most disgusting bum, said. His hair was stringy and thin, appearing wet on his peeling scalp. He reached under his gut and grabbed his crotch.

Jack could smell the cheesy odor that wafted toward him.

"Look, answer my questions, and there's a twenty in it. For each of you," Jack said. He took his wallet out with his left hand, his right stayed firm on the black jack.

The black bum took another step closer. His blade was extended and his yellow eyes glimmered with violence in the firelight. "Hand it over, or I swear to God I'll open your fucking gut."

He stepped closer to Jack. Too close.

Jack hadn't lost a step. In fact, he felt down right fast. The black jack snapped in a blur, breaking the back of the man's hand. Tiny bones shattered under the brute force of the impact. The knife clattered to the ground, and the bum opened his mouth to scream.

The vagrant choked on his own teeth and blood as the black jack smashed him in the mouth. The bum fell with both hands trying to hold in his ruined teeth. Jack wound up and kicked him in the balls. The tip of his boot tagged a testicle—hell, it might have been both of them. It was a good kick.

The bum writhed in pain, slithering into the darkness. It was the first smart thing he'd done since Jack arrived.

The other two miscreants put their hands up in surrender.

"Now, answer my question," Jack said.

"Sure, sure," the fat fuck said. "Whatever you need."

Jack's grin glowed in the fire. "There was a man—a man in your current predicament—named Garrison. He used to run with a woman and a younger girl. The woman I don't give a fuck about, but I need to know about the girl."

The bums looked at each other. "Now, mister, that's not a normal girl. Trust us, you're better off leaving that alone."

Jack sucked at his teeth and looked down at the black jack. "Try me."

THE REUNION

Red looked at the address in the light from his dashboard. His car bounced along uneven ground as he drove to the junkyard. An old clothing donation bin sat abandoned, covered in graffiti of various forms. His headlights cut through the darkness, stopping at the hole in the fence.

"What the fuck?"

He flipped on the dome light and re-read the address. It was right. He had a feeling Jack Tunney had fucked him, but there was only one way to find out.

When the PI had called and told him he'd found his daughter, Red was elated. When he'd given Red the address, and told him the location was an abandoned junkyard, it made Red scratch his head. He'd questioned Jack over and over, hoping the man would slip up, but he hadn't. The PI was confident—willing to bet his reputation on it—that the girl would be there.

Red killed the lights and engine. He sat in his car listening to it tick and cool. His heart was thudding with fear and anticipation. It had been years since he'd seen his daughter and this wasn't quite the reunion he was expecting.

Red exited the car, taking a small flashlight with him. He didn't know who owned the junkyard and the last thing he wanted was to stunt their reunion by being arrested for trespassing.

The cut in the fence was small, but more than large enough for him to squeeze through. Red used the light of the moon to navigate as best as he could, but the deep shadows further along would require the use of the flashlight.

Around him, towers of crushed cars rose. Statues to the auto industry, relics of the past, sat dead and abandoned. Broken glass littered the ground, shimmering in the moonlight. The air stunk of animal and old automotive fluids—each with a sickly-sweet aroma.

Something moved in the stacks to Red's right. He snapped his head, looking into the darkness, but nothing was visible. He fumbled with the flashlight, clicking it on. The white beam danced off a busted up Ford, but nothing moved.

There!

Something small ran behind the car, leaving a long shadow before disappearing again.

"H—hello?" Red muttered. "Please, I'm not here to hurt you. I'm looking for someone."

Another flash of movement and Red saw what it was: a stray dog.

The dog wandered out into the light and sat in the beam. It was a mangy, wiry looking thing, with protruding ribs and a scarred face. The dog stared at Red, holding his gaze. Something else moved. No, more than one thing moved around the dog. Red's flashlight wavered.

Dogs—lots of dogs—came out from behind the cars.

Red's light was low, monitoring the pack of feral animals. A few of them issued a low growl, but that was it. They all stopped next to the first and sat, as if waiting.

Then, he saw her.

Her dirty jeans were the first thing he noticed among the cars. The flashlight traced her tiny body up to her face.

Red recoiled when he saw her lips. Or lack thereof.

"D-Dessi," Red muttered. Her face was a mess of scar

tissue and teeth. Someone—well into the past—had cut her lips off. Her rotted teeth—the ones that remained—were exposed, locked in a corpse-grin. But her eyes were alive. Oh, were they ever. Her dingy hair was pulled back into a ponytail.

He stared at her, not wanting to approach. Red took her in. She may not have been the little girl he'd lost, but he was certain it was her. The one he'd watched over and cried with on those dark nights when Mommy had lost her mind. The girl he'd nicknamed to make her feel special. His ex saw her as Desiree, but that name had too many bad connotations attached. She would always be Dessi to him.

Tears stung his eyes.

"It's me, Dessi. It's daddy."

A glimmer of realization flashed over the girl's face. Her dark eyes squinted, but she knew. The ruined flesh around her teeth flexed, trying to close enough to form syllables.

"Daddy?" she muttered.

Red moved closer. The smell of the dogs and her unwashed flesh welcomed him. He didn't care about any of that; after all his doubts, he'd finally found her. He was grateful to get a chance to absolve his sins of the past.

"Yes, baby, it's me. I've found you. I'm here to take you home. To give you the life you've always deserved."

Dessi's eyes told her story, painted on her face. "Home?" she asked. "This is home."

Red stepped up to her. A big dog—a one-eyed, mean looking motherfucker—growled and stepped forward. Dessi stopped the dog with a quick raise of her hand. The mutt obeyed her.

"No, this isn't," Red explained. "This is no place to live. Please, come with me. I have a nice apartment and money now, sweetie. I can take care of you. We can take care of…" he pointed to her mouth. "There are doctors that can make you whole again. Just please, come with me."

Dessi stared at him. The emotions danced over her face. Red could've sworn he'd seen her eyes misting up.

Red took a chance—he'd taken a lot of them up to that point—and opened his arms for a hug. He didn't know how she'd respond, but it felt right. He'd waited years and done horrible things to get to this moment. Full-circle redemption was within his grasp.

Dessi shuffled back a little but didn't run. She looked at Red's open arms, and then his face, before giving him a slight nod.

Red nearly broke down and moved in to hug his long-lost daughter. He was so caught up in the emotion that he didn't see her right hand slip behind her back.

Red finally broke the embrace and looked at his daughter. Dessi was smiling, as best as she could.

"Daaaaaaddddddy," she growled and removed her hand from behind her back.

Red's smile wavered as he noticed the crude, glass knife in her fist.

Desiree's cheeks widened, her grin stretching broader and wider. And then, she struck.

DOG DAYS

"You think he's got the cash on him?" Buggs asked.

His smell and general lack of hygiene was making Dane nauseous. For as long as he'd been working with Buggs, the smell was something that he'd never gotten used to.

"Well, after what that PI was spouting at the bar, I would certainly think so," Dane said. "If not, I'm sure we can convince him to tell us where it is."

His window was down, and he puffed on a cigarette. They weren't his brand, but the cancer stick helped mask the odor of Buggs. The paper crackled as he inhaled. A thin finger of smoke ran up to the roof of the car and slithered out of the window.

Both men watched Red sneak into the junkyard. He wasn't the stealthiest of people. Using a flashlight was a dead giveaway to the cops. Or the other creatures of the night.

"Ready?" Dane asked.

"Oh yeah," Buggs replied. He grabbed the baseball bat from the floor of the car. It was the same one they'd planned on using on Mrs. Blanchfield's body if her son didn't pay up. Luckily for her, he did. But Red didn't deserve that money. He didn't fucking earn it. Playing casino games? Ha, that was hardly worthy of the stack of cash he supposedly had stashed away.

They closed their car doors quietly, just enough to hear the locks engage. Together they walked toward the hole in the chain link.

"What the fuck is that sound?" Dane whispered.

"What sound?" Buggs asked.

They continued walking.

"That," Dane said, looking at Buggs. "What the fuck are you wearing?"

He peered at his partner's pants. Dane didn't know how he didn't realize it earlier, but Buggs was wearing windbreakers.

"These?" Buggs pulled at the elastic band around his waist. "These are my hooker pants. I love tearing off a piece of pussy after a job. You know that. These stupid pants just make it easier. I slide 'em down and let that fucking skank suck my cock."

Dane shuddered at the thought.

"And ah, you know," Buggs continued, "if I get a little pussy slime on 'em, I just wipe it off or throw them away."

Dane frowned. "Jesus Christ, I wish you would've worn a quieter pair, but whatever."

Buggs held open the piece of fence and let Dane through. Red had been generous with his flashlight, giving them a beacon to follow.

"Dumb fuck," Dane muttered.

Closer they crept, using the broken-down cars as cover.

"Are you fucking seeing what I'm seeing?" Dane asked.

Buggs was close to him—too close. "Yeah, what the fuck is going on?"

Red stood in front of a deformed young girl. It was hard to tell in the moonlight, but it looked like the girl was missing her lips. Not only that, but she was surrounded by dogs. Mangy junkyard dogs flanked her like she was their queen or they were under her spell.

Red moved closer to the girl, arms out as if he was going to hug her. Dane saw her slip her hand behind her back.

"She's going for a piece," he said without taking his eyes

off her.

They hugged, and sure as shit, Dane saw the girl draw a haggard blade.

"She's gonna cut him," he continued.

"Oh shit," Buggs muttered. He had the head of the bat resting on the glass strewn ground. "Should we move in? If she kills him, we'll never know where the money is."

"Fuck, you're right," Dane said. "But what about the dogs?"

"Fuck the fuckin' dogs," Buggs said. "Come on, you got a piece. But don't be firing shots unless we need to. You understand?"

Dane nodded.

Buggs looked back at the melee. "Let's go."

When they stood, Red screamed.

"Too fucking late." Dane ran around the car and into the open.

Red stumbled back, falling away from the girl. His hands—which were already bandaged—clutched at his bloody stomach.

"Hey, you little cunt!" Buggs snarled. He raised the bat in front of him like a magic wand. "He's ours, ya hear."

The mutilated girl smiled with her rotten teeth and no lips.

"Get 'em," she said.

Three dogs—medium size and nasty looking—rushed forward. Red tinted saliva flew from their jaws as they ran. They bared yellow teeth, some of which were broken and decaying but still deadly.

"Oh, fuck yeah," Buggs said and pulled the bat back like he was getting ready for a pitch. "Come get it, you little fucks."

The bat took the first dog in the mouth. Its jaw crunched, hanging loose and oozing blood. Teeth flew, but the momentum carried the dog forward and into Buggs' legs.

"Ah, fuck," he snarled.

The injured dog still tried to bite. It couldn't, but the others certainly could. The second and third dogs leapt, teeth bared.

Buggs grabbed the throat of the mutt, but its jaws bit his left breast. "You motherfucker!"

His fingers sunk into the flesh and fur of the beast, as he used the bat to brush the third dog aside.

Dane pulled a knife from his pocket, heeding Buggs' suggestion about keeping things quiet. He slid a set of brass knuckles over his opposite hand.

"Come get it, you fucks," he said.

Dane bobbed and weaved, trying to watch the ever-increasing host of dogs.

The girl giggled and covered her mouth with both hands; the bloody knife still in her grasp. "Get 'em," she growled.

More dogs emerged from the stacks of cars, this group larger and fiercer. They didn't rush in, rather stalked forward, watching.

Buggs was screaming as more dogs joined in on the attack. One dog had a grasp on his shin, tearing flesh and fabric. He kicked and tried to push the thrashing beast from his leg. It did nothing, except rip his pants and skin even worse.

The dog on his chest had gone limp. Its tongue lolled from its dead mouth and eyes bulged red and bloodshot.

"Fuck!" Buggs turned, and swung at a new attacker, this one attached to the back of his thigh. His balance was compromised. He staggered like he was drunk, swatting at the dogs. He tripped over one, feeling something break as it yelped and ran away, limping. Buggs fell hard, hitting the dirt in a puff of filth.

Dane's blade sunk into the flank of an attacking dog, but a second bit him in the arm. When he saw Buggs hit the ground, he immediately realized they'd underscored the seriousness of the situation. The gun in the holster under his jacket did him little good then.

White hot pain shot through his nerves, making his hand

snap open. With the knife still buried in its flesh, the mortally wounded dog pushed the attack. It bit Dane on the leg. Sharp teeth, now slick with internal bleeding, entered behind his kneecap. Tendons snapped like high-tension wires as the chunk of bone was disconnected.

"Jesus fuckin' Christ!" Dane screamed. He fell to the floor, looking at the horrors unfolding upon Buggs.

The dogs ripped and pulled, tearing Buggs' pants off. The fabric was shredded and bloody and it was quite clear the disgusting man wasn't wearing underwear. The bat was long gone, but Buggs was a fighter. He punched, kicked, bit, and snarled, but the dogs kept coming. Rising to all-fours, Buggs covered his neck and kicked out as best as he could. Fear and panic flooded his core when he felt a heavy weight on his back.

"No, fucking bad dog!" he screamed and looked over his shoulder.

The Alpha—the big, one-eyed beast—had its paws on his back as it mounted him. Buggs screamed as the slick, pink dog cock probed his butt cheeks. Buggs thrashed, but the dog's resolve was strong. A cry ripped through the night air as the dog dick entered his tight asshole. The Alpha bit Buggs in the back of his neck, sinking its yellow teeth into his spine as it fucked him with feral rage. Paralyzed and on the verge of death, Buggs's limp body shook with every pump of the dog's enormous hips.

Dane tried to roll away. He couldn't watch what was happening to Buggs, and he knew his fight was far from over. Dead and injured dogs lay everywhere. He kicked at the ones still attacking him. Yet they continued biting and oozing froth.

"Red, you fuck. Get up!" Dane yelled.

A dog bit his hand, ripping two fingers off in a bloody crunch. He pulled his mangled hand back—a few fingers less—and leaked gore. Another dog rushed in, snapping at his gut. Dane punched but quickly had forgotten about his injury. The stumps of his missing fingers met canine fangs.

Pain shot through his arm as the dog brushed past the attack, biting into Dane's bicep.

Buggs was limp—paralyzed from the bite to the neck. Except he could still feel pain. His anus tore as the dog fucked him, still biting and ripping at the ruined flesh of his neck. The dog thrust deeper than before and shuddered. Buggs wished for death as the big mutt emptied its ball sack into him. The dog withdrew, leaving him bloody and leaking.

The cum and blood ran pink, creating a hellish slurry in the dirt. Buggs couldn't move, frozen to the whim of the beasts, as a cold nose probed his rectum. A tongue lapped his shame, aggressively eating the spunk of the Alpha. More dogs joined in, yipping and snapping at Buggs' gaping asshole. And then, one bit. His throat still worked, bellowing out a primordial scream. The word flashed into his brain—

Prolapse

—as his ass was ripped out and devoured. The pink snake of his intestines was thrust into the air in snapping jaws. Shit and blood-coated snouts chomped what they could, as the dogs fought over every morsel of filth. Cold noses sought after warm guts as they all fed, plunging deeper and deeper into the body of the doomed man.

Dessi stood on one of the destroyed cars watching the dastardly act play out, her permanent grimace of gore shining in the moonlight.

WORTH IT

Red was cold and hurt.

His blood was still running from his perforated stomach, but with each second, more and more heat left his body. Desiree—*his* Dessi—had stabbed him. She cut him without a second guess, sticking her blade into his belly.

Guess she takes after her mother.

If it hadn't been for Dane and Buggs, whom he knew were there for nefarious reasons, he'd already be dead. That he was sure of. It was only a matter of time before the dogs grew bored with the other two men and turned their attention to him.

Dane bled, but he fought on. His strikes grew weaker as his voice grew hoarse and the dogs circled him. Each bite took something from the man, part of his resolve. It snatched away a piece of what made him a fearful monster. He wasn't a monster anymore; he was a scared man, who knew his death was coming and painfully so.

"Ahhhh!" Dane groaned.

His arm had gone slack from blood loss, and his face was the color of the moon. A dog came in low, aiming straight for his crotch.

Dane punched and pushed, keeping the snapping jaws

from his cock and balls. He never saw the dog heading toward his face.

Jaws closed over his throat, entering his soft flesh and windpipe with a gentle pop.

Red winced at the sound, almost feeling the man's pain. The coldness was growing, as was the puddle of blood underneath him. He smelled the stench of shit and figured his daughter hit his gut in her attack.

Red looked away from Dane. The man had stopped moving, but the dogs hadn't. They pulled, fighting over his meat and blood. His body shook with each snarling rip as if he were dancing.

Red looked up at the sky. It was clear and beautiful. Not like Shadows, the hellhole he'd barely escaped from. It was perfect. It was calming. He coughed up blood.

Dozens of paws shuffled in the dirt, surrounding him. Then he heard the tell-tale sound of human footsteps.

Dessi. How long have I looked for you? How many nights have I gazed upon this very moon, wondering where you were? If I should find you? If I would find you? I would do it all again, just to relive that hug. To hold you—my baby girl—in my arms, one last time.

Red wanted to speak, to tell her every word and scream apologies, but he couldn't. He knew he had a hand in what she'd become. In a way, he'd stabbed himself.

The coldness dominated, sapping his energy. Red shivered and caused more blood to leak from his wound.

Dessi stood over Red, looking down at him. There was no remorse in her macabre face. No love for a father who'd made mistakes and had many regrets. Just the glare of a queen—a black widow in her own right—who looked down upon a peasant.

Red's tongue was dry, even though his mouth was wet with gore. It was rough and tasted of dirt and blood. The moonlight was fading, the edges of his vision growing black.

"D-Dessi," Red's parched throat was on fire. His speech wasn't much more than a weak croak. "I love—"

"Get 'em," she growled.

The dogs—every single one—attacked. There was no screaming, only the wet sound of death, of entrails being liberated and consumed—the yip and snarl of a bigger dog taking its place at the feast.

A girl stood with no lips yet with a giant grin across her face, watching. A girl who, in the moonlight, looked like a grinning Jack O' Lantern.

A FINAL FAREWELL

Jack Tunney sat in the back seat of the car. The cigarette smoldered between his fingers, unsmoked for a few minutes.

Cee didn't mind letting him smoke in her car. She knew he needed it. Over the last few days, she found herself smoking more than usual, so she knew the feeling. It also made her laugh when she told him he could smoke in a car that cost more than most people's houses. He put the butt to his lips and inhaled.

The big sedan purred quietly in the dark. All of the occupants sat in silence, staring at the junkyard ahead of them. Cee and Jack sat in the back seat, each looking at the scene in front of them. Marty was behind the wheel, with Rachel in the passenger seat.

"You're sure this is the place?" Cee asked. She didn't bother to turn toward Jack.

Jack took a final drag on his cigarette and tossed it from the car. It hissed as if it landed in some kind of liquid.

"Yeah, this is the address I gave him." Jack reached into his pocket and pulled out his pack of smokes. His hand shook as he extracted a cigarette. He glanced over at Cee, who was looking at him.

"Relax. You're not the one we're interested in," she said.

Jack put the cigarette in his mouth and cradled his lighter with both hands in a vain attempt to stop it from shaking.

Marty looked at him in the rear mirror with a shit-eating grin on his face.

"There!" Jack mumbled. The cigarette bobbed as he spoke. His hand shot between the driver and passenger seat, pointing toward the junkyard.

Cee leaned forward to get a better look. The night was dark, but there was just enough moonlight for her to recognize the man she'd given a second chance to.

Red. Her pulse quickened as she looked at him. His birthmark was visible in the moonlight. In her mind, she could see the blood pumping from her father's destroyed skull. This was it: Red's chance at redemption. Finally, he would be reunited with his daughter. Cee didn't know what she hoped for. Did she want a storybook ending that so many wish for? Or did she want the girl to snub him and yell in his face? She didn't know, but thinking back to her childhood, she wished she'd had this chance. Just a shot at forgiveness that didn't come in the form of a bullet.

All eyes in the car locked on the man. And suddenly, he wasn't alone.

A pack of dogs began to emerge from the cars. Slowly, they spread out, circling Red. Behind the dogs came another figure—a girl. She couldn't have been older than eight, but it was difficult to tell in the dark of the night.

More dogs came out and Red looked around, clearly frightened. Cee didn't blame him. She wasn't a fan of dogs either, and she was behind the fence, not in front of them. There was something wrong with the girl's face. It was as if she had a permanent sneer or some kind of weird smile.

Red moved closer to the girl and opened his arms like he was going to hug her. But, from the angle of the car, they all knew that wasn't the case. The girl reached behind her back and drew a weapon. Then, she struck.

Jack winced as the blade entered Red's gut. The wounded man stepped back clutching his abdomen as two other men entered the fray. "That's Buggs and Dane." He didn't address anyone in particular, rather just spoke aloud. "A couple of psychos that do the dirty work for Mad Dog."

Cee didn't recognize the names and didn't care.

Buggs rushed forward with a baseball bat and into the waiting jaws of the dogs.

The night was filled with the sounds of death, a sound they were all too familiar with. They watched as the scene in front of them devolved into full-on depravity. Men died, dogs screamed, and blood spilled, but not a single person in the car, except Jack, flinched.

Cee watched the massacre beyond the fence. She produced a cigarette and lit it. It was subtle, but her hand shook ever so slightly. *Sometimes you win, and sometimes you lose. I hope this was worth it, Red.* She puffed on the cigarette, letting the creamy smoke slither from between her lips.

Finally, the killing was over. A pack of dogs, bloodied and mangy, stood by the girl. In her hand was a glass shard, which she'd used to stab Red. Her mutilated face was twisted in a rictus grin as the dogs circled her, watching for any more danger.

With the eyes of a predator, Cee watched as well. There was something about the girl. Something *familiar*. They were the eyes of a girl who'd seen death and who'd taken life, the eyes of a little girl who'd killed two of her classmates by a brook when she wasn't even old enough to drive. They were eyes they'd all seen hundreds of times: eyes of desperation.

"What do you think?" Cee asked no one in particular.

Marty looked at her via the rearview mirror. "She'd be a good fit." It was as if he'd read her mind.

"Agreed," said Rachel. "Little bitch has some spunk."

Marty held the eye contact with Cee. "Kind of reminds me of someone I know."

Cee nodded in agreement. "Pay him."

Marty jumped out of the car and pulled Jack's door open.

The dome light had been deactivated because the car remained dark. A rough hand grabbed Jack's collar and yanked, pulling him clean out of the backseat. Jack hit the rocky ground and looked up as Marty's hand went into his jacket.

The fear in Jack's eyes was comical. It was clear he thought he was about to catch a bullet, not a stack of cash.

Marty's hand came ripping out of his jacket, holding an envelope.

Jack sighed, looking as if he were about to piss himself. He held firm as the fat envelope hit him in the chest. It didn't register that it was money—quite a bit more than the agreed-upon amount—until he realized he wasn't being shot.

"Find your way home," Marty said.

Jack cradled the envelope, pressing it to his chest. He didn't dare take his eyes off Marty, as he stood, still clutching the money.

Cee leaned out of the car, looking at her man. "Bring her to me." She looked at Rachel, who was already exiting the vehicle.

"Consider it done," Marty said, this time drawing a gun. The woman pulled her piece as well and produced a pair of bolt cutters in her other hand.

Jack stumbled away, posting up beside an old building a healthy distance from the shady people. He stood there and watched.

In the dark quiet of the night, gunshots broke the silence. They were followed by the death wails of dogs, each put down in a flurry of bullets as they tried to protect their master.

Cee sat in the back of the car, smiling. The glow of her cigarette lit her face as her goons killed the dogs and disarmed the girl. She took a deep drag and threw the butt out of the window as the trio made their way back to the car.

The girl was bound, gagged, and thrown into the trunk.

THE END

R

THE RED ENDING

RED

The coin was a blur. Red looked like he was going to puke. Red and black glimmered in his eye as his fate was about to be decided.

"I said call it!" Cee yelled.

It was do or die. Cee knew what color she would pick, but would Red be smart enough to realize it? Red—the color, that is—had failed the man all night. Would he be stupid enough to stick with the color that had fucked him so many times? Cee certainly hoped so. She loved a good comeback story, but the deep, dark side of her wanted him to fail. The Red Room was begging for him to fail.

Red's lips pursed, puckering like he was about to kiss the air.

"Red," he spurted. Red looked exhausted, slick with sweat. He held his gorge, but Cee knew the man was on the verge of vomiting.

Serpent-quick, Cee snatched the coin out of the air and slapped it down on her hand. The black side with a red 'S' in the middle, stared back at them.

Cee looked up at him. Her face was calm, but inside she wanted to shout. She rolled the coin off the back of her hand and into her palm. With deft fingers and years of practice, she slipped the chip back into the locket.

Red could only stare. Everything he'd endured and fought for was for naught. His last chance at redemption, at finding his daughter and saving his mother, was spent. The luck he seemed so full of had run out.

"Poor choice," she said. "Always, and I mean always, bet on black."

Red collapsed. He stumbled back, hitting his ass against the execution table, and slid to the floor.

"Fuck me," he muttered.

Red's head hung low. Deep sobs made him shudder. He ran his bloodied fingers through his hair.

Cee walked over to the door and knocked. It opened, and she saw Rachel had joined the men.

Marty looked past his boss at the crying man on the floor. "Rough luck, I take it?"

Cee nodded. Her eyes blurred, but the tears didn't fall. Not for Cee. Not anymore.

Manx and Rachel moved in and pulled Red from the floor of The Red Room.

"Where are we taking him? Or do you want him on the table?" Manx asked.

Red didn't fight. He didn't yell or scream. He did nothing, which was somehow even worse. The desperation in his eyes was gone, replaced with a look of loss. There was nothing left for him. It was well enough known that he'd die there, and his mother would suffer a fate potentially worse than what awaited him.

Cee locked eyes with the destitute man. "I think I have the perfect place for you."

"C'mon," Manx said, pulling Red toward the door. The bodyguards and doomed man left, pushing the door closed behind him.

"Are you gonna put him in the new spot? The one you told me about?" Marty asked.

Cee nodded. "Yeah. He's the perfect candidate for it. Especially with his nickname and birthmark."

"That was an awfully generous sentence," Marty said, with just a hint of pride in his voice.

Cee looked at him. The brief exposure of softness had disappeared. Again, the granite hardness had returned. "Maybe I'm getting soft in my old age," she joked.

Marty huffed and smiled. "Doubtful, but I don't disagree with the punishment." He ran his hand over the lethal injection table where so many souls had perished. "It shows character and compassion. Plus, it gives others hope."

Hope? There is no fucking hope in Shadows. Not for any of them and certainly not for me.

Now, it was her turn to laugh. "Yeah, lots of hope flowing through these walls. Gotta smoke?"

On cue, Marty handed a cigarette to his boss.

Cee smoked, her vision blurring with the blue tinge in her eyes. The cigarette burned and crackled. The fire consumed all.

DAMAGED GOODS

The Doll House never closed. Like every good carnal house, the doors were always open. Men and women—some losers and some winners—needed to fill or release their needs all hours of the day and night.

While the girls were on stage or performing for a client, they kept up the act. It wasn't about money, of which there was little, but about survival. They knew what would happen to anyone if they didn't perform. They'd all heard about the recent events involving Lilly and Porsche. The atrocities neither began nor ended with them.

The living quarters for the girls wasn't the best thing in the world, but compared to many of their former residences, it wasn't the worst. In the bowels of the mine, behind the whorehouse, was a bunkroom. It resembled a military barracks more than anything, with bunks stacked three high, and a small footlocker assigned for each bed. At the end of the room was a door that led to the small bathroom. Inside were two toilets, with just the bare minimum in privacy, a few mirrors, and two shower stalls.

Girls filtered in, just finishing their shift. They were tired, sweaty, and oozing secretions, some from their ailments, others from the johns. A mixture of squeaky wheels, the clacking of crutches, and the limp of ruined limbs echoed off the walls. The end of the shift was usually met with a sigh of relief, but for them, it was a bittersweet event.

Three of their girls weren't coming back, and Melinda was left without a scalp and a ruined eye. She'd come back to The Doll House earlier with her head wrapped in bloody gauze. It was easy to see Melinda's losses, but no one had seen the absolute torture Juicy had to endure. She was dead and gone.

Everyone knew about Porsche's fate. Her oxygen tank was left there as a reminder to the girls. She too was on ice.

It didn't take long for word to travel about the fate of Lilly, one of their more beloved coworkers and friends. Her brutal death at the hands of Calypso the Cunning, orchestrated by The Black Widow, spread through the casino faster than a case of syphilis. None of them saw it coming.

Lilly wasn't a top earner, but she pulled her weight. Her death was just more proof that no one was safe in the casino. No one. And that thought alone put everything in motion.

Akari wheeled herself over to her bunk. She wanted a shower, but the girls with legs beat her there. As long as there was a little hot water left when it was her turn, she wouldn't mind.

She'd taken more cock up her ass than she'd intended at the start of her shift and desperately needed to bathe. The slimy feeling of spunk in her shitter was making her writhe. After the last guy, who pumped a load the equivalent to that of a horse into her ass, she'd put in a bigger buttplug. Akari was grateful that was the last john of the night, as her ass felt like it had a poker buried in it.

With her strong arms, Akari grabbed the bars of her bunk and yanked herself onto her bed. She fell heavy onto the thin mattress, looking up at the one above her. It used to belong to Lilly.

"Fucking bullshit," she said. The conversation she'd had with Lilly only hours earlier was still fresh in her mind.

After hearing about her friends' deaths, Akari powered through the night. It was as if their deaths had given her a boost of grief energy, willing her to perform to the max to not suffer the same fate or worse. But what could be worse than getting sawed in half with a chainsaw to the sounds of a cheering crowd?

Maya leaned her crutches against her bunk and sat down across from Akari. Even though she didn't have any ears—only nubs of scarred flesh with dark holes in the center—she could still hear just fine.

"I hear ya on that," she said.

Maya pulled the eye patch from her face, revealing an area of ruined flesh. Her eye, a bet that she'd lost when she first arrived at Shadows, was long gone.

There was no need to elaborate on what they were talking about. Both of them knew. Every girl in the room and those who had taken their places in The Doll House had known.

"What the fuck did Lilly do to deserve that?" Akari asked. What did any of them do to deserve their punishments?

"Oo, da fug knows," Carly interjected. Her scarred face and lack of lips made her a bit hard to understand, but all of the girls had been around her long enough to get the gist of it. It was like having a toddler and translating their gibberish to the other parents. "I jus know it wis fugged uh." Carly stood next to Maya's bunk, resting the nub of her severed arm on the frame.

Akari rolled onto her side and looked at the other girls. The ones in the showers had come out, dripping wet and wrapped in towels.

Bonnie, the oldest and heaviest of the bunch, rubbed at her scarred tits with the towel before pulling it over her shoulders. She stood nude, with her rolls of fat covering the stubble of her abused pussy.

The scarred burns covering her body left her flesh smooth in random patches. Deep pockets of past torture decorated her skin, leaving her with craters. She lifted a roll of fat and sopped up some water.

Reina, the newest girl, dropped her towel as well. She bent at the waist, letting her hair hang in front of her face. She wrapped her wet locks, twisting them in the towel, and flung her head back. Her small breasts still had the perkiness of youth and good genes.

A thin strip of hair was all that remained on her vagina. Her body was damn near flawless, unlike her face. Many of her missing teeth were a result of a poor bet made at poker. The broken ones were from her insulting a john's small cock. And the black eyes were courtesy of Cee's goon, Marty. The players were the most valuable assets at Shadows, and if they weren't happy, the house wasn't happy.

"I'm sick of it," Akari said.

She sat up, looking at the girls. Each of them watched her, hanging on her every word. Suddenly, she realized they'd put her up as their leader. There was nothing said, or implied, but the looks in their eyes were more than enough. They needed some hope, something to keep them going. They were looking to her to provide it.

"It can be any of us next. She doesn't have a rhyme or reason." She didn't shout, but her voice was raised. "We can't just sit back and let it happen." Akari looked at all of them. "Lilly was the best of us. Always willing to help, even with the shit hand she'd been dealt." The girls knew one another's stories and how they'd arrived at Shadows. Lilly was no different, another discarded human life that floated on the river of despair.

They all nodded, gathering closer to hear how far Akari would go.

"Yeah, but what can we do?" Maya asked. Her eyeless socket began to leak a tan fluid.

"Yeah," Bonnie said. "We're trapped in here, at the

whim of that crazy bitch and her fucking thugs. There's no escape, no hope.

Akari let her gaze rest on each of them, taking their measure.

Tired.

They were all tired and done with the casino.

Was life worth living in such conditions? Of being fucked in the worst ways, treated like freaks, used and abused for the pleasure of the sickest individuals alive? And then, even when you're playing by the rules like Lilly was, to have it all snatched away in the most brutal of ways?

No.

The gears in her brain were turning. A plan was forming. Freedom was coming and with it came bloodshed—the sweet release from the casino or the release from life. Either way, Akari wouldn't waste any more time under the thumb of The Black Widow.

"I have a plan," she said.

THE CALM BEFORE THE STORM

Alex clenched his cigarette tightly between his fingers. A curl of smoke rose in the camera room. The light of the monitors gave the tendril a bluish glow as it gathered on the ceiling before being sucked away in the exhaust fan.

The last few days at Shadows had been quiet. Almost too quiet. The Red Room had been unoccupied, and the last guy who was in there was now a slave to the newest station at the casino, The Blood Bank, an area where patrons could drain their veins for a few chips to use at the tables. So far, The Black Widow's latest concept was a hit. The blood was flowing like wine.

A calm of sorts had descended on the casino, but something felt off like a bubble ready to burst. The place was holding its breath.

Alex scanned the monitors but almost always found his way back to watching The Doll House. The girls there weren't his type, but nudity was always welcomed, especially when the people didn't know they were being watched. Of course, the hundreds of cameras spread around the casino was a good indication that the eye in the sky was always looking.

After being under their watchful eye, most people forgot they were being recorded. Even if they did, the atrocities at the casino far outweighed a little fucking.

Alex flicked back and forth between the numerous cameras at the whorehouse, looking for some of his favorite girls. Maya, a black beauty with missing ears and a missing eye, was his favorite. He'd never fucked a black chick before, and if he didn't think he'd get in trouble with the boss, he'd drop by The Doll House and pay her a visit.

It wasn't against the rules, but he doubted Cee wanted the employees fucking. Nothing good could come of that. Alex found his girl. She was getting fucked from behind by a fat, pasty-skinned man. He couldn't help but watch as the john humped her furiously. Maya's tits shook with each plunge. The light in the room reflected off the smooth skin that was once her ears.

Alex put his hand down his pants, rubbing at his erection.

"That's it. Fucking take it," he said, using a glob of pre-cum as lube.

Alex stroked his cock to the rhythm at which the guy fucked. And then something happened that stopped not only his stroking but the man's fucking.

Maya shit.

It wasn't a tight log, either. A wet mix of chunky shit sprayed from her anus, coating the man's cock and pubes with rancid filth. He pushed her away, smashing her face into the wall.

That didn't stop Maya. Feces poured from her, covering the bed in a brown mess. Alex didn't have the speakers on, but he could tell the man was angry. He punched Maya, who was trying to get off the bed and presumably to the toilet. His meaty fist caught her in the stomach, causing yet another wave of shit to spew.

Maya clenched her gut, but the man didn't stop. His next punch came in on her blind side, catching her in the empty eye socket.

She fell onto the bed dazed but conscious. The man grabbed the blanket and wiped his filthy pecker with it. He put himself away, and Alex thought the worst of it was over. He was wrong.

The man, already soiled in shit, climbed onto the bed. He mounted Maya and began beating her like he was in a cage match.

Alex, his erection long gone, had seen enough.

"Hey, Marty," he said into the mic. "I think you need to get over to The Doll House right away."

DISTURBANCE

"What? What is it?" Cee asked.

She walked alongside Marty through the casino floor. They'd just watched a desperate bettor have his face pummeled for losing a hand of blackjack.

Marty pressed his finger against his earpiece, listening to Alex giving him updates. He was torn on whether to send Manx and Rachel over or give Cee an update first. Marty chose the latter.

"Trouble at The Doll House," he said.

He switched the channels on his radio and keyed it up.

"Manx, Rachel," he said, "head over to The Doll House ASAP. We have a disturbance with one of the girls and a john.

There was a hiss of feedback in Marty's earpiece, which caused him to wince. Cee had already started in the direction of the whorehouse. Even in a pair of heels, she could move fast. Marty was right behind her, doing his best to get in front just in case anyone decided to block her path.

"Copy," Rachel said. "We're en route… about a minute away."

"Copy, we'll meet you there," Marty said.

He looked over at Cee. "We can handle this if you want."

Cee exhaled a huff of annoyance. "I'm aware. But these whores need a talking too. Things have been weird around here lately, and I don't like it. They need to be reminded who they answer to."

Marty nodded and grinned. "Understood."

The last few nights had been quiet, so having a little action would be fun. He reached down and touched the baton on his belt. Lots of fun.

A MINOR MALFUNCTION

Manx and Rachel walked into The Doll House looking to crack some skulls. Whether it was the face of a john or that of a girl, someone was getting an ass-whipping.

"Alex, anything on camera?" Manx asked over his radio. "Where exactly are we going?"

The club was booming with loud music. Johns and dancers were clustered up at the bar and in private booths, but nothing seemed amiss.

"Ah, it was room six, but the camera isn't working."

Manx heard the sound of keys being clicked over his earpiece.

"It looks like something is covering it," Alex continued.

"Copy," Manx said.

Akari was rolling toward him in her wheelchair. The nubs of her severed legs peeked out from beneath her skirt, a pleated fabric that resembled a schoolgirl's outfit.

"Did someone call you?" she asked, squeaking to a stop.

Manx looked around, then at Rachel before gazing at the private rooms. "Yeah, there's some trouble in room six with one of the girls and a john."

Akari was taken aback. "Oh shit, that's Maya's room. She went in with some heavy guy a little while ago."

Akari looked around as if making sure the girl hadn't miraculously appeared on the floor. "Come on. I'll show you the way."

Manx and Rachel followed the wheelchair-bound prostitute, hardly noticing the others following in their wake.

ROOM 6

Maya couldn't stand the smell of shit. Even though it was her own, it was still difficult to inhale. But it was all part of the plan, one that would give them freedom or death.

"Here's room six," Akari said from the other side of the door.

That's the signal.

Her heart was pounding. She looked at Bonnie, who stood alongside the door, hidden in the shadows of the room.

After her shit-show with the john, Bonnie had come in and helped tie him up with his clothes. Maya stood up on the bed and took a generous pile of shit and smeared it all over the camera. That was part one of Akari's crazy plan. Part two was about to begin.

The door unlocked and swung open.

"Jesus Christ, it stinks like fucking shit!" Manx said as he walked through the door.

"What the actual fuck?" Rachel chirped, walking right behind him.

Maya was on the bed. Her face was a mess from the beating she'd taken. She didn't know what took Bonnie so long to get in there, but they'd address that later.

Now wasn't the time for past indiscretions.

Maya let out a whimper. Her left hand covered her non-existent left eye, but her right hand was hidden in a tangle of blankets.

Manx saw the bound and gagged john as Maya's right hand came free.

The wet shit flew perfectly, hitting Manx in the face. His open mouth took a semi-solid nugget down the throat, causing him to gag. The rest—the mush—hit him in the eyes.

"What the fu—" was all Rachel said before Bonnie smashed her in the face with a crutch. The metal flattened Rachel's nose, which had seen its fair share of damage over her years of fighting. Blood ran as she stumbled back, tripping over Akari.

Without hesitation, Akari pulled a steak knife—she traded a stump-fuck for it—from under her seat and wrapped an arm around Rachel's throat, pulling her onto her lap. She had locked the brakes on her wheelchair, holding her and her captive in place. Akari held Rachel tightly as she reached around the front of the injured woman and stabbed.

The serrations on the blade scraped bone as it entered Rachel's chest. Over and over, Akari stabbed. Each time her fist came back wetter and wetter. The fight, along with most of her blood, was out of Rachel. Akari released her grip on the blade leaving it buried in the corpse and pulled Rachel's sidearm from her holster. She threw the mutilated body from her lap. It hit the hard ground with a wet slap.

Manx clawed at his eyes, but a crutch strike to the back of his head sent him sprawling. Maya rolled as he landed on the bed.

Manx spun to his back and blinked. He cleared excrement from his eyes as his hand went to his gun.

Akari rolled into the room. She was a golem of gore. Rachel's blood soaked her white blouse and skirt. She raised the gun, aimed at Manx's shit-covered face, and fired.

The hollow-point bullet entered just above his left eye, causing the orb to bulge. Overpressure filled Manx's cranium as the hollow point filled with bone and brain matter, causing blood to trickle from his ears and nose. The lump of lead exited his head, taking with it a shower of gore.

The room stunk of cordite and shit, but the prostitutes had succeeded with the first part of Akari's plan. "Grab his shit and get ready. That shot is going to bring us some company soon," Akari said.

Maya, still on the bed, frisked Manx's corpse, pulling his gun and baton from his belt. She plucked his earpiece out, wiped the blood from it, and stuck it in the left hole where her ear used to be.

"They're coming," Maya said, looking at the other women.

"Good." Akari smiled.

She spun her wheelchair around and headed back out toward the stage. The trap was set, and they were ready to catch a black widow.

UPRISING

"Fuck," Marty said. His gun was in his hand as he rushed into The Doll House. House music blared and strippers continued dancing as if nothing had happened. In Shadows, gunshots and screams were common enough.

Cee was in tow, right behind her bodyguard. Something was off. The girls were dancing, others engaging in various sex acts, but their eyes were on her. Reina, a girl missing a healthy amount of teeth with a permanently swollen face, was giving a john a sloppy handjob in one of the booths. While stroking the man's cock, Reina seemed to be watching Cee, giving her a Jack 'O Lantern smile. For the first time since her ascension to power, Cee was nervous. All around her were the same glares and smirks, even a few giggles.

"Get the fuck out of my way!" Marty yelled, pushing a mutilated amputee named Carly. The girl's face was smooth with scarring. She liked to bet on fire, and a few hot hands melted most of her face off.

Marty stood outside of the room Alex had identified. He could smell shit wafting from under the door. Something else stunk to him: an ambush. There was no way Marty had survived overseas tours only to be ambushed by a few freaks.

Marty tested the handle, finding it unlocked. Slowly, he turned the knob with his gun at the ready.

Speed, surprise, violence of action were the words he was visualizing. Marty always thought back to the mantra one of his commanders had preached before heading into a dangerous situation. Despite being outnumbered, his enemies had no chance against a trained killer. But then again, where were Manx and Rachel?

Marty kicked the door open.

He'd seen a lot during his time at war and in his employment at Shadows. Not much could surprise him, but when he saw his friends on the floor, mutilated and defiled, he stuttered for a second. And that was all it took.

Bonnie rushed from the left, smashing into Marty. Her flabby arms wrapped around his, pinning them to his sides.

Marty didn't panic. He knew he was stronger than the behemoth, but it still wasn't an ideal situation. Nor was it perfect when the black girl rose on the bed with a gun in her hands.

"Fuck," Marty said.

He could smell the rancid breath of Bonnie on his face, as he squirmed to get the gun angled properly. With the muzzle pointed in a direction away from his legs, he fired.

The shot was loud, but Bonnie's screams were louder as the bullet destroyed her knee. Butter-yellow fat and gore protruded from the exit wound. Her grip on Marty loosened as she fell to the ground holding her ruined leg.

Marty didn't have time to worry about her, at least for the time being. Maya, the earless, one-eyed girl holding the handgun, was his priority.

Moving, Marty saw a flash erupt from the muzzle of her gun. The bullet whizzed by his face, smashing into the wall. With years of training behind him, Marty snapped his gun toward her, not needing to aim. He fired three shots in quick succession, all of which took Maya in the chest.

She dropped to the filthy bed, blood oozing from the gunshot wounds. Maya wasn't dead yet—that would come in a few seconds—but her fight was over. Blood bubbles rose from the holes in her chest, popping with a strawberry milk-like froth. She took one last hitching, agonal breath and died.

Marty turned back to Bonnie, who was holding her ruined leg and shot her twice in the head. Both bullets cracked her skull open and ruined her already scarred face. Marty's ears were ringing and his nose burning from the combination of offensive odors. He didn't even hear the squeak of the wheelchair.

TO THE DEATH

Cee was unarmed. There wasn't a recent time when she needed a gun or even a knife. Marty was her weapon, but at that moment, with the girls of The Doll House surrounding her, she wished she had a weapon.

Akari, one of her favorite girls, was wheeling herself toward the slaughterhouse. The wheels of her chair left streaks of blood on the floor. Gore soaked her white shirt, sucking it tight to her braless breasts. With a Kabuki mask of blood, the Japanese girl smiled at Cee and pulled a gun from her lap.

"Marty!" Cee yelled, as Akari raised the gun toward her loyal man.

Marty turned as Akari fired.

His gun fell from his paralyzed hand as the bullet entered his gut, hitting his spine upon exit. Akari fired again, this time taking Marty in the chest as he was beginning to collapse. Her third and final round struck the top of Marty's head.

Cee knew she was fucked. She didn't have to turn around to know the remaining girls had her surrounded. Something hard smashed her in the back of the knee. Cee stumbled forward as smooth hands, some still covered in lube, grabbed hold of her.

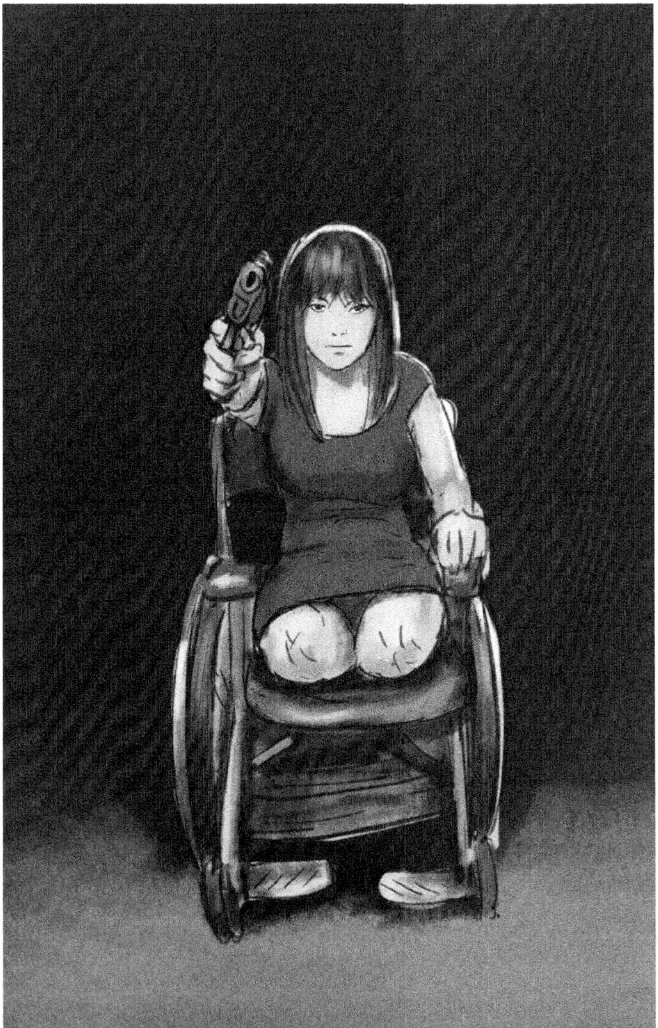

An oxygen tank—the one belonging to the dead whore, Porsche—lay on the ground. Cee wanted to fight, but still hoped for an escape.

Akari tucked the handgun into the side of the wheelchair and rolled over to Cee.

"Well, it seems we've caught ourselves a black widow," she said. Akari reached up and snatched the locket from around Cee's neck, snapping the chain. "Let's see how lucky you truly are."

STRENGTH IN NUMBERS

The girls escorted Cee through the casino. Gasps mixed with the sound of music and screaming as bettors stared. Cee kept her head up as if she were still in charge. The guns pointed at her and the two women holding her arms were good indications she was not.

Cee had no plan of escape. She was lost. The only hope she had was that her death would be quick. But if that were the case, Akari or one of the others would've shot her in the head already. They were going to make an example of her.

A few of the pit bosses—men and women who were loyal to the casino—watched their boss being led at gunpoint. They looked around, probably searching for Marty and his goons, likely realizing what Cee already knew: she was on her own. One locked eyes with Cee, then snapped his gaze elsewhere. It was clear he wasn't willing to die for her.

"You know, I've been waiting for this for a long time," Akari said. Her wheelchair squeaked behind the entourage of death. "Ever since I bet away my legs and witnessed the disgusting pleasure on your face as you sawed them off. Not to mention the fucked up things you did to me and the others *after* our bets. But you were always the star, weren't you, Cee?"

Cee didn't speak. She followed as they left the casino floor and headed into the backrooms toward The Red Room.

The door stood like a red sentinel. How many people had entered this room and never left? Would Cee be one of them? Would the smooth leather of the executioner's table be the last thing to caress her flesh?

Carly, holding the keys in her only hand, opened the door.

The smell of the room was the same, but to Cee it smelled like Hell. What was once comforting now made her pulse thump with fear. The centerpiece of the room—the lethal injection table—sat cold and waiting. Cee's heart thudded against her chest. A cold sweat broke out in her armpits and crotch. She didn't feel like a black widow but more like a fly caught in one's web.

Part of her knew she deserved this. Whatever the girls were about to do to her, she deserved. It was easy for her to say she was a product of her upbringing. That was a cop-out. She loved it. All of it. From the day she'd killed Jade and Maria, she knew that murder was her calling. Deeper she fell, becoming more and more like Gianni, something she never thought possible. In the end, she was right where she belonged.

Akari was the last one in the room. She pushed the door shut behind them.

"Okay, you've made your point," Cee said. She shrugged out of the grasp of Reina but made no move to escape. "Someone give me a fucking cigarette."

Carly looked at Akari, who nodded.

"Heah," Carly mumbled, tossing Cee a pack.

Cee opened the pack and took one out. She lit it and set the rest on the lethal injection table.

"So what now?" Cee asked.

Akari wheeled around the room, touching the various tools and instruments along the tables. Tools that had been used to torment innocent people. Shards of steel that had ended lives and made people beg for mercy.

"Strip her," Akari ordered.

Reina yanked the cigarette from Cee's mouth.

"Hey!" Cee shrieked.

Her cry was cut off with a punch in the mouth. A piece of tooth snapped off, shooting down Cee's throat.

"Doesn't feel so good, does it?" Reina asked.

Cee reached up to her bloody mouth. Red drool ran from her lips.

"Et is fugging thin off!" Carly shouted. Using her stump, she pushed Cee hard against the table. With her remaining hand, Carly pulled at Cee's dress, ripping it from her shoulders.

"Get your fucking hand off me!" Cee yelled, fighting back against the one-armed woman. Blood ran down her chin as she scratched at Carly's deformed face.

Reina threw another punch, hitting Cee in the cheek. It glanced off her smooth skin, causing little damage.

Carly fought back, but with one arm, it was challenging.

Reina pulled Cee's hair, yanking her head back. She dug a finger into her mouth, pulling it open like a fish on a hook.

Akari had seen enough. She grabbed the rubber mallet—a favorite weapon of Cee—and wheeled into the fray. The three women were intertwined. Bites, punches, and scratches were exchanged. Akari swung the mallet, connecting it with the back of Cee's arm.

The crack of her joint snapping echoed in the room. For an instant, there was silence. And then, Cee screamed.

Her elbow bent the wrong way. Manicured fingers hung limp as she grabbed her damaged arm.

"Put this bitch on the table," Akari ordered.

Carly and Reina were bloody and gasping for air. They both snatched Cee roughly and forced her onto the table.

Cee kicked and spat. One of her high heels caught Reina in the gut, gouging her skin.

"Fucking whore!" Reina yelled. She threw a hammer-fist at Cee's face, crushing her nose.

Cee's world went blurry with tears. Her good arm was yanked and secured to the table. Pain like nothing she'd ever felt before lanced through her body when her ruined arm was pulled.

"Fuck!" she screamed. Cee kicked as the women grabbed at her feet. "Fuck you, you fucking freaks!"

Akari wheeled over, the mallet still in hand, and smashed the toes on Cee's right foot. Little bones cracked and bent, some poking from the skin. Her heel flew off, landing on the ground.

Another visceral scream erupted from Cee's throat as both of her legs were secured.

"There. That's much better," Akari said. She set the mallet down and picked up a pair of sheers. "Now, we can begin."

***

With Cee secured, Akari cut her dress off.

Cee lay nude on the table. Her nipples were shriveled nubs, and goosebumps made the fine hairs on her belly stand tall. Blood ran from Cee's nose and mouth. She took deep breaths.

Akari stared at her, looking at the woman who'd tormented them for years, the woman who'd caused countless deaths and disfigurement. She ran the closed sheers over Cee's stomach. "You know, I used to be afraid of you. We all were. Anyone that took the trip down to this hellhole knew about you. The Black fucking Widow and her goons. Kill first and ask questions later, right? Well, now look at you."

Akari teased Cee's left breast with the tip of the sheers. She opened them just a little and snipped, allowing the metal to take a bite of flesh.

Cee winced. A drop of blood ran down the crease under her breast.

"I heard a rumor that you have the cock and balls of Gianni Lito—creator of Shadows—on your desk. Is that true?" Akari asked.

Cee stared at her. Her nose was grotesque, bent, and bloody. Her eyes flicked to the jar on the desk.

Akari followed Cee's gaze, seeing the floating genitals and smiled. She scraped the sheers over Cee's stomach again, this time heading toward her pussy. The blades scratched through the strip of pubic hair above Cee's slit.

"Have you ever wondered what it would be like if the gyno opened you with scissors instead of forceps?" Akari guided the tip of the sheers to the pinkness of Cee's pussy. Slowly, she pushed them in.

Cee gasped as the cold steel entered her. The sharp tip slid in but didn't cut. Deep it went, finding Cee's cervix. She shuddered and looked down. There was still more steel to go.

Akari smiled at her. Her face was flecked with Rachel's dried gore. Slowly, she pushed, digging the sheers into Cee's sex.

"No!" Cee grunted.

Sharp pressure tore through her guts as the metal blades punctured the soft flesh of her cervix.

"Yes," Akari growled.

She twisted the blades as she opened them, burrowing further into Cee.

Carly and Reina watched with emotionless glares on their faces.

Blood ran from Cee as Akari continued to fuck her with the sheers.

"See? Don't you like it?" Akari asked. She smiled and laughed at Cee's screams. Gore and chunks of Cee gathered on the leather of the table.

"Oh, you don't?" Akari pulled the sheers from Cee with a wet slurp. "Then why the fuck would you have thought we would've liked it?"

Her eyes went back to the table, looking at the rest of the tools of torture Cee had used. Another one stood out to her, a tool that had brought them to this moment: a hacksaw.

"Reina, hand me the saw," Akari ordered.

She'd slid into the role of boss rather quickly, and the remaining women followed right behind her.

"Which one?" Reina asked.

Akari hadn't noticed the variety of power saws as well. She pursed her lips, as if in thought but ultimately settled back on her first idea.

"I want the hacksaw." Akari looked back at Cee but still spoke to Reina. "I want this bitch to feel every cut."

Many of the girls who resided and worked in The Doll House had felt a saw blade in their time. Now, The Black Widow would know the feeling.

"Get those straps, too," Akari said. "Wrap them above her knees."

Carly and Reina did as told, ratcheting tourniquets around Cee's upper legs. The Black Widow had been pleading through the entire process, but the girls were so focused on the task at hand they just continued to follow their script.

"When her leg comes off, I don't want any part of her unsecured." With Cee better fastened to the table, Akari placed the teeth of the saw against her shin. "Now try to hold still. This is gonna hurt," Akari said with a smile.

The dried blood cracked and flaked off as her face contorted. Cee screamed as the teeth of the saw bit into her flesh. A jagged, crimson line wept as the saw hissed across the bone. Cee thrashed, causing Reina to grab onto her leg, better holding it for Akari to do her work.

Sweat slicked Akari's brow, wetting her dark hair, as she cut. Chunks of Cee's shin mixed with the mangled meat gathered in the teeth of the blade. Still, Akari sawed. Blood ran from the table as the shock of it all put Cee into a daze.

Finally, the lower leg was removed. The cut was the quality of a Civil War surgeon. Ragged muscle and cracked bone peeked out of the gushing wound.

Akari knew Cee was fading. The blood loss from the shear-rape and the amputation were getting to the woman. But Akari wasn't done. Not yet.

She tossed the saw on the floor and brought her lips close to Cee's ear. Akari breathed heavily from exertion, but she wasn't tired. It was like the exertion of good sex, and she had plenty more left in her.

"That was for Lilly and my legs, you cunt," she said, in almost a whisper. "Reina, the filet knife, please." She looked then back to Cee. "And this… this is for me."

She took the offered knife and grabbed Cee's left breast, pulling it taut. With the grace of a chef slicing a fine steak, Akari put the flat of the blade on Cee's ribcage and sliced, taking her flesh off in one cut.

The lucid shock Cee was in disappeared with one of the vestiges of womanhood. Akari threw the lump of flesh and fat onto the floor with a splat. She wheeled around to the other side of the table, the squeaky tires singing the whole way.

Cee's cries were ragged. Her ribcage was visible, having been cut to the bone. Akari grabbed her right breast and gave it the same treatment.

Cee stopped moving. Her cries ceased, and the rise and fall of her chest slowed.

"I ink shis ded," Carly muttered.

Akari wheeled over to the table and grabbed a pair of pliers. "Too bad, because this next part would've fucking hurt."

With the knife and pliers on her lap, Akari rolled back to Cee and began cutting.

REUNITED

There was no way to track time at Shadows. To Red, he'd felt like he'd been trapped in The Blood Bank for an eternity. He was tired and empty, both physically and mentally. Death was the only thing he thought of, knowing escape from the underground hellhole was not an option.

He stood in an office. The room was large, furnished with lavish couches, chairs, TVs, and a wide desk.

When a pit boss had come down and grabbed him, Red didn't know what he was in for. Would he finally be awarded a gift of death and released from his contract? He had no idea. The only thing he did know was that he was summoned to the boss's office.

Some time ago—what was time really in a casino?—Red heard rumors that The Black Widow had been killed, overrun by some of the employees and deposed. Even if that pipe dream was true, what did it mean for him? Besides, he knew better than to get his hopes up, knowing that evil bitch would always find a way to win.

Behind him, the door slowly opened. Red's back stiffened, bringing him to attention. He didn't dare turn to face The Black Widow. Instead of footsteps, Red heard something else—squeaking. Curious, he tried to decipher the sound, but it didn't take long for the source of the sound to come into view.

"Hello, Red. I'm Akari," she said, wheeling her chair past the stunned man. Without looking back, Akari rolled behind the desk. "Please, join me." Akari gestured to a chair.

Red approached the desk and hesitated for a moment. On the desk was a large jar, in which floated two breasts that appeared to have been hacked from a very unlucky woman. He stifled a smile, knowing whose chest they *used to* reside upon.

"You were a friend to Lilly, yes?"

Red thought back to the woman with whom he'd become close in such a short window. Their time together was brief, but their bond was real. As was the grief he felt when that psycho cut her in half.

"Yeah," he croaked, not realizing he was getting choked up. "Yes."

Akari smiled. "Good." She removed a cigarette from her desk and lit it. "Come, push me while we smoke. I have an offer for you." Akari rolled away from the desk.

Red stood and grabbed the handles of the wheelchair. "Ah, where are we going?"

A jolt of fear made Red's stomach clench. He couldn't read Akari's emotions. She might tell him they were going to the bar for a drink or a room for a fuck, but he wouldn't be surprised if she told him he was going to be executed either.

"Just take me to the floor," she said.

Red wheeled her to the elevator, not speaking. He just listened to her inhaling the cigarette. The casino floor was alive with death. Bells rang, whistles blew, cheers rose, and the screams never stopped. Fingers were severed, teeth pulled, eyes removed, shit eaten—Shadows was still alive and running.

Akari looked around with glee in her eyes. Most patrons smiled at her, shooting a quick nod, while others avoided her glare.

"This is all mine now," Akari said. "Turn here. This whole thing is mine but what the fuck do I know about numbers." She pointed with her cigarette toward the entrance to the casino. "That way."

Red pushed, feeling the eyes of his fellow employees on his back. The entrance to the casino was ahead, but something was different. There was something new.

"That bitch sure knew how to build a business, but I need someone to help me run it," Akari said. "Stop."

Red obeyed and put the parking brake on the wheelchair. He looked up and smiled.

Gianni Lito's skin hung at the entrance to Shadows, but it wasn't alone. In a perfect glass case next to his was another sheet of flesh, this belonging to a woman. A woman with no breasts.

"She screamed." Akari smirked. "A lot."

She smiled staring at Cee's flesh, on display for all to see. If there was ever a doubt as to who was in charge of Shadows, it was answered immediately.

"I'm sure you were hoping that I'd release you, but that's not going to happen. At least not right now. No, I need someone good with numbers, someone who has a strong stomach for the perversions of this place. And more importantly, someone who is loyal. What do you say you leave The Blood Bank and work for me?"

Red stared at Cee's skin.

I hope it fucking hurt.

He stepped in front of Akari and offered his hand. "When do I start?"

THE END

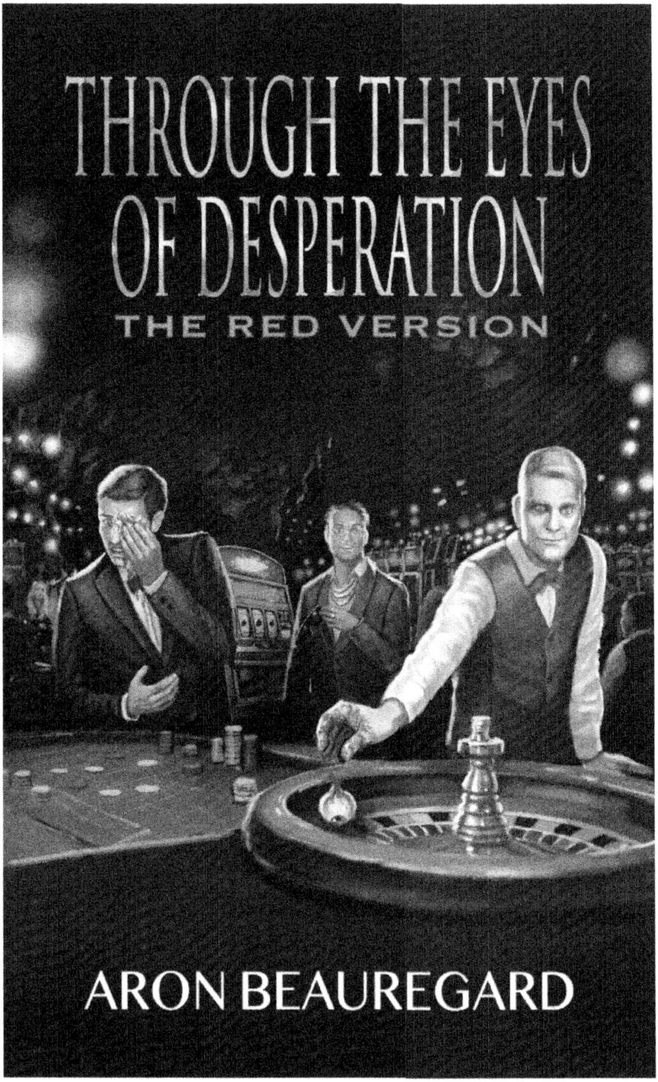
THROUGH THE EYES OF DESPERATION
THE RED VERSION
ARON BEAUREGARD

To learn Red's full story
and reveal many other Easter eggs read:

THROUGH THE EYES OF DESPERATION:
THE RED VERSION

By Aron Beauregard

Both novels are completely different stories, each with two completely different endings transpiring over a simultaneous timeline.

To learn more about Dessi read:

SEW SORRY

By Aron Beauregard & Daniel J. Volpe

ABOUT THE AUTHOR

Daniel J. Volpe is the Splatterpunk Award-Winning author of *Plastic Monsters, Talia, Left to You, and A Story of Sorrow series.* He's not much of a gamblin' man but routinely eats lunch meat past the expiration date. He can be found on the major social media platforms and reached by email at DanielJVolpeHorror@gmail.com. Signed books and other merch can be found at DJVHORROR.COM

WHAT HIDES WITHIN
JASON PARENT

"...a masterpiece of literary violence and filth"
—Curtis M. Lawson, author of It's a Bad, Bad, Bad, Bad World
WHITE TRASH AND DIRTY DINGOES
a novella
Jason Parent